JOSHUA REM

THE RUFINO FACTOR: BOOK ONE

ALL RIGHTS RESERVED

No part of this book may be reproduced or transmitted in any form or by any means, electronic or mechanical, including photocopying, recording, or by any information storage and retrieval system, without permission in writing from the author, except in the case of brief quotations embodied in reviews.

Publisher's Note:

This is a work of fiction. All names, characters, places, and events are the work of the author's imagination.

Any resemblance to real persons, places, or events is coincidental.

Solstice Publishing - www.solsticepublishing.com

Copyright 2016 Joshua Rem

To Linda:

I hope you enjoy reading this book as much as I enjoyed writing it.

Sincerely,
Jason B.

Leap of Faith
Joshua Rem

Dedication:

Leap of Faith is for anyone who's known the soul-sucking emptiness of depression, as I once did. May today be the first day of the rest of your life.

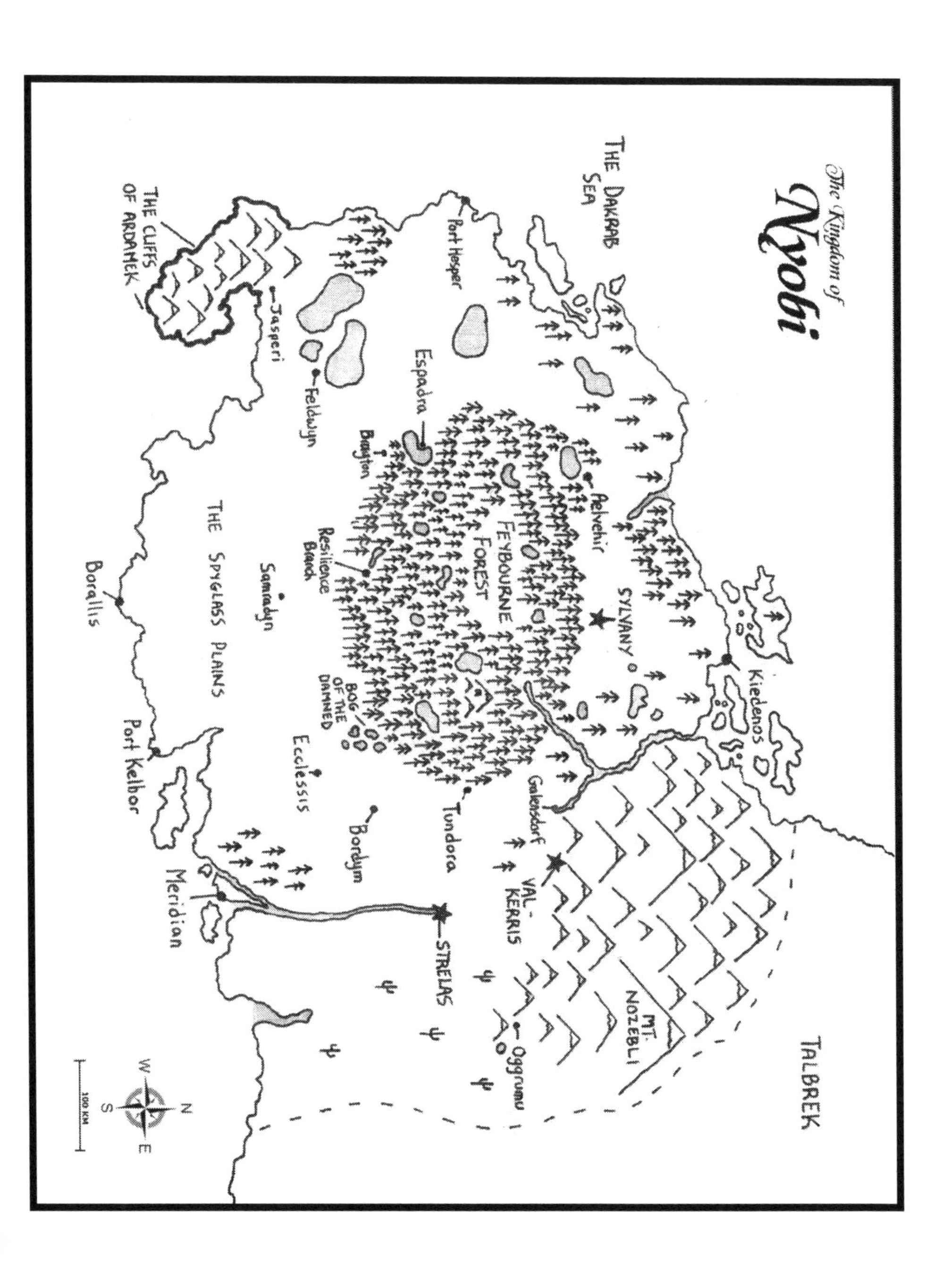
The Kingdom of
Nyobi
THE DAKRAB SEA
THE CLIFFS OF ARDAMEK
Port Hesper
Jasperi
Feldwyn
Espadra
Bragton
Aelvehir
FEYBOURNE FOREST
Resilience Beach
Samiadyn
THE SPYGLASS PLAINS
Borallis
SYLVANY
Kiedenos
BOG OF THE DAMNED
Ecclesiss
Port Kelhor
Galendorf
Tundora
Bordym
VAL-KERRIS
Meridian
STRELAS
MT. NOZEBLI
Oggrumu
TALBREK
N
S
E
W
100 KM

Chapter One
A Glimmer of Hope

12 July 1511N

Rufino Endicott seldom woke up in the same place twice. His mobile coffin, hidden away in the underside of an art merchant's trade cart, went wherever the old businessman thought he could close a sale. Sales could be difficult to find in niche markets such as this, so the two of them spent a lot of time on some *very* bumpy roads. This was a headache, to be sure, but it was a headache that Rufino was more than willing to endure if it kept him hidden from those who hunted his kind. He hadn't survived for six years as a vampire by being conventional.

His unsuspecting host's long-established pattern was to load up on merchandise at the country's coastal trade hubs and then haul it to the major inland cities. The city of the moment was Borallis, one of three major port cities along the south-central shores of Nyobi—a peninsula nation located at the southwestern tip of West Vendraca. Rufino loved port cities—harbours meant *sailors*, sailors meant *taverns*, and taverns meant *victims*. Whether he felt like swindling some coins or chomping some necks, a tavern was an oasis in the wasteland of restraint.

Sitting on prime real estate in the heart of the Borallean Docks District was *The Salty Squid Tavern*, the marquee oasis for many miles around. That being said, the *Squid* was actually something of a dive, as sailor bars so often were. Rufino wasn't picky about such things, though, and he did respect the people of this town for not trying to be what they weren't. They were salty, to be sure, and some of them were even a little slimy, too, but they were proud of what they'd built here in Borallis and they weren't going to let anyone rain on their parade. If the *Squid* wasn't classy enough for some people, then that was just too bad.

Borallis didn't attract many nobles.

Preparing himself for a night on the town was a simple affair. Once darkness fell, Rufino would slip out of his coffin in the form of a black bat, and none but the owls would have a hope of spotting him. Then, upon locating suitable concealment, he'd assume his humanoid form and blend in like a chameleon.

Or rather, he'd blend in like a three-foot-two-inch halfling with a green mohawk haircut. But that wasn't as bad as it sounded. Yes, his humanoid form stood out like a T-bone steak on Vegetarian Night, but people tended to focus so much on his wild hair and his lack of height that they missed his fangs completely. He was hidden in plain sight, and all the more so from women because they were so easily blinded by the rest of his physical attributes. He'd heard the word "cute"—the most despised word in the halfling vernacular—more often than he cared to remember, but he'd long since learned how to tolerate it. It was enough for him to know that the ladies *would* be calling him a walking slab of raw sex appeal if not for the fear of making their own men feel inadequate.

The little dreamboat fed once per week on average, though it could actually be plus or minus several days depending upon his activity level. He'd spruce up a bit before embarking on a hunt, of course, but only a minimum of sprucing was ever necessary for one as sexy as he. He didn't sweat, so he seldom needed to bathe—all he really needed to do was to keep his clothes clean and his hair vertical. His charm would take care of the rest.

***

"Get lost, creep!"

Now dripping with what had once been the woman's drink—with nasty thoughts about religion in general and abstinence in particular running through his mind—Rufino's indignant gaze fell upon the knowing smirk that was glued to the young bartender's face. With the crystal clarity of hindsight, Rufino suddenly knew what the other man's earlier expressions had signified. "You knew?"

"Sure," the bartender, a reasonably handsome six-foot-tall human man, admitted easily as he watched the woman leave. "She's been coming here every Friday night for the past three or four years now."

Rufino shook his head slowly, cursing his own rotten luck. "Lemme guess: vice night at the temple?"

The bartender nodded toward the exit through which the priestess had taken her leave. "I'll admit it's strange for a religious babe to show her face in a place like this, but Ishiirites consider it very important to integrate—they don't feel they can do their jobs otherwise. I've always assumed her once-a-week drink has something to do with that."

Rufino ran a hand through his mohawk to brush away some of the rum. The goddess Ishiira had followers from all walks of life, but she had very few priests because they had to be women and they were required to emulate The Maiden of Virtue's mortal life as she'd lived it twelve hundred years ago. That meant a selfless, often-thankless existence with no sex, no drugs, no creature comforts, and very little fun. The little vampire would have expected booze to be a no-no as well, but apparently it wasn't—not in Borallis, anyway. "You know her name?"

The other man hesitated briefly. "I don't know if they even have names. When she speaks of her colleagues, she refers to them only by title." He then set a full mug on the bar and presented it to his disgruntled patron. "Anyway, here you go."

Rufino stared at the mug of rum, half-expecting it to explode in his face. "What's this?" he demanded.

The bartender grinned. "It's the drink you paid for," he explained. "I couldn't in good conscience *sell* the drink you ordered for her, since there was never much of a chance she'd actually drink it." He was trying really hard to keep from laughing. "As you now know," he added a bit lamely. "So as far as I'm concerned, this one's bought and paid for."

This scene must have played itself out before. Rufino wondered if the priestess had any idea she was part of the entertainment bill around here. "What about a refund?" he demanded pointedly.

"That's still an option," the bartender conceded quite gracefully for such a conniving bastard, "but I figure you could use a drink right about now, hey?"

Rum was still dripping down Rufino's face and into his lap, so there was no real point in denying it. "True, that," he admitted with a snort as his hooks went for the mug.

It wasn't simply the necessity of keeping up appearances that drove Rufino to drink. His undead condition did rob him of the ability to become intoxicated, but his taste buds still functioned normally, and from this standpoint he was still able to enjoy many foods and beverages. Most of his vampiric body, in fact, still functioned more or less as it had before his conversion, with two significant exceptions: his heart no longer beat, and though his stomach did still process traditional food, he no longer gained energy from it. Only the blood of others could sustain him now.

One might believe that a being with no heart would be similarly bereft of emotions, but Rufino had learned over the years that emotions came not from the heart, but from the soul. And he certainly still had one of those. *I feel embarrassment in the wake of rejection*, he thought to himself as he drank, *just as I did before I died. I'm drawn to distraction when I'm feeling down,* he went on, *just as I was before I died.*

A loud curse sounded from near the billiard tables, and he looked over his shoulder just in time to see an enormous tattooed man strike his much smaller opponent in the head with a cue stick. The victim dropped like a sack of potatoes—clearly unconscious—which elicited a wince of sympathy from Rufino. *I even feel pain more or less normally,* he reminded himself. *So did I ever truly* die, *or did I just* change*?*

He turned back to the bar wearing a deeply conflicted expression on his face that the bartender misread. "Fighting's not your thing?" the other man asked dryly.

Rufino glanced back over his shoulder, more for the other's benefit than for his own. The battle was heating up now—two of the fallen man's buddies had jumped on the behemoth and were attempting to wrestle him to the stained hardwood floor. The big man eventually lost his balance and all three of them went down in a heap, much to the chagrin of the small wooden table that had the misfortune of being in their path. Rufino shed no tears for the table, but it was somewhat distressing to watch two plates of food get flattened along with it—one of those sandwiches would have gone a long way toward making him feel better.

The little vampire returned his attention to the bartender and shook his head casually. "Not enough blood," he replied.

The man chuckled and turned away, which brought an amused smirk to Rufino's face. *He thinks I'm kidding.*

After draining the rest of his drink, Rufino began his mark-selection process for the second time that evening. As he typically did, he immediately eliminated all men from consideration. He'd chomp the neck of a man if it was the only alternative to starvation, but women tasted so much better. His opinion was not a universally held one, though—the vampire who'd chomped his neck had been a female, and she'd been very insistent that *men* made for the tastiest snacks.

That seemed perfectly natural to him. Whoever had invented vampirism had really thought things through.

He also ruled out all women in the company of large men, because getting one's face rearranged was a steep price to pay for a nice meal. He then made a note of the handful of ladies who were accompanied by skinny, nerdy-type men. Although a small human was still much larger than he was, that was fine—he was well practiced in the art of upending larger foes. Occasionally he even did it on purpose.

There was, of course, always the possibility of getting his ass handed to him by the woman herself in a nerdy-man scenario, and in such situations he had no palatable choice but to eat the whooping and move on. But though they seldom admitted it out loud, many of the tougher ladies were quite satisfied to be "rescued" from their useless dates by an alpha like him. It was well worth the risk, because gratitude was about as open a doorway to seduction as he was going to find.

Single women were his favourites, of course, but the *Squid* was fresh out of those now that he'd finished running off the priestess. There were also no elves. Rufino had a love-hate relationship with elves, far more so than he had with the other races of Ch'ulu—the draconic word for Earth. On the bright side, elven necks were closer to the ground than their human equivalents, and the elven lack of thickness meant they were relatively easy to get drunk. On the not-so-bright side, elves had terrific hearing; under the correct set of circumstances, they were capable of hearing that Rufino's heart wasn't beating. One of those circumstances, obviously, was that the room needed to be almost silent.

Rufino smiled to himself and once again turned to regard the noisy carnage behind him. *Carry on, gentlemen.*

The little vampire had long suspected that random brawling was just another part of the entertainment bill around here —one that didn't cost the owner much money beyond providing his bouncer with combat training. To the joint's credit, however, it did offer several alternatives to fighting and drinking, which was probably a significant part of why the place was still standing after almost a century. The *Squid* had three pool tables near the front door on the south side of the building, two dartboards to the west of those, and just past the boards were several rows of chairs facing a stage that occupied the entire west wall of the building. There was a three-man band on that stage tonight, and they were actually pretty good, so the owner was clearly making an effort to appeal to a wide variety of tastes. In a different town, the *Squid* might have evolved into a classy establishment.

Rufino had been here before, of course—he'd been to most of the watering holes in the country by now. As a general rule, though, he did everything he possibly could to make things difficult for those who sought to do him harm. Since Nyobi was a nation largely comprised of individual city-states whose authorities didn't communicate well with each other, he used this to his advantage by feeding in as many different jurisdictions as he could. It'd been four months since he'd gone hunting in Borallis, and it had been a year since he'd targeted the *Squid* specifically.

This hunt wasn't going as well as that one had. Though this was cause for irritation, it was hardly the end of the world—his need to feed wouldn't become urgent for several more days. Failure was always a bitter pill to swallow, but Rufino believed such pills were best taken with food. Now that seduction seemed to be out of the picture this evening, there was nothing stopping him from spending the last of his pilfered coin on one of those juicy steak-and-cheese sandwiches he'd been craving a few minutes ago.

He was five seconds from doing just that when a lone woman came through the front entrance.

The first thing he noticed was that she was six feet tall. That was a bloody nuisance, but it could also be considered a *challenge* by one who chose to see it as such. Though she wore a hooded cloak, he could tell from both her posture and from the way she ignored the brawling idiots at her feet that she owned herself and her surroundings. *That* was an attention-grabber, for Rufino had long since learned that the most difficult necks to chomp were also the tastiest.

Okay, Rufino, he told himself sharply, *don't get ahead of yourself, now. This could be your only shot at a good meal for the next few days. Wouldn't it suck if you had to chomp a dude because you couldn't keep your composure around an attractive lady?*

He made no particular effort to be subtle as he watched the newcomer remove her cloak. Beneath it she wore a dark-green, short-sleeved blouse of an unfamiliar but strangely appealing design, and her form-fitting black pants were also unfamiliar insofar as the fabric was concerned. They looked expensive, though, as did her laceless black shoes with relatively thin soles. Either the *Squid* was a nicer joint than he gave it credit for, or this lady was slumming.

The former seemed unlikely.

But while the clothes *were* pretty nice, they were merely the tip of the iceberg as far as first impressions were concerned. What was curious was that he was actually taking the time to soak them all in. Yes, she was a beautiful woman by his definition of the word, but he probably would have said the same of that Ishiirite priestess if he'd stopped staring at her neck long enough to notice. Necks were important to him, for obvious reasons, but despite being hungry, he'd made no effort as yet to predict this new woman's blood type. For him, this was atypical with a capital A.

With a concerted effort, he attempted to fixate upon the aforementioned piece of prime real estate. It was an attractive neck, to be sure—with a couple of downright *bodacious* jugular veins—but within seconds, his attention was once again ripped away by something that had nothing whatsoever to do with sustenance. This woman—whoever she was—had hair the colour of blood, and a lot of it, too. Rufino the vampire was only mildly interested in such details, but the vampiric side of him didn't seem to be the one holding the reins right now.

That was both exciting and puzzling at the same time—puzzling, because he'd not looked at a woman like this since a few hours before his unfortunate conversion. It did occur to him that this might be happening because of the questions he'd been asking himself a moment ago, but he quickly dismissed the possibility. This would have happened *dozens* of times over the past six years if it could be triggered so easily.

The second thought to cross his mind was that he'd somehow begun some form of vampiric puberty in the last five minutes, but this notion also failed to hold up to scrutiny. Though it did feel a lot like he'd just discovered the appeal of women all over again, the onset of adolescence resulted in many symptoms and thus far he'd seen no evidence of the others. He certainly wasn't getting any taller, nor had he developed an insatiable appetite or an abnormal compulsion to rebel against figures of authority. On top of all that, his complexion was still perfect as of twenty minutes ago, according to the more-or-less-intact mirror in the *Squid's* men's room. The notion that vampires couldn't use mirrors was quite absurd, really—not as absurd as his debunked puberty theory, but close.

Rufino was a smart guy, as were most of his kind, and he needed only seconds to realize he could not solve this puzzle on his own. There was something about this woman that was making him want to ignore the fact that he was a vampire, and there was only one way to find out what that something was. He probably would have attempted a pick up anyway, but he would have preferred to do so with a clearer mind—figuring out what a woman wanted was difficult enough without having to answer those questions of himself as well.

First things first, though. "Tell me that's not another priestess of Ishiira," he demanded of the bartender, gesturing toward the new arrival with his eyes so as to maintain at least a small measure of discretion.

The young man took a not-so-quick look, his eyebrows lifting slightly. "Never seen her before," he declared after a moment.

"You sure?"

The bartender nodded microscopically, a smirk returning to his face. "I'd remember," he said simply.

That was all the little vampire needed to hear. He grabbed the nearest napkin, cleansed his hair and face of the remaining rum, then hopped off his stool and trotted over to his new crush. That they were complete physical opposites had been apparent from the moment she'd walked in the door, but the differences could not be fully appreciated until they were standing right next to each other. Some men, in his position, might have attempted a more subtle approach, but that wasn't his style. He was three feet tall. He had a green mohawk. Rufino Endicott was many things, but he was *not* subtle—his approach to women best resembled a bear's approach to beehives.

"Hiya, baby," he greeted her cheerfully.

Though her attention had been elsewhere during his approach, she didn't seem terribly surprised to hear a voice coming from the general vicinity of her butt. She turned halfway around to regard the owner of that voice and lifted her eyebrows upon making eye contact. "Nice hair," she remarked.

Not exactly an auspicious beginning, but it could have been worse. She could have ignored him completely, which would have denied him the opportunity to put his legendary charm on display. "Thank you," he neutralized her sarcasm by twisting it into a compliment, "you too. You must get that all the time, but it's not every day that I meet someone sophisticated enough to recognize abstract artistic expression when it's standing before her."

There was nothing artistic or expressive about his hair, but she didn't know that. She couldn't know that he'd actually done this to himself on a dare, to win a front-row seat to the gladiatorial Tournament of Champions in the year 1505N. She also couldn't know that his life as a vampire had begun two days later, long before his hair could have possibly grown back. She wasn't going to find out, either—if ever he dazzled the world with the story of his life, this was one of the details he would omit with great prejudice.

"So you're an artist, then?"

Lying convincingly took a lot of truth, so Rufino typically posed as a merchant since it was the only profession that came close to matching his crazy lifestyle. He was just fine with being mistaken for an artist, though—ladies seemed to like those. "I expect my work to become renowned the world over," he proclaimed ambitiously, "but only after I'm dead and people start to miss me. Until then I put food on the table by connecting foreign art to local buyers. I'm waiting for a ship as we speak—one with a box full of soapstone carvings from Agnarach in the south."

The woman was starting to look less disinterested. If she *was* slumming, as he strongly suspected, then there was a more-than-respectable chance that she actually knew what he was talking about. Unfortunately, she neglected to respond, which left Rufino with no way of measuring where he stood. "I'm pretty useless when it comes to visual art," he attempted to keep the ball rolling, "but my wordplay can knock the ugly off an ogre. I..."

"But can it pick up the girl at the bar?" the girl at the bar broke her silence in a very pointed manner. "That is the purpose of this exercise, is it not?"

Rufino was a bit taken aback by the lady's bluntness. His interpretation of her tone was that she'd been through this song and dance enough times to be sick of it by now, but it simply was not easy to understand how one could tire of being approached by men like him. He'd have made a terrible female. "The idea right now," he crafted a careful response, "is merely to strike up a dialogue with the girl at the bar. I..."

The woman's attention was then diverted by the fight behind her, which appeared to be nearing a conclusion in the bouncer's favour. "I understand that you probably don't want your book to be judged by its cover," he attempted to make himself heard over the loud cheers of encouragement being directed toward the combatants, "and neither do I want my book judged by its cover." *Though perhaps for different reasons.* "What I want is to open both of our books—over a drink, perhaps—and see if we share anything in common. That's all."

She turned back to face him, and it was clear from her expression that she wished she'd gone somewhere else. To Rufino it was an obvious case of grass-is-greener complex, because things didn't *get* any better than the *Squid* in Borallis, but perhaps the lady was new in town and had yet to absorb the local knowledge. "A 'wordsmith', huh?" she finally spoke again.

The little vampire shrugged, wondering if she'd heard a single word of his eloquent proclamation a moment ago. "Mostly short stories—a few poems here and there," he bent the truth very carefully. "Much of my work is inspired by what I see in the world around me."

"Do you have an example to share?" she decided to test the story that he was weaving.

He did have a few random verses, but nothing concrete. Unfortunately, the woman's attitude toward him was clearly going to be decided by how well he handled this challenge, so he needed to come up with something quickly. "Story or poem?" he tried to buy himself some precious seconds.

"Doesn't matter," she replied way faster than he would have liked.

"Okay," he murmured. Then, after a few seconds of furious improvisation, he launched himself into what would surely be remembered as the most awkward pick-up poem in history. "*Although thou art so bloody tall, dost interest me more than that brawl.*" He pointed toward the heap of exhausted bodies for emphasis, though in fact he was just stalling for time again. "*If sweaty brutes are not your style, why not hang out with me a while?*" He was quite proud of that one. "*You've naught to lose and much to gain, by viewing me without disdain.*"

She lifted her eyebrows in surprise, but he took little comfort in that because he could feel his train of thought jumping the rails. "*I know Borallis is kinda sleazy, but...* ummm..."

He was then bailed out in a most unexpected way. ..".*And blood on the floor might make me queasy,*" the woman breathed some life back into his awful poem.

Rufino perked up instantly. When a halfling female started going out of her way to match wits with a male, it informed the male that a steamy sex scene was almost within his grasp. Since this was only the second time he'd pursued a human woman for reasons other than blood, he didn't know if halfling rules were going to mean anything here. It would sure be nice if they did, though. "Indeed," he nodded in agreement before switching to flattery. "So what's a brainy knockout like you doing in a place like this?"

She shrugged, though it was clear she was holding

back a bit of a smile. "I seem to be watching a strange-looking halfling pull some strangely endearing poetry out of his backside."

Rufino smiled a little in return. "I never said it was improv," he pointed out.

"I know," she told him as her full smile came out of hiding, "but I'm a schoolteacher, so it's part of my job to be able to tell recitation from improvisation. What I'm wondering now is why you didn't want me to hear one of your existing pieces."

She was quick, no doubt, but he'd been expecting this question and already had an answer prepared for her. "Were you in my shoes," he challenged her, "would *you* try to woo a non-halfling woman with political satire, even if it does rhyme?" *Gods, I miss home sometimes.*

"Try me," she minced no words. "You might be surprised."

Rufino sighed. "Okay," he didn't even try to hide his unease. He'd never shared this limerick with anyone. "From the perspective of King Augustus V, here goes nothing."

Well, my country ain't looking so bright,
But I still have my military might!
This won't fix a thing,
But it'll make me some bling,
So a war with the orcs we must fight!

The woman's response was not immediate, but it was decisive. After standing in place for a handful of seconds, she lowered her voice to a whisper and said, "Let's not discuss such things whilst we're within earshot of everyone. There's an empty booth over there, in the corner."

He might have felt a rush of adrenaline over having been accepted, but the seriousness of her words dulled the sensation. The noise level in the tavern was returning to normal now that the fight was over, and Nyobian humans were notorious for harassing anyone who dared to slander their king in public. Slandering him in private had become something of a national pastime, but King Augustus V still had the sympathy of most of the populace, due in large part to the queen's assassination three years ago. It remained to be seen how long that sympathy would last, but for the moment the man could screw up with relative impunity.

Rufino counted himself among those who liked to make fun of the king, but he liked to make fun of everything else, too. Vampires had little use for politics, so he'd not taken the time to figure out where he actually stood on recent events. All he cared about at the moment was that his mystery woman had agreed to sit down with him. The first battle had been won, but he could still lose the war with ease if he misplayed his cards now. "May I get you a drink?" he attempted to improve his fragile standing. "I can't imagine you came in here for any other reason."

She shrugged again. "I didn't know what to expect," she told him before gesturing toward the bar with her head. "As he already told you, I've never been here before."

The little vampire stopped himself before asking who she meant, but he couldn't stop himself from voicing the second question that came to mind. "How the…?"

She stopped him with an index finger, then used that same finger to brush the hair around one of her ears back just enough to show him a pointed helix, which signified that she possessed some elven blood. He was dimly aware of her pierced lobe, which was surprisingly empty, but it seemed an insignificant observation in lieu of the revelation that her senses were far stronger than he'd given them credit for. He'd have to be extra careful from now on. "I'm sorry," he scrambled to save face, "it didn't occur to me that a woman your height cou…"

She was starting to smile again, which shut him up

as soon as he noticed. "Don't worry," she assured him, "I know as well as anyone that these ears don't show up on this body very often."

She wasn't going to let him off the hook that easily, though. "But what was all that about an Ishiirite priestess?" she poured some salt all over his wound.

Rufino sighed in frustration. "There was a woman in here not long ago," he explained slowly and painfully. "I was apparently the only man in Borallis who didn't know she was a priestess, so I offered to buy her a drink. She didn't know that I didn't know she was a priestess, so she took the drink. Things went downhill from there."

"Is that why your clothes smell like rum?"

Again, truth was the only way out of this one. "Let's just say she returned the beverage rather emphatically," he tried to paint his rum shower in the best possible light. "I didn't mean to make her feel uncomfortable, but if she'd just *told* me what the problem was, things never would have gotten out of hand in the first place. We halflings sometimes forget that it's difficult to find honesty and open communication out here in the big man's world."

It was also difficult to find those qualities in him right now—six years of undeath could make a lying snake out of even the most virtuous. On the off-chance this ridiculous mismatch of a relationship extended beyond a single evening, he promised himself he *was* going to tell her he was a vampire. He didn't know how he was going to do that, or when—he just knew he had no choice. The only way their budding relationship had *any* long-term potential was if she could somehow accept what he really was.

The open and honest part of him knew he had a better chance of getting a dwarf to shave. But he could dream.

"A bottle of peach cider, please," she spoke up once it was clear that his rant was over. "I'll hold the booth for us."

He observed for a moment as the woman claimed the booth. He didn't doubt she'd be able to hold her own seat, but he *was* concerned that some other dude might try to slip into the seat across from her before he could claim it for himself. He barely knew her. Though she'd told him she was a schoolteacher—and she'd responded to political satire, of all things—that told him precious little about what she looked for in men, or if she'd consider upgrading on the fly. Sure, he could give her plenty of eye candy, but if she was one of those material girls, his boat would capsize before he even had a *chance* to sort things out in his head.

He took a few controlled breaths and started back toward the bar. *Calm down, Rufino,* he told himself sternly, *if she was a material girl, she'd almost certainly be wearing earrings.* As a general rule, he tried not to stare a lady's chest until he at least knew her name, but he had stolen a brief look at the conservative but very enticing V-neck of this woman's blouse and did not recall seeing a necklace, either. Maybe *I should take another look,* he decided in good humour, *just to be sure.*

The bartender saw him coming. "Doing better this time?"

"Not a priestess this time," the little vampire answered dryly as he hauled himself up onto the same stool as before.

The man grinned. "You're in luck, then. So what can I getcha?"

Rufino didn't have much money left, so he had to make his own drink a memorable one. "A peach cider for the lady," he requested as he scanned the selection with his eyes. He'd reviewed the bar's arsenal of alcohol earlier, of course, but his mood had improved considerably since then and he was seeing things with a fresh perspective. "And, hmm, and an Arcane Explosion for me," he decided. He didn't know what in the hells an Arcane Explosion was, but it sounded interesting.

"Coming right up."

As he waited for the drinks, his attention fell upon a group of sailors at the end of the bar nearest the stage. They were playing cards, and though Rufino couldn't identify the game from where he sat, it was clear from the outset that they were playing for money. Heavy drinking toasted every victory and washed away every defeat. Conventional wisdom suggested that gambling whilst intoxicated was pure folly, but in the real world, things weren't always so cut and dried. A storm at sea was not something to be tackled whilst sober, lest a man start having second thoughts about his career. Alcohol was the only comfort some of those men had ever known.

And I don't even have that anymore. When Rufino stopped to think about it, his unlife thus far had been bereft of any form of comforting influence. His mobile coffin was the closest thing he had to sanctuary, but even tucked away in there, he was never more than one gnarly wagon wreck away from being barbequed. It was a sorry existence: he had no lovers because they were his primary source of food, no friends because vampires were hunted so relentlessly that they needed to stay hidden even from each other, no family because he was legally dead and they'd probably no longer see him as kin, and no way to dull the emotional pain that he often felt because he was no longer affected by alcohol or drugs.

A handful of absent heartbeats later, his attention was back on the blood-haired woman who'd indulged him thus far. He wanted very much for things to be different this time, but his own fear of failure kept this desire from being any sort of comfort. Already his body was beginning to remind him that feeding time was just around the corner, and already his mind had visualized a dozen different ways in which the woman might freak out upon learning the awful truth about him. The only way he could protect her from the truth was to walk out the front door right now and pretend this had never happened.

But, as was usually the case, taking the easy way out would teach him nothing. In two months he'd be asking himself all the same questions as before, but with one more doozy thrown into the mix: *how could you have been such a bloody wimp?* That whole "protect her from the truth" shtick was naught more than an excuse, and he knew it. She was a big girl—a *really* big girl, in fact. It might take her a long time to get over a sexy vampire like him, but she could probably do it.

And maybe, just *maybe*, she wouldn't have to get over him. Maybe this would somehow work out. He doubted he had more than a snowball's chance in the hells with a woman like this, but as wise men throughout the world were fond of saying: "a slim chance is better than no chance at all."

He was repeating that line to himself, over and over again, when the bartender returned with the drinks. "Just what the doctor ordered!" the man proclaimed with enthusiasm.

Rufino slapped the rest of his money on the counter, save for a few silvers. "Thanks, Doc."

He made it back to the booth without incident. The woman welcomed him back with what started as a warm smile but quickly became a frown when she noticed the second drink. "What's that blue thing?"

Rufino slid the drinks onto the table and then hopped into his seat. "Barkeep called it an Arcane Explosion," he explained, "and curiosity killed the halfling."

The woman stared inquisitively at the hissing blue froth. "What's in it?" she asked.

"No idea," Rufino replied honestly, shrugging and reaching for the mug in one smooth motion, "but I know a good way to find out."

"Hold it," the woman instructed, grabbing the mug with a hand of her own. "This mug is the size of your head—if you try to drink it all yourself, you're going to demonstrate how this thing earned its name." With her right hand, she withdrew a straw from the jar at the far end of the table and dropped it into the mystery beverage. "Let me help you with this… whatever it is."

The little vampire smiled as he leaned against his backrest. Things seemed to be going well. "Help yourself."

Chapter Two

Worst-Case Scenario

Rufino let his date do most of the talking, but since nobody got that tall by hanging out with halflings, he doubted she recognized the significance of his sacrifice. When one of his people gave the verbal reins to someone else, it signified that he either feared for his life or that he was making a desperate effort to impress. It seemed like he'd already made a favourable impression with his creativity, but he had a long way to go yet.

The woman's tale wasn't boring, per se, but her lack of storytelling prowess was evident from the beginning. She taught at the primary level, which was a fortunate thing because she'd probably have to flunk teenage boys at an alarming rate. She hailed from Samradyn—a small human village roughly 160 kilometres to the north of Borallis—and she was here because she didn't want to wait ten years or more for one of Samradyn's two full-time teachers to retire. That sounded perfectly reasonable, though the evidence of her ambition did reignite his concerns over money, and whether his own lack of it would ultimately drive her away.

Perhaps he was looking at this the wrong way. *You should be looking forward to the money issue,* he told himself, *because it's not going to come up until* after *the vampire issue does. If you last long enough to hear the words, "whaddya mean you're broke?" it means you're doing great.*

Such thoughts kept a dopey little grin on his face whilst they conversed. At first, she only seemed interested in determining if their politics were compatible, but after downing half of his Arcane Explosion, her agenda became decidedly sexual. This was not usually a distressing situation for an unattached male to be in, but Rufino was no closer to explaining the *why* behind his own sexual urges than he had been when he'd first laid eyes on this woman. Vampires were supposed to think with their fangs, not their wangs; yet here he was, doing exactly the opposite even though feeding time was just around the corner. It made no bloody sense!

He was still lacking answers by the time the *Squid* closed at 01:00. The only thing he did know for certain was that he *really* liked this woman. Unfortunately, this meant he couldn't allow the seemingly imminent sex scene to play itself out under false pretenses. He had to tell her what he was, and he had to do it *before* she jumped on him. Not only was it the gentlemanly thing to do, but it was the only chance he had of keeping her in his life beyond this one night. If she didn't run screaming to the undead-hunters at the first mention of the word "vampire," he'd tell her what was happening and then ask for her help in determining the why of it all. With a bit of luck, she'd be willing to partake in this very awkward social experiment; with a bit *more* luck, she might decide his tale was incredibly romantic and jump on him anyway.

He wanted to be optimistic, but he also realized it was a darned good thing that he was pulling this stunt in Borallis. In the likely event that she did freak out and force him to flee the country, then hey, there were a bunch of ships not two kilometres away. If he was lucky, he'd end up in a place like Minta Cadra—one of several progressive nations on the other side of the Dakrab Sea to the west. They did things a bit differently in Minta Cadra—and on the continent of Rajatan as a whole—but Rufino was confident he could make the adjustment. He was a *very* adaptable dude when his life was on the line.

It was a splendid night for some neck chomping: the sky was overcast, the dirty streets were all but deserted, and the lighting in this district was dreadful to begin with.

Figures it would be so perfect the one time I'm not interested. "I don't have a room," he explained apologetically, "I usually sleep in my cart." *That may be the first honest thing I've said all evening.* "So I…"

"I have a room," she cut in, "just off the docks." After taking a moment to gather her bearings, she pointed toward a cluster of lights emanating from the small hospitality district just east of the docks. "That way."

"Which way?" Rufino asked, pretending he couldn't see in the dark.

"That way!" the woman insisted.

She took off, paying no mind to the fact that a brisk walk for someone her size was a brisk jog for a halfling. He didn't care, though, for the exercise provided him with a distraction from the difficulties that would soon be upon him. He was *way* too smart for his own good, and seldom was that statement more accurate than at times like this, when the hundred different ways his latest plan could go wrong were all painfully obvious to him. There was nothing more he could do, though— she'd either freak out or she wouldn't, and the former outcome was far more likely than the latter. He could only hope that his feelings for her originated from an instinct of some sort that...

His musings were derailed by the spectacle of his companion misjudging her surroundings and smacking into a lamppost just before an intersection. What was most noticeable was the half-second of lag time between the collision and her reaction to it. He'd given her credit for being reasonably sober thus far—as someone her size should have been after only two drinks—but perhaps her elven blood was more incompatible with alcohol than he realized. Or maybe she just didn't drink often enough to have any tolerance for it.

She was still sober enough to be embarrassed, though. After taking a moment to rub where her right shoulder had collided with the post, she turned to him and said, "Nobody saw that."

There was only one possible response that wouldn't land him in the doghouse. "Saw what?"

She nodded approvingly. "Good man." She then turned and stepped into the crossroads.

"Look out!"

It was probably the first cart to roll through this intersection in half an hour, but there it was; and if not for her reflexive leap backwards in response to his warning, she would have been clobbered by it. But though her inebriated reflexes *had* been up to the challenge of saving her from some serious blunt-force trauma, they weren't up to the challenge of keeping her upright. She fell backwards onto the ground; as she did so, the driver of the speeding cart decided to make his unwanted opinion known. "Watch where you're going, you stupid bitch!" he yelled in passing, either not knowing or not caring that he'd just blown a stop sign.

It was fortunate for the driver that he didn't stop, because Rufino would have delighted in kicking the man's ass for insulting his new girlfriend. As things stood, though, he was impotent—unable to chase down a horse in either of his forms. "You okay?" he approached his date with some concern.

Her reaction was surprising. She wasn't angry; hells, she wasn't even upset. She just broke out laughing, and after a few seconds Rufino joined her, if for no other reason than to lend his support. There was no question about it now: she was drunk. "How about this," he proposed after a moment, "I'll flush out the traps, and you just tell me where to go."

After reining in her hysterics, the accident magnet heaved an exaggerated sigh, then looked at her companion and smiled. "I like the way you think."

They made it to her inn of choice without further

incident, though Rufino did make a point of stumbling once or twice over objects that he could see perfectly well. The woman may not have been in much of a condition to notice his fine performance, but he had no intention of dropping his act until they were away from prying eyes and ears. *It's not paranoia when everyone wants you dead,* he often told himself.

Her lodging of choice was small—only sixteen suites on two floors—but it was a pretty nice place: the windows were intact, the graffiti had been painted over, and the flowers in the garden were still alive. Luxuries like these cost a premium in Borallis, which suggested that the woman was at least fairly well off, but Rufino had no energy to waste on money concerns right now. He'd never believed he would part with his deepest and darkest secret of his own free will, but here he was, seconds away from doing just that. Hopefully it would somehow be worth it.

The woman seemed to sense his unease, because she turned to face him upon reaching the door to her second-floor room. "Don't worry," she attempted to soothe him as she removed her cloak and draped it over one shoulder, "I don't bite."

That was an awe-inspiring choice of words, under the circumstances. "I'm not worried about you," he told her in a voice that sounded just as awful as he felt. "Not about you as a person, anyway."

She turned the key and pushed her door open. "Then what *are* you worried about? Your apprehension is written all over your face."

His resolve faltered, but only briefly. Yes, he was scared of the coming few minutes, but he was terrified of how the rest of his life would play out if he took the coward's way out now. "I need to tell you something about me," he choked out with considerable difficulty, "and you aren't going to like it."

"Oh, gods," she cursed somewhat lightheartedly,

"your name's Bubba, isn't it?"

In spite of himself, the little vampire smiled as he stepped past her into the room. The floor plan was that of a perfect square, and it wasn't very big, but the furniture had been arranged to make efficient use of the space, and the air carried the scent of roses. With two of the candles on the overhead four-point chandelier lit, Rufino could see that there was actually a rose sitting on the desk to his left. This came as no surprise whatsoever—just as the conditions outside had been all but ideal for feeding, so too were these conditions perfect for a steamy sex scene with the most desirable woman he'd ever met. Carnal paradise was his for the taking, and all it would cost him was his one chance for a brighter future. *Someone up there is having a good laugh at my expense.* "No, it's Rufino," he told her, painfully, as he looked around. "Rufino Endicott," he spoke his birth name for the first time in six years, reaffirming his resolve to come clean with this woman. "What's yours?"

She shut the door softly behind her and applied both of the locks. "Kiralyn," she responded casually.

But there was nothing casual about the fear that had suddenly wrapped itself around his dead heart. "Carolyn?" he asked, hoping he'd heard wrong.

"No," the woman corrected him decisively, "Kiralyn."

This was not good at all. "Keira Lynn?" the besieged vampire took one last shot in the dark.

"No," she repeated with razor-sharp enunciation, "Kiralyn."

And just like that, Rufino was in deep trouble. Kiralyn was a very uncommon name, but it was a name that everyone in this country had heard at least once. There existed a community of druids within the borders of Nyobi, and their most infamous member—by far—was a rare sorceress who called herself Kiralyn Frostwhisper. She'd only been on the scene for three years or so, but in that short time she'd established herself as Nyobi's Most Wanted—*ostensibly* for multiple counts of attempted murder. But this was where the story got intriguing. The reward for her capture was *fifteen million* gold coins, which was a *ridiculously* high bounty for her relatively minor rap sheet. The country's previous record-setting bounty had been less than half that size, and *that* bounty had been for a cold-blooded serial murderer and demonologist whose body count was longer than the castle's servant roster.

One of the rumours floating about the country was that the sorceress was an elite spy who got her kicks from exposing the ethical and financial corruption of the upper classes. When one stopped to consider the societal landscape of Nyobi at the moment, this particular rumour made a lot of sense. There was an industrial revolution taking place, which gave the upper classes a golden opportunity to expand upon their already-ludicrous wealth. To do so, however, they had to deal with a bunch of anti-industry druids who—thanks to Frostwhisper—suddenly had more teeth than they'd enjoyed in a long time. It seemed quite obvious that a bunch of her potential targets had collaborated to post her astronomical bounty. Rufino didn't know if those people actually expected someone to catch her or if they only wanted the bounty hunters to keep her off their backs, but he would have bet money that it was one or the other.

Whatever the plan was, it hadn't worked. In addition to being one of the major players in the world of Nyobian politics, Kiralyn was also one of the country's biggest mysteries. Nobody seemed to know anything about her background, and the many descriptions of her appearance often failed to agree with one another. Unfortunately, in spite of the lack of corroborating evidence, Rufino had a *very* nasty feeling that he was dealing with the genuine article. He'd never heard anything about Frostwhisper being a half-elf, but reports of her being approximately six feet tall were pretty consistent. More telling than that, though, was the fact that she didn't seem to be drunk anymore—druids were famous for being able to cleanse bloodstreams. This ability was typically used to remove poison, but Rufino had little doubt that it worked against alcohol as well.

That meant he was dead. The mantra of the druids was to protect nature from mankind's interference, and since vampirism was man-made, it fell well within their self-appointed jurisdiction. "Nice knowing you," he bid her a hasty farewell as he pulled a hard 180 and made for the door.

His escape route had a critical flaw, though, in that he had to go through the druid-sorceress to reach that door. She made no discernible effort to obstruct him as he scooted past, but before he could even start to wonder about that, she dashed his remaining hope by encasing the door's chain lock in a small block of ice. His only way out of this room now was to jump through the closed window, and since they were on the top floor, it would be a coin-flip as to whether he'd even survive the fall.

"Not so fast, *art merchant*," the wolf in sheep's clothing drove a stake through his heart with her words, "we need to have a little chat."

In that moment, for possibly the first time in his life, his mind blanked, and he just stared at the frozen door lock in paralyzed terror. He was dimly aware that he wasn't helping his own cause by doing nothing, but *nothing* seemed to be about all he *could* do. He couldn't run, and he certainly couldn't fight—he was powerless against even an ordinary druid. The fact that it was Frostwhisper herself was just so much overkill.

After ten seconds, however, it started to dawn on him that he wasn't dead yet. *We need to have a little chat,* she'd said. Conversation was good. He suspected she just wanted to gloat a bit before finishing him off, but if there was a way to talk oneself out of a death trap, a wily halfling could usually find it. "If you wanted to place an order," he choked out as well as he could, "you could have just waited until standard business hours."

The woman was somewhere behind him now, though it was anyone's guess as to where. He had no recollection of the room's layout, which served as evidence that he was still a little stunned. "I was wondering," her unassuming voice broke the silence again, "about that shipment of yours from Agnarach."

Rufino blinked a few times in confusion. Was it possible she hadn't yet figured out what he was? "What about it?"

"How long since you last met with your contact?"

The little vampire collected his wits and turned to face the sorceress. She was standing in the middle of the room, just in front of the bed, with her arms folded across her chest and her weight slightly on her left side. Her expression was perfectly neutral, betraying absolutely nothing—the polar opposite of the exuberant woman he'd spent the evening with thus far. "Not long," he replied, his mind scrambling to come up with a believable lie. Agnarach was two weeks away in a fast ship, so… "Maybe five weeks ago. Why?"

The woman averted her eyes. "Well, there's the first problem," she said with a sigh before looking back down at him. "Nyobi's ports have been closed to Agnaran ships for the last two months, so," she paused for a second to shake her head, "you didn't meet with an Agnaran merchant five weeks ago."

"That shifty bastard," Rufino tried to hide his fear with an indignant snarl. "Where do you think he's from?"

She smiled, but though it *was* the same smile he'd thought was so beautiful five minutes ago, it wasn't the same. It wasn't the same at all. "If I had to guess," Kiralyn replied coolly, "I'd say he's from somewhere between your left ear and your right ear."

Lucky guess. "Well, no point in my hanging around Borallis, then," he suggested as casually as he could, which wasn't very. "If you'll unfreeze this lock, I'll be on my way."

Kiralyn looked away and tilted her head again. Unless his memory was totally failing him, that was the precise gesture she'd used before lowering the boom on him a few seconds ago. "Well, that brings us to our second problem," she declared with another theatrical sigh. "When I realized you were lying to me, it made me wonder why. There's always a reason, you know."

Rufino *really* didn't like where this was going. "So, what, you're the one woman in the world who can't believe a man is lying just to get into her pants?"

She smirked, knowingly. "That's exactly what I did believe, at first," she admitted. "It wouldn't have been the first time." Her smirk then pulled a vanishing act. "I was almost right, too, because you definitely wanted me—just not the part I thought you wanted." She presented two of her fingers, held together, for him to scrutinize, then she placed them on the right side of her neck as if to measure her own pulse. *Shit.* "Seventy-two," she reported her heart rate after five seconds. "What's yours?"

She knew, all right, and not even a wily halfling could talk his way out of this one. His mind frozen once again, he fell silent, and after a moment the druid-sorceress tired of waiting for a comeback. "You're good, vampire," she made her discovery official, "but I'm better."

So there was to be some gloating, then. Fine—she could be that way if she wanted, but he was determined not to give her the satisfaction of seeing him break. Halfling men were the smallest, slowest, and weakest humanoid men on the planet, so they'd long since figured out how to cope with being taunted and ridiculed. "Do you always play with your prey before you kill it?" he filled his voice with as much conviction as he could muster. "They call that cruelty in some parts of the world."

"And rightly so," she agreed.

She fell silent again, leaving the little vampire to wonder what in the hells was going on. "So you're saying you're a cruel person, then?" he demanded in frustration. "Cut the mind games and get this over with."

She shook her head slowly. "No, I don't think I can follow those instructions," she screwed with his head some more. Then, after letting him stew for another brief moment, she spoke again. "You see, I didn't bring you up here to kill you."

The first glimmer of hope wormed its way back into his dead heart, but after being duped so easily, he was far from willing to just take her word for it. "Is that right?" he put voice to his skepticism.

"Could I make that up?"

That was an easy one. "Do fish swim?" he retorted with an emphatic snort.

The sorceress opened her mouth to respond, but nothing came out for a moment as she appeared to rethink her response. "Okay, I could," she admitted with grace as she took a seat at the foot of the bed, "but if there's one thing you should know about me before we proceed, it's that the unbelievable will be true more often than you think. I have a proposition for you."

The delivery of her last sentence was so casual that Rufino almost missed it completely. He didn't know what to make of this unexpected development, but the words "kinky vampiric fantasy" did spring to mind. Here he was, trapped in an intimate bedroom with a vampire-hunter who just happened to be gorgeous, and now he was being *propositioned*. What could such a woman possibly want from him, other than his outrageous sex appeal? "Oh, really?" he replied, his voice full of suspicion but his mind full of steamy images.

As it turned out, though, life wasn't a kinky vampiric fantasy. "My people have a job we need done," the druidess explained matter-of-factly, "a job we don't want traced back to us."

The little vampire let out the breath he hadn't realized he'd been holding. Suddenly this was all starting to make sense. "A murder," he concluded out loud.

She immediately shook her head. "An *execution*," she corrected him before he could get his hopes up, "for crimes committed against the land."

"Like what, littering?" the retort just kind of dribbled out before he could stop himself.

Kiralyn didn't seem certain how to react to that. She started by rolling her eyes, followed that by looking up at the ceiling, then she finally settled on burying her face in her left palm and shaking her head slowly. Under other circumstances, he might have apologized for the cheap shot, but this time he figured she deserved it for letting him assume the worst for so long.

She needed only a few seconds to collect herself, at which point she favoured him with a sort of cynical sneer. "So you think we want to kill everyone who cuts down a tree, is that it?"

Rufino hesitated briefly. Her accusation was incorrect, but he didn't want to allow her to put him any more on the defensive than he already was. "Your reputation does precede you," he riposted after some careful consideration.

She merely lifted her eyebrows. "You grew up in Galensdorf, did you not?" she asked.

It wasn't really a question. Galensdorf, located in east-central Nyobi—about five hundred kilometres to the north-northeast of Borallis—was the only halfling village in the country. It was an agricultural community—the greatest in the land, since halflings were closer to the dirt than anyone—and it was the home of nearly all of the country's four thousand halflings. If one fancied some good food and some splendid arguments, there was nary a better place to find either. "Sure," he admitted with pride, "why?"

Kiralyn wasted no time. "Are you aware of the relationship between your community and mine?" she asked. "We're able to se…"

"Oh, no you don't," the son of Galensdorf cut her off rather courageously. He waggled a finger at her for emphasis before going on to say, "This isn't about random druids predicting the weather for a bunch of farmers." He then pointed his active finger directly at her. "This is about one *specific* druid. This is about a woman who's already wanted for attempted murder, for whom violence seems to be the rule, not the exception. Ho…"

Now it was her turn to interrupt him. "It never ceases to amaze me how readily people gobble up every morsel of misinformation the king puts out there. I expected better of you after all that talk of activism earlier." She stood up and walked over to the large rectangular window. "Do you want to hear my version of the 'attempted murder' story, or are you content to wallow in your ignorance?"

Getting a little defensive, are we? "You've been lying to me all evening," he reminded her with the delicacy of a rhinoceros. "Why should I trust anything you tell me now?"

"You shouldn't," she replied immediately without turning to face him. "Do you want to hear my side or not?"

Rufino blinked a couple of times. *That was an interesting response.* Either she was lying again and he *should* trust her, or she was telling the truth and contradicting herself by doing so. Either way… "Sure," he decided, "but you can skip the stuff I already know about. Westbrook Lumber Co. tried to deploy some steam-powered 'shredder' machines at the old Brayton Ranch near the south-western tip of your forest, but they were stopped rather forcefully by a female druid who's since become a household name in this part of the world."

She nodded, though she still didn't turn to face him. "That's all true," she admitted softly, "but it's just a fragment of the complete story. When I first arrived at the Brayton Ranch, I delivered an ultimatum on behalf of my people: Westbrook could either remove their shredders from protected lands, or they could watch me turn their machines into scrap. I gave them forty-eight hours to obtain the authorization they needed in order to withdraw." She took a slow breath and finally turned to face him again. "When I returned two days later, the shredders hadn't moved; and when I demanded an explanation from the foreman, I was promptly attacked by five men wielding two-by-fours."

Rufino winced. "Not exactly my weapon of choice against a mage."

"No one knew I was a sorceress at the time," she reminded him. "Anyway, the brutes with the boards never had a chance against my magical shield, so I was content to let them whale on it until they exhausted themselves. The foreman then attacked me verbally, and for the next several minutes, we just stood there screaming at each other. When I heard the words, 'I don't recognize your authority, you ignorant bitch,' for about the tenth time, I decided enough was enough and told him in return that I didn't care if he recognized my authority or not. I then walked over to the nearest shredder and began the process of turning it into molten slag. Unbeknownst to me at the time, the machine was manned, which is where the attempted murder charges come from."

"Remind me never to piss you off."

Kiralyn took her seat at the foot of the bed again. "It was the disrespect that upset me more than anything else," she went on. "Druids have been the caretakers of this land for over ten thousand years—since long before the political body of Nyobi even *existed.* Now we're supposed to surrender our charge because some self-important royal wants to claim land that does not belong to him?" She shook her head slowly. "Over my dead body."

Rufino didn't want to comment about the political situation, so he decided to see if there was a way he could use her words to his own advantage. "You make it sound like you're in a battle for your very lives," he suggested.

"We are," she told him. "In the long term, we are."

Just the response he'd expected. "Okay, so how is your struggle for survival any different from my own?"

"The difference is what's in our hearts," she was quick to reply. "We seek to preserve the natural order of things, whereas you only seek to preserve yourself."

The little vampire favoured her with a sardonic smile. "Maybe you shouldn't be so quick to knock self-preservation. You are, after all, counting on that very trait to make me go along with this scheme of yours."

She sat up a little straighter. "I don't negotiate like that. You can say no and still walk out of here; you simply won't get a second chance to turn this particular enemy into an ally."

He wanted to believe her—he really did—but it was impossibly difficult to trust someone who was as skilled at deception as Kiralyn. "Tell me about this person," he stalled for time to think. "Who is he? What did he do?"

"You don't need to know his name yet," she cleverly reinforced her story that she intended to let him go if he said no, "but I can tell you that he's responsible for the negligent slaughter of tens of thousands of animals by ignoring every single guideline we've laid out in regard to sustainable logging. He's been issued warnings on four separate occasions, and his defiance has gotten measurably worse in response. Our complaints to the king have likewise gotten us nowhere, so the arch-druids have decided that our only remaining option is to take the offender out. Quietly."

Rufino wondered how many times she'd rehearsed those lines in front of a mirror. "Correct me if I'm wrong, Kira, but your people have never been all that reluctant to do their own dirty work. Why the secrecy this time?"

"You don't need to know that, either," she further demonstrated how bloody irritating she could be. "The less you know, the less you can reveal if you're caught."

The argument made sense, but what she didn't realize was how much he already knew. "Might it have something to do with the diplomatic games your people are constantly playing with the king?" he asked without really asking. "You know: you druids end up on his shit-list for whatever reason, he issues the appropriate threats, you pretend to cower in horror for a while so he can feel all high and mighty, then you do one of your good deeds and all is officially forgiven until the cycle begins anew. We're in the threatening and cowering part of the cycle, aren't we?"

The druidess shrugged, as though she didn't have a clue what he was rambling on about. But she did, and they both knew it. "Yet this mission must be of critical importance," he filled in the blanks with confidence, "because we wouldn't be having this scintillating conversation otherwise."

She remained silent, but it made no difference—he'd seen the superiority of his bargaining position and now he was going to milk it for all it was worth. "You know, for such an important mission, you sure aren't offering very much."

"Excuse me?"

Rufino could feel the temperature in the room cool a few degrees as she challenged his assertion. "Your offer is basically for druids to turn a blind eye to my activities," he spelled it out slowly, "but I've been a vampire for almost six years now, and this is the very first time I've run afoul of your kind. There's no guarantee that I'll ever bump into one again."

She lifted her eyebrows again, though he had to believe she was doing it deliberately—a good spy was always in control of such things. "It only takes one," she pointed out ominously. "Are you really so willing to gamble with your life?"

Rufino smiled a little as the argument came together inside his mind. "I gamble with my life every time I leave my coffin, babe," he informed her with a snort. "That's not going to change if one small group of people decides to stop looking for me." He took a deep breath and braced himself for what promised to be a difficult sell. "Now, I *am* willing to help, but I won't do it for less than a *legitimate* quality of life upgrade."

Kiralyn responded by standing up and folding her arms across her chest. "You're in no position to be making demands, vampire," she tried to intimidate him.

"Oh, I think I am," he corrected her with the unbridled glee of a halfling who knew he was winning. "You see, vampires are *rare*," he lowered the boom without mercy. "I've heard it said there are seldom more than a couple dozen of us in Nyobi at any given time. How long do you think it'll take you to find another one? Weeks? *Months*, perhaps?"

She didn't respond, so he kept going. "And while you're doing all that unnecessary searching, your dangerous offender will be hard at work. How high do you think the body count will go before..."

"How much?"

Rufino winced. The druid may well have recognized the disadvantaged position she was in, but convincing her of that was the easy part. The tough part was coming up right now. "You may not believe this," he began, "but…"

"You're right," she cut in rather abrasively, "I

don't."

That was not entirely unexpected, but Rufino pretended to be hurt all the same. "How do you know?" he demanded indignantly. "You don't even know what I was going to say."

"I don't need to," she retorted immediately. "You've been lying all evening, just as I was. The validity of your current argument doesn't change that."

He couldn't deny it, so he didn't bother trying. "No, it doesn't," he agreed, "but it *pains* me to think about all the time you'll waste trying to find deception in this honest request."

"It may not take as much time as you think."

Rufino smiled. "Let's find out, shall we?" He braced himself again. "I don't want money, and I don't want blood. What I *do* want is a second date. I..."

"*What?!*"

The look of stunned disbelief on her face was everything he'd imagined it would be. "A date," he repeated, though he was certain it wasn't necessary. "How can you be deaf with ears like those?"

Kiralyn took a moment to gather her thoughts. "Let me get this straight," she pondered aloud as she returned her attention to him. "You want me to believe that you *like* me?"

Rufino grinned and nodded earnestly. "What's unbelievable is what's true around here, remember?"

Kiralyn didn't respond verbally, but she did throw her arms in the air before dropping back onto her seat at the foot of the bed with one of those "why me?" expressions on her face. "Oh, come on," he half-argued, half-teased in response, "this can't be the first time you've heard something like this."

"Oh, I've heard it many times," she admitted, "but it's seldom been spoken to *me.* You see, the person you liked doesn't exist."

The little vampire blinked a few times in surprise. “Sure she does,” he argued, his arms outstretched toward her, “she’s sitting right here in front of me.”

“Don’t be naive,” she scolded him with a renewed edge in her voice. “It was a persona—I have twenty others just like it. You don’t know the real me, and you don’t *want* to know the real me.”

Anyone who’d once been a halfling child had a saying: “if your parents tell you there’s nothing good inside the cupboard, there’s something good inside the cupboard.” Kiralyn obviously didn’t have much experience with his people, else she’d not have attempted to deter him in such an ineffective manner. “With all due respect,” he smiled sweetly before putting on his best hard-bargaining look, “that’s my call. Unless you’d *rather* I walk away and forget this whole thing?”

She didn’t react, verbally or otherwise, but she didn’t have to. The pot had been called, and her cards sucked. “Something unprecedented happened to me tonight, and you’re going to help me understand the why of it.” He paused for a second to take a deep breath, not knowing what to expect of the coming moments. “That’s my condition—my very reasonable and non-negotiable condition. Take it or leave it.”

Her response was anticlimactic. “I’ll take it,” she told him as she stood up again.

Rufino blinked a few more times in surprise. “You’ll what?”

“You heard me,” she retorted confidently.

It was fortunate he didn’t have elven ears, else he got the distinct impression she’d have thrown his earlier remark back at him in full. “Yeah, I guess I did,” he admitted as he scratched the top of his head. “I just wasn’t expecting you to surrender so easily.”

She just shrugged. “Your condition was acceptable. We’ll be spending a few days together anyway, so there’s no reason we can't kill two birds with one stone."

That wasn't really an expression he would have expected a druid to use. What was more bothersome, though, was her assumption that his objective could be resolved in only a few days—he wasn't at all certain that his persistent attraction to something so life-threatening could be explained so quickly. "What if a few days isn't enough time?" he demanded.

"A few days should be plenty," she was casually confident. "It usually takes me only a few seconds to figure out why a man is looking at me."

He didn't doubt that, but he also didn't believe it was relevant. "In case you hadn't noticed, Kira," he said with a smile, "I'm not a 'man' anymore. I'm asking you to help me figure out why a *vampire* would be having such feelings."

"To bail himself out of what he thinks is a life-threatening situation, perhaps?"

So she hasn't conceded anything after all. "If I wanted to do that," he murmured under his breath, "I could have just smiled and nodded in all the appropriate places."

"You could have," she agreed as she folded her arms across her chest once more, "but I'd have been suspicious all the same." She paused for a brief moment before continuing. "You aren't going to earn my trust with words, vampire—I spend too much time around nobles to take *anything* at face value. If you want me to believe you're serious about any of this, you have no choice but to help me. Now, are you in, or are you out?"

Rufino sighed. As much as he hated to admit it, she was right to mistrust him, as he was equally right to be suspicious of her. Words alone could not build a bridge between historical enemies—it took hard work and sacrifice to make any meaningful difference. It also took a good deal of faith, because there was never a guarantee that the other side would reciprocate. *Someone* needed to take that leap of faith, and Rufino decided that someone was going to be him. He could always change his mind later if it felt like the goodwill was only flowing in one direction. "I'm in," he put a note of finality into his voice. "I don't like what you want me to do, but I'm in."

She turned and took a few steps toward the window. "None of us like it, Rufino," she told him, using his name for the first time, "but these are desperate times. If you could see the world through my eyes for even a day, you'd understand why these regrettable measures are sometimes necessary."

There didn't seem to be much to say to that. He understood more than she gave him credit for, but he wasn't about to show her all of his cards until it was in his own best interests to do so. "Where are we going?"

She didn't turn to face him. "I'm going to assume you know where Tundora is, since it's not far from your old home. How long will it take you to travel from here to there?"

Tundora was a logging town on the eastern edge of Feybourne Forest, about four hundred kilometres to the north-northeast of Borallis. He could cover that distance in four and a half summer nights, but the travel time wasn't what was foremost on his mind. "Wait a minute," he demanded, "we're not going together?"

She turned to face him again and shook her head. "No—I have a meeting to attend between now and then, and we don't have an extra seat. You may consider this your first test: if you're there when you say you'll be there, you will have earned some trust. If you're a no-show, th..."

"Yeah, yeah," Rufino really didn't want to listen to threats. "Trust me: I'd much rather be your boyfriend than your enemy. Give me..."

She buried her head in her left palm and shook her head slowly. "Give me 'til the eighteenth and I'll be there," he continued. "I might even wash my hair."

With a visible effort, Kiralyn removed her palm from her face. "There's an establishment called the *Killer Cocktail* in the heart of Tundora's commercial district," she explained. "If you're there at 22:00 on the eighteenth, I promise I will not care if your hair is dirty or not." She then appeared to scrutinize it briefly. "Do you wash it often?"

The little vampire shook his head. "I don't sweat anymore, so there's seldom a need."

She exhaled through her nose for a short moment, then pinched a few strands of her own hair and held them up where she could see them. "Must be nice," she murmured.

If Rufino hadn't known better, he would've sworn he was looking at the schoolteacher from Samradyn again. "No, it isn't," he disagreed, at which point he fell silent until he had her undivided attention. "I'll admit there are one or two really cool things about being what I am, but I'd give those things up in a second if it meant getting my old life back."

Kiralyn didn't respond to that, but after a moment she did dispel the block of ice that she'd placed over the chain lock. "You're leaving?" he asked.

"There doesn't seem to be anything left to say," the sorceress replied softly as she walked past him to the room's only exit. Before leaving, though, she found something to say after all. "I can't give you your old life back," she told him slowly, "but I *can* help you make something of the one you still have."

She paused again, her hand on the door handle, as her captive audience stared weakly up at her face. At her beautiful face that at first he'd adored, then feared, and was now somewhere in between. "*Killer Cocktail*; eighteenth; 22:00," she made sure there was no room for error. "I'll be waiting."

At that, she opened the door and left, shutting it softly behind her.

Rufino stared at the closed door for a long minute thereafter as a strange combination of relief and regret pervaded his mind—relief because she was gone; regret for the very same reason. This wasn't exactly what he'd had in mind when he'd gotten it in his head to start a new relationship, but it was too late to back out now. *You bloody idiot,* he sighed to himself. *Of all the women in the land to develop a crush on, you choose* that *one. Unbelievable.*

He couldn't deny his feelings, though, as much as he might like to—there was something about Kiralyn that he found absolutely irresistible. He just didn't know what that something was. Fortunately, his course of action was relatively clear, even if his feelings were not—there was only one way he would ever learn what, exactly, had happened to him this evening. "Okay, Kiralyn," he whispered into the silence, "I'll meet you in Tundora," he paused to take a deep breath, "but I won't show up unprepared."

There was little time to waste. He left Borallis in his own flight form, hoping to find some shelter before sunrise. It wasn't imperative that he find some—he could build himself a little shelter in the dirt if need be—but it would be nice if he could catch a snooze in his humanoid form. He didn't get to do that very often.

Before leaving town, however, he chomped the neck of a passed-out drunk in one of Borallis' many back alleys. The man's blood tasted like glue, but it was better than nothing. Besides, the last two women he'd crossed paths with had been an Ishiirite priestess and a druid-sorceress—if *that* wasn't a sign that he should steer clear of women for the next few days, he didn't know what was.

With that thought in mind, the manblood didn't taste so bad. As paste went, it was actually pretty palatable, though it could have used some salt.

Chapter Three
The Road Less Travelled

Rufino had his work cut out for him. It was within his ability to cover roughly ninety kilometres per night at this time of year, but it would be thirsty work—finding a nice, juicy neck to chomp wasn't going to be easy in the middle of nowhere. To make matters worse, if he *did* find a neck, it would probably belong to a dude since not many of the wandering merchants were women. *Bleh.*

He didn't find a cave on that first night, but he did stumble upon something that was almost as good: an abandoned cavity in the side of a large tree, perhaps forty feet off the ground. If a cave was a luxury resort, a north-facing tree cavity was a comfortable apartment with a nice view. If the undead-hunters wanted to find him up *here*, they'd have to start climbing trees, which was no mean feat in the heavy armour they usually wore.

He still would have preferred a cave, though, if for no other reason than because they were often inhabited by bears. Resorts needed bouncers, after all, and who better to fill that role than a half-ton grizzly bear? Maybe a dragon, but if they weren't extinct by now, they were only hanging on by a thread. They'd charge too much for their services, anyway.

As Rufino made his way across the Spyglass Plains—the vast swath of grassland that separated the southern coast of Nyobi from Feybourne Forest—during his second night of travel, he found his thoughts dominated by a single soul-searching question: *why in the hells am I flying halfway across Nyobi for a secret rendezvous with the most dangerous druid in all of Vendraca?* Now that the adrenaline rush from meeting the infamous Kiralyn Frostwhisper had worked its way out of his system, flying to Tundora didn't seem like such a brilliant idea. The sensible course of action, he knew, was to leave the country altogether.

He was usually one to do what was sensible, but there was one thing that was keeping him from stowing away aboard a boat to Anywhere But Nyobi in this case, and that one thing was fear. Kiralyn was frightening, yes, but what was *more* frightening was his belief that the surge of humanity he'd experienced in her presence might never happen again. For all he knew, this could be the only chance he'd ever get to break his endless cycle of isolation. He couldn't count on being able to meet someone else because he simply no longer saw women—or men, for that matter—as he had before his conversion. There had been comfort in that certainty, as damning as it may have been.

Now he wasn't certain of anything. His infatuation with the druid-sorceress was not so severe as to blind him to the coming dangers, but he didn't see that he had any way out of this. The day a man said "no" to a chance for a brighter future was the day he signed his own death certificate. Rufino wasn't ready to do that just yet.

That being said, the opinion he'd given Kiralyn about vampirism had been an honest one. He believed in making the most of the cards he'd been dealt, but if given the choice, he'd swap his flight form for some more hair in an instant. Having to choose between mohawk or skinhead was a gruesome fate for one who thought of the words "hairy bastard" as high praise. If he ever saw the vampire who'd chomped *his* neck again, he'd have some extremely choice words to say about her timing.

It wasn't just the hair, though—it was also the crushing weight of the secret he was forced to carry. He couldn't let anyone know what he really was, lest he bring a firestorm of fear and hatred down upon his head. Yes, he did need to drink human blood to survive, but having one's neck chomped was not exactly an undeath sentence. It took twelve hours for the vampiric virus to overwhelm a normal person's immune system, and during those twelve hours, the virus could be defeated by the intervention of a divine healer, a nature healer, or even a skilled alchemist. Wielders of nature magic were rare and mistrusted, but priests and clerics were as common as dirt in every town larger than a fruit stand, so within city walls there was very little to fear from vampires.

Loathing was easier than understanding, though, so vampires had to remain hidden from civilization if they wanted to survive. This should have been a simple task because a vampire looked just like a humanoid whilst in humanoid form and just like a bat whilst in bat form, but certain folks—paladins, undead-hunters and druids—were capable of sensing even disguised undead creatures if they got close enough. The effective range of this undead-sense was a closely guarded secret, so Rufino didn't know exactly when Kiralyn had pegged him as a neck-chomper, but he couldn't dismiss the possibility that she'd known what she was looking at right from the get-go. *That* was an unsettling thought, for it meant his whole hide-in-plain-sight strategy could be blown to the hells by a casual glance from the wrong person.

Unfortunately for paladins and other holy warriors, the higher forms of undead creatures could sense *them* in return and flee before any unpleasantness could transpire. The king's undead-hunters couldn't be detected in this manner because they were just ordinary soldiers with extra training, but since they almost always wore armour, Rufino had a very obvious countermeasure: dodge anyone in armour. It wasn't the most courageous of strategies, but it was wonderfully effective.

Then there were the bloody druids. From a vampire's perspective, the only good thing about druids was that they were few in numbers. They were neither good nor evil, so sensing abilities didn't work on them; and they wore no standardized garments, so they were all but impossible to pick out of a crowd. Rufino hadn't suspected Kiralyn at *all* until she'd told him straight up who she was, and even *then* he hadn't completely believed her until he'd realized she'd gone from drunk to sober in two seconds flat.

She wasn't the first druid he'd laid eyes on—they dropped by Galensdorf with helpful advice from time to time—but she *was* the first one he'd actually met. Curse his rotten vampiric luck that his first tree-hugger would turn out to be this one. He couldn't be too hard on himself, though—he'd heard several different descriptions of Kiralyn Frostwhisper, and none of them had drawn a picture of the actual woman. She was *supposed* to have white hair, light-blue eyes, a fanatical disposition, terrible table manners, and a willingness to turn anyone who beat her at chess into a frog. Tavern gossip wasn't always accurate by any stretch of the imagination, but it was usually closer to the mark than this.

To be fair, the blood-red hair and emerald-green eyes of the woman he'd met could have been fakes, but he'd argue that it was more likely the *white*-haired look was the disguise. Did it not make sense that Nyobi's Most Wanted would disguise herself whenever she intended to drop her real name in public? Of course it did. The real question was: would she bother with another disguise when all she wanted was to buy a drink at the *Squid*?

Maybe. *Arrgghhh...*

There was little distraction from these thoughts to be found in the Spyglass Plains. The little vampire couldn't see all that well in his bat form, so he relied upon his echolocation to get him from A to B without bumping into things. Echolocation was, without doubt, a useful ability, but it did have its weaknesses, not the least of which was that it was exceptionally difficult for his ears to "see" the difference between dead grass and a dirt road. For this reason, he maintained an altitude of only ten feet—he did want to follow the road for as long as it was reasonable to do so. He'd never been very good at using the stars to navigate, so he needed landmarks—not only to keep his compass properly calibrated, but also to reassure himself that he was still making forward progress. Vampire or no, he was still very much a halfling, and halflings *hated* it when nothing interesting was happening.

His bat form also had some difficulty differentiating between dim light and total darkness, which necessitated that he shift forms periodically to ensure that dawn wasn't sneaking up on him. This was another reason that he preferred low-level flight when he wasn't in a city. His sense of time was extremely good, but when the penalty for being wrong was death, it made a person want to err on the side of caution.

He couldn't depend on locating a convenient cave or tree in the middle of the Plains, so his second night of travel came to an end roughly forty-five minutes before sunrise so that he could dig himself a protective shelter. A tunnel in the dirt didn't offer the glamour and comfort of a cave resort or a tree hotel, but after flying for eight hours straight, Rufino could have slept comfortably on a cushion of thumb tacks. Within minutes of completing his shelter, he was fast asleep.

***

Shortly after abandoning his shelter at the beginning of his third night of travel, the little vampire decided he was going to make a quick stop in Samradyn. The town was more or less along his intended route anyway, and there was something he needed to know before this madness went any further.

Samradyn was located roughly equidistant between the northern edge of the Spyglass Plains and the southern edge of Feybourne Forest, and only a few kilometres west of the highway Rufino was following. The town had been constructed in a concentric manner: city hall and the other government buildings comprised the geographic centre of town; a commercial district fully encircled the administrative district, and two distinct residential districts comprised the town's perimeter. Not a single building was over two storeys high, but what the architecture lacked in technical prowess, it made up for in aesthetic splendour. No two buildings were exactly alike—each one had been personally designed by either the original resident or proprietor as appropriate, with assistance from the town architect. Naturally, the buildings had been decorated over time, but there had clearly been a communal focus in this individualization because the designs and paint schemes complemented each other very well. The result was a town as beautiful, in its own way, as the renowned elven cities of Sylvany and Aelvehir in northern Nyobi.

He wasn't here for the scenery, though. This place had been Kiralyn's cover story, and it had been a damned seductive cover story, at that. He needed to clear his head, and he figured this was the best place to do it. Here, where he could separate the truth from the lies.

Of particular interest to Rufino was the schoolhouse, or perhaps the schoolhouses, since there were two residential districts. The druid-spy had spoken of her "former job" in considerable detail, and now it was time to see how much thought she put into her masquerades. He could decide how to proceed once he had some verified information in hand.

Fortunately, schoolhouses weren't difficult to spot, even at midnight. Within five minutes, he'd found the first site, in what appeared to be the nicer of the two residential districts. He doubted there were any truly wealthy people in a town like this, but one could find income disparity anywhere.

Kiralyn had been very specific: there were two full-time teachers plus one substitute teacher who doubled as a tutor in Samradyn. At first glance, Rufino could believe this part of the story was true. The schoolhouse was smaller than some of the nearby private residences—single storey, one entrance, maybe two rooms. He also noticed that the schoolhouse and the surrounding homes were all made of wood—there wasn't a brick building within his line of sight. Samradyn was undeniably beautiful, but he imagined the local firefighters had some complaints about the place.

All that remained now was to find the other half of the puzzle. Within ten minutes, he'd located the other schoolhouse, which was situated in the heart of the less-affluent residential district. One would have expected this schoolhouse to be a bit larger than its counterpart—seeing as how the majority of the populace lived on this side of town—but in fact the reverse was true. This was a genuine, old-fashioned, one-room schoolhouse, smaller than Rufino's own schoolhouse in Galensdorf had been. *How do they expect kids to learn anything in a cage like this? There's no workshop, no kitchen, no...*

No fun. Therein lay one of the fundamental differences between humans and halflings. This wasn't to say that *all* humans devalued education, because some of them were very well learned, but in general, humans seemed to place the physical above the cerebral. Athletes and warriors were celebrated, whereas scholars and philosophers were marginalized or ignored until society caught up with them a few hundred years later. Rufino hadn't the faintest idea how someone whose talent was shooting balls into nets could be more revered than, say, a doctor whose mission in life was to help people put their broken lives back together.

He was a halfling, though, and halflings saw the world from a unique perspective. Though Nyobian halflings were excellent farmers and were as tough as their work implied, it was generous to call them "lousy" at every physical sport ever invented. "Utterly hopeless" was more accurate, and this would never be otherwise because halflings were just too small to compete against humans at a game of football. The original settlers of Galensdorf had known this, so they'd decided to build their little society around something halflings *were* good at—academics.

That had been easier said than done, though. There was simply no way to get a congenitally hyperactive halfling child to do *anything* unless it was fun, so halfling schools had to be fun. This was accomplished through the liberal use of home economics, woodworking, metalworking for senior students, arts and crafts, drama, and other programs that were either optional or non-existent at most human schools. "Basic" stuff, like geography and math, was in the curriculum too, but even these programs had been spiced up with puzzles and games and contests and whatnot. The halfling school day was two hours longer than the human school day, but the kids never complained. Why would they? This was their big chance to play with saws in the workshop and burn some water in the kitchen without being harassed by their parents! They loved school.

Galensdorf was not proof, in itself, that engaging children with education led to an abundance of brilliant young adults, but neither was it a fluke. Visitors sometimes questioned the point of having a farming community full of geniuses, but Rufino figured it was better than having a farming community full of idiots.

By halfling standards, Rufino had never been the best of students. He was a hands-on kind of guy—excellent at building and cooking but average at best when it came to math or foreign languages. He'd also been a frequent recipient of detention: mostly for practical jokes, but he'd suffered a few episodes of having his homework stolen by reptiles, too. Nevertheless, he'd been well liked, for he'd been ferociously loyal to the halfling community as a whole, and he was always the first to offer words of encouragement to a person in need.

He'd been in need of such words for the last six years, but he'd had nobody to turn to for them. Kiralyn's offer to help him build a new life would have been exactly what he needed, if only he could trust its legitimacy. If checking on the druid's cover story had told him anything, it was that she used truth to conceal her deceptions, just as he did. The difference was that she was a lot better at it. *Every single detail* of her cover story—the size of the town, the number of teachers and students, the beauty of the architecture, and everything in between—was spot on, so it stood to reason that her next deception was going to be equally strong. *She wasn't kidding,* he realized soberly. *I'm a nobody compared to the fish she's used to frying.*

He didn't believe she was looking forward to committing murder, but that was hardly comforting because doing the same to him wouldn't be recognized as such. To some, skewering undead was a career; to others, it was sport. He didn't know what it was to Kiralyn, but he highly doubted she'd turn out to be a champion of undead rights. As he'd noted back in Borallis, his condition was *unnatural*, and druids had been the most consistent opponents of the unnatural since the birth of druidism over ten thousand years ago. That wasn't going to change just because he was sexy.

This had little to do with Kiralyn, though. This was about his powerful need to explain what was happening to him. He'd lost a lot six years ago, and this was his first tangible opportunity to get some of it back again. Yes, the fear that he felt was very real, but so too was the other emotion that had surfaced in the wake of his encounter at the *Squid.*

Hope. It had been a long time since he'd had something to hope for, but he had something now, and he liked it. He'd spent so much time and energy on survival over the years that he'd forgotten how exhilarating it could be to take a wild gamble such as this. The explorers of old hadn't known what they were going to find on the other side of the ocean, but they'd gone anyway, and so too would Rufino. As of right now, he was a *social* explorer, setting sail for parts unknown. The odds were most certainly against him—and he didn't even know what to expect from success—but the status quo was killing him and he was no longer able to pretend otherwise. Wherever he was going, it had to be better than where he was coming from.

Perhaps the explorers of old had felt the same way.

***

He managed to cover another thirty kilometres on that third night before he had to shut down, which put him approximately 180 kilometres from Tundora with three more full nights available. Continuing to follow the trade route—which cut east to the towns of Ecclessis and Bordym before curling back north—would take more time than he had to spare, so he decided to continue flying north-northeast until he reached the perimeter of Feybourne Forest. He could then follow the forest's edge to his ultimate destination. This would mean going another two days without food, but Bordym's resident dwarves didn't make for very healthy snacks anyway. Dwarves were the pastries of a vampire's palette: very easy and very tasty, but more fattening than a bowl of fat.

The little vampire reached the southeastern tip of the forest a few hours into his fourth night of travel. He knew the geography of Nyobi like the back of his hand, so he was aware that Feybourne's almost-circular perimeter would guide him to within a kilometre of Tundora's walls. The tedious part of his journey—flying virtually blind across a seemingly endless sea of nothingness—was now over.

He was in druid country now.

This should have been no cause for alarm, seeing as how he was the new instrument of druidic justice, but that was assuming Kiralyn had found the time to tell her people about him. Maybe she hadn't. She seemed to be a very busy lady, as people with her skills so often were, so it was within the realm of possibility that she hadn't had a chance to report in yet. It was *also* possible that the details of this operation were being deliberately withheld from the other druids for the purpose of preserving plausible deniability. Rufino didn't believe such measures were necessary in this case, but since nobody had asked for his opinion, he decided to keep a respectful distance from the treeline. Just in case.

As he proceeded northeast, he found himself wondering what the druids had done to upset the king as much as they obviously had. Kiralyn could be as tight-lipped as she wanted, but there was simply no way her people would be pulling a stunt like this if they had any choice in the matter. They weren't just breaking the king's rules, here; they were breaking their own rules as well, which told Rufino they were desperate. What was curious was that he hadn't heard any rumours of druidic activity in recent months. Whenever the druids did something flashy, they made themselves the subject of rarely intelligent discourse and slander at every tavern in Nyobi, but he'd visited enough of those in recent weeks to know that nobody was talking about "tree-huggers" right now. *This implies what, exactly?*

He didn't know, so he made a mental note to ask Kiralyn about it when the opportunity arose. There was little to no chance that she'd actually indulge his curiosity, but at least he'd get to observe how a pro slipped away from an awkward question. Maybe he'd learn something.

The southeastern region of Feybourne Forest—often referred to as the *Bog of the Damned*—was one of the worst vacation destinations in the entire country. As if Feybourne's ordinary threats of ferocious predators, poisonous vegetation and territorial druids weren't bad enough, the deep swamps scattered throughout this region made for an absolutely perfect troll habitat. Trolls were green-skinned carnivorous monsters that could reach fifteen feet in height and up to six thousand pounds in weight. Their skin resembled thick leather armour, and this natural armour along with their redundant *and* regenerative internal organs made them exceptionally difficult to kill. A trio of stomachs made their appetites equally difficult to satisfy, and to *further* disqualify them from being invited to any good parties, they smelled quite terrible and tended to leave puddles of saliva wherever they went. If trolls had one redeeming quality, it was that they were awkward and slow—their dinners could usually outrun them if given a head start. Trolls knew this, so their preferred tactic was to wait in ambush—often underwater—for their meals to serve themselves.

Yeah, once in a blue moon, a troll would hide under a bridge, which was how that story had become so ingrained in popular culture. Ninety-nine times out of a hundred, though, they'd pick a lake or a swamp. Why wouldn't they? With their redundant lungs, they could hold their breath for hours. Water helped conceal their overpowering body odour, too.

Of course, nobody would care about any of this if not for the fact that trolls were known to eat people. Statistically, a person was more likely to be trampled to death by a horse than to be eaten by a troll, but such things didn't seem to matter to the average Joe. If Joe had the *illusion* of control, as he did with domesticated animals, he seemed quite oblivious to the fact that his beloved pets caused more carnage and mayhem than trolls, vampires and dragons *combined.* Rufino hardly thought of himself as a numbers man, but he'd come to respect statistics over the years—it was one of the only pursuits in which a person could find a pro-vampire perspective.

Statistics were dangerous, though, in that they could be used to justify all sorts of twisted agendas. Many would correctly point out that on a strictly per-capita basis, a vampire was far more dangerous than a horse. Rufino had become a big-picture guy, though, so he just didn't see how a handful of honest vampires could be worth all this mistreatment. If people would just stop worrying about being eaten by exotic beasts, they'd find themselves with more energy to spend on *constructive* pursuits. *Like finding a cure for vampirism!*

But perhaps that was asking too much.

It was about two hours pre-dawn on that fourth night when Rufino noticed a metallic reflection of moonlight just beside his intended path. He didn't think there was supposed to be any metal out here, so he decided to use this as the excuse to stop and rest for a few minutes that he'd been looking for.

A strange scent assailed his nostrils as he drew closer, but a halfling with an idea in his head was seldom deterred by such things. It was probably just a troll, though he couldn't be certain because he'd never actually run afoul of one. As a normal halfling, he wouldn't have welcomed such an encounter; but as an exotic undead beastie, he probably didn't have much to fear from the so-called "bog monsters." If grizzly bears were smart enough to know that vampires weren't edible, then hopefully trolls would be, too.

Upon landing, it was immediately obvious that his find wasn't just metal: it was the lower half of a suit of human-sized undecorated full plate armour. Not only that, but it was *steel* plate—not iron—which meant it had once belonged to a knight. In keeping with the tradition established by his predecessors, King Augustus V only forged suits of steel plate for his knights, as a means of symbolizing the great respect they had earned. Knights weren't the only people in the country with steel armour, of course, but civilians in Nyobi were required by law to paint their armour so they could not be mistaken for soldiers. The penalty for noncompliance started at five years in prison and it applied to both the wearer *and* the blacksmith, so Rufino was fairly confident the stuff he was looking at was genuine.

This was when the uneasy feeling in the back of his mind began to make itself known. *If you know what's good for you,* it was telling him, *get out of here. Now.* There were only a handful of ways a knight's armour could have gotten all the way out here, and none of them were good. Did he really want to get caught up in whatever had happened here? *Am I not in enough trouble already?*

He stared at the armour for the next minute or so, trying to work things out in his mind. Foul play wasn't just suspected in this case, it was guaranteed—there was no way in the world that a knight would have been wandering the *Bog of the Damned* alone whilst on duty. This had to be an evidence dump. Why had the armour been dumped *here*, though, so far away from everything except the forest? Could *this* be why the druids were so eager to escape the king's notice for a while?

That was a question that needed answering, lest he find *himself* dumped out here once Kiralyn was finished with him. Unfortunately, the armour itself probably couldn't tell him much. In his experience, any unique inscriptions would have been carved into the breastplate, or perhaps the gauntlets—probably not the thigh-guards or the greaves. All he could hope for now was to find some distinctive damage. There had to be something—nobody would dump undamaged steel plate, not when it was but one underground paint job away from fetching five figures. *It will take some good fortune*, he told himself as he reached for the thigh-guard, *but if I can identify...*

His train of thought made it no further, for his outstretched hand had just made a discovery—a discovery so gruesome that his reflexive recoil was violent enough to send him tumbling backwards onto his butt. Not only was this the lower half of a knight's armour, it was the lower half of the knight, too. Rufino had known all along that the man was probably dead, but it was still something of a shock to have his suspicions confirmed so graphically. *You bloody idiot,* he berated himself emphatically. *Why can't you ever listen to those instincts of yours that are so often right?*

He couldn't answer that, but after a moment of laboured breathing, he regained his courage and crawled back over to inspect the knight's remains. It was immediately apparent that *this* was the source of the unusual smell he'd noticed a few minutes ago—what remained of the man's flesh had been very badly burnt. One of the thigh-bones was missing, too—the work of a hungry troll, perhaps? Trolls seldom left their meals unfinished, but it wasn't difficult to imagine why an exception had been made in this case.

He forced the thought aside, for a more important concern had just sprung to mind: *how is it this man was burnt to a crisp, yet his armour is spotless?* His earlier point about the value of undamaged steel armour was still very valid—it made no sense at all to murder an off-duty knight and then suit him up for disposal. Such a twisted errand would be nigh impossible anyway, because military armories didn't permit civilian access. *Could this be an inside job?*

The little detective reluctantly shifted his attention back to the fallen knight's remains. It hardly seemed appropriate to call the stuff *flesh*—in its current state, it could only be described as *organic residue*. He was reluctant to touch it again out of fear that it would crumble.

Nobody could have equipped a body in this condition, he realized. This didn't preclude the possibility that the murderer was someone in the military, but right now Rufino would have bet his life savings—five silver coins—that the victim had been wearing his armour in his final moments.

That nagging voice in the back of his mind was screaming at him again. It believed it knew what had happened to this man, and it *really* wanted to leave; but before Rufino could pass this information along, he needed to be certain. He needed to be *dead* certain, because he was approaching a very frightening conclusion, and there was no way he was going to share this theory with *anyone* unless he knew the ensuing panic would be entirely justified.

His attention shifted back to the armour. It seemed that the stuff was the key to the puzzle after all, just not in a way that was immediately apparent. To validate his theory, he needed a good look at the inside of the armour, and he'd have to separate the organic residue from the steel in order to get that look. *I'd cut the rest of my hair for a good pair of gloves right now.* He wasn't in any danger—his vampiric immune system could handle just about anything sans garlic—but the circumstances of this victim's death were more than a little creepy. If there was one thing worse than death, it was suffering, and fire could always be counted on to take its bloody time to kill someone. It was a marvelous tool, but an unthinkable weapon.

Ten extremely delicate minutes later, the little vampire had the remaining armour components separated from the organic residue. Not enough of the latter remained to tell him anything useful, but the metal was another matter. As there were two sides to every coin, and two sides to every story, so too were there two sides to every suit of armour. Unfortunately, the second side of this armour told the story Rufino had been afraid of. It was severely scorched—as the exterior should have been—and some of the organic residue had burned onto the metal, not unlike how food might burn onto a frying pan.

He sniffed the air again, paying close attention as he did so. It was a difficult odour to describe, but it was somewhere between decaying flesh and moldy bread. *If you ever smell this again, Rufino,* he carved into his permanent memory, *challenge yourself: see how far away you can get in two hours.*

This wasn't a normal fire.

Rufino stood up, his skin crawling all over. It was certainly *possible* for a man to catch fire whilst wearing full plate armour, and it might even be possible for him to do so without warping or scorching the exterior surface of that armour—improbable and impossible were two very different things. The creepy smell, however, told Rufino he was looking at the work of either a warlock or a demon. It was within their ability to combust a person's blood and burn him from the inside out with what was commonly called *demon's fire*. He was unclear as to the specifics—and he desired to remain that way for the rest of his unnatural life—but he'd been told that demon's fire didn't burn nearly as hot as regular fire, which could explain why the armour had sustained no visible warping. It would also explain the smell.

Rufino took a few steps backward. Poking one's nose into the affairs of warlocks and demons was extremely unhealthy, and he was in over his head already. The smart man's course of action was to return to the sky and forget he'd ever seen anything. The authorities could deal with the warlock.

It wasn't until a few minutes and one very hasty kilometre later that Rufino realized the authorities were already on the case, and that the knight back there had been one of them. *Fiddlesticks.* They needed to know what they were up against. The sun would be up soon, so he couldn't do anything this morning; but since he was running ahead of schedule, he could probably detour to the nearest police station later today and still make it to Tundora on time. Someone was undoubtedly searching for this missing knight, so if Rufino delivered an anonymous tip to the authorities in Bordym…

...No, that wasn't going to work. He hadn't succeeded in identifying the victim, after all, so if he wrote an unsigned letter to the Bordym police and dropped it in their mailbox, he could probably retrieve it from their garbage can the following evening. *A warlock murdered a human knight and dumped him in the Bog.* Even *if* an investigator believed such a story, he or she wouldn't have enough information to act on. Rufino knew he was just over half a kilometre from the treeline, but he didn't know his precise co-ordinates. Without those co-ordinates, he'd essentially be asking a search party to comb an entire troll-infested swamp on the word of an anonymous note that they *might* find something. Pigs would fly before this would happen. *He* could take his chances on the ground out here, but no living search party had the benefit of his built-in immunity to being eaten. They'd need precise information and a *lot* of heavily armed personnel before they'd even *consider* coming out here.

Unless...

In a moment that would have been brilliant had it not taken so long to manifest, Rufino recalled why he was out here in the first place. *I'm flying to a rendezvous with a freakin' druid-sorceress.* If there was one living person in Nyobi who had nothing to fear from trolls, it was Kiralyn Frostwhisper. Ignoring her sorcery for a moment, there was a more than respectable chance that an encounter between her and a troll wouldn't come to violence at all. Her kind got along remarkably well with wild animals, including the ones that would usually consider attacking humanoids. Trolls weren't animals so much as they were extremely feral humanoids, but a druid could probably talk one down all the same. *The only question is: will she give a damn about one of the king's knights even if she does believe my story?*

It was a valid question, given the elevated level of tension between her people and the Crown. But maybe it didn't matter—maybe the demonology angle alone would be enough to grab her interest. Any demonic presence in this plane of existence was a result of *mankind's interference*, so if her people believed that *vampires* didn't belong in this world, then they weren't going to be warm and fuzzy about demons, either. Yes, this was a much better idea than flying to Bordym: he'd report his discovery to Kiralyn, and then she'd bury him in an avalanche of praise. The ice between them would melt like a snowball in the hells. Maybe, if he was *really* lucky, she might even…

Might even *thank him*.

No, probably not, he sighed to himself. For one of his kind, even getting the correct time of day from a druid would be an accomplishment. He had to be patient. If there was one way for him to melt the ice between them, it was to be the polar opposite of what she expected, and he'd have to do it over a prolonged period of time. The actual timeframe was up to Kiralyn, but he did have the power to influence her thinking, and perhaps telling her about this knight would help assuage some of her doubts about him.

It remained to be seen whether his grisly discovery would be a stroke of good or bad fortune. One thing was clear, though: the *Bog of the Damned* no longer seemed as friendly as it had thirty minutes ago.

Chapter Four
Brushes with Death

Rufino wasn't able to escape the *Bog* before bedtime, which presented to him the unique challenge of finding suitable housing in the heart of a troll habitat. He ended up choosing a tree den on the scary side of the treeline, not because he wanted to but because he had no reasonable alternative. He didn't trust that one of his pitiful tunnels in the dirt could survive a trollquake, nor did he believe there were any luxury suites to be found at ground level. The *Bog* was rich in insect, songbird and amphibian life, but it was sorely lacking in species that could save him the trouble of building his own shelters.

That left Feybourne. The cavity of his choosing was adequate in and of itself, but the neighbours left a *lot* to be desired. Rufino spent the rest of the morning wide awake, watching in paralyzed horror as a forest's worth of monstrous snakes slithered past outside. None of them took any particular interest in him, but that wasn't even *remotely* comforting. Snakes creeped him out to begin with, and snakes that were twenty feet long would have scared him half to death if that didn't already describe him to a tee. How the druids could live in a place like this was completely beyond him.

There was nothing he could do about the snakes, though—the oppressive sunshine had him pinned down. Even knowing this, it took him until almost 13:00 to build up enough courage to try to doze off. Tundora was still just over one hundred kilometres away, and it was beginning to feel as though he'd overestimated his ability to make this arduous journey without so much as a single drop of blood. Energy management was the name of the game now. *I have more than enough time,* he attempted to soothe his beleaguered mind. *There's no need to panic—if I need to slow down a bit to conserve my strength, I can do so.*

After a few minutes of positive reinforcement, the little vampire started to nod off. *That's it,* he approved wholeheartedly, *take some deep breaths and feel the tension escape your body. You'll be in Tundora in thirty-six hours, and then...*

And then the biggest bald eagle he'd ever seen set down on the branch five feet in front of him. It turned to stare at his trembling form; and though he trusted *most* animals to recognize his absolute lack of nutritional value, he wasn't at all certain he could trust an eagle. It was quite a majestic bird, but he knew from his childhood education that it was essentially an enormous crow, willing to eat just about anything if it couldn't find what it wanted. Were eagles clever enough to realize he was poisonous? Or would this predator's ignorance doom them both?

He assumed the gargantuan bird of prey was a female, since the largest eagles always were. *As if I didn't have enough woman problems already.* It was difficult to believe that a bird could have gotten this big without knowing a thing or two about healthy eating, but this was even less comforting than being ignored by the snakes had been. Rufino could only handle so much torture, so when the eagle neglected to take action—hostile or otherwise—he decided to see if he could persuade her to leave. He made eye contact with the menacing bird, showed his fangs, spread his tiny wings, and tried to snarl.

It came out as a cross between a hiccup and a squeak, which left him with an eight-inch wingspan and a couple of fangs. The eagle was twenty times his size, and she knew it—her initial response was a kik-kik sound that probably wasn't mocking laughter but it may as well have been. She then spread her own wings, which were wide enough that the poor vampire couldn't see the tip of either one of them from inside his prison. *So much for persuasion.*

He did have one more card up his sleeve, though, and if this feathered monstrosity took so much as one step toward him, he was going to use it. Sure, he'd be risking exposure to the sun by shifting forms, but one thing was dead certain: the eagle wouldn't be expecting a tiny bat to suddenly become something as big as she was. He didn't think he'd be able to squeeze his torso through this shelter's opening, but that was fine because he didn't want to fight something with as many pointy ends as the eagle had, anyway. He'd be counting on the gambit's shock value to scare the eagle away, and at the same time, he'd be counting on this massive tree trunk to shelter his legs from direct exposure. That was a lot to count on. *If I don't make it,* he pleaded to nobody in particular, *just make it quick. That's all I ask.*

The eagle chittered some more in her incongruous voice, which would have been better suited to a seagull than to an apex predator. She then returned her wings to their folded-up positions and tilted her head to one side. Had a human made such a gesture, Rufino would have assumed she was trying to figure out what he was; but for all he knew, the bird was just trying to identify which parts of him were the meatiest. He didn't believe his miniscule bat form *had* any meaty parts, but if this giant crow was hungry, she wasn't going to care. In fairness, he wasn't all that picky after a week without food, either.

When the bird of prey spread her wings again, a desperate struggle seemed imminent. Perhaps it was, but it wouldn't be fought here. Without so much as a parting taunt, the eagle took off, exiting his life as quickly as she'd entered it.

Or rather, she exited his life in the physical sense—the fear stayed with him long after the bird herself had departed. During these hours, he asked himself a hundred times if he'd have survived this latest encounter if not for his vampiric condition. The answer he arrived at was a resounding "no," but he also decided this conclusion was irrelevant because if not for his undeath, he wouldn't have met Frostwhisper and he wouldn't be in this accursed tree. He'd be in Galensdorf, working a stove or running his sword through some vermin, or something.

Hells, he might even have a wife and kids by now. That should have been a frightening prospect, but at the moment it sounded pretty darned good. He'd take some impish halfling children over the denizens of Feybourne Forest any day of the week.

***

Rufino finally managed to nod off at around mid-afternoon, but his beauty sleep was interrupted shortly thereafter by a rather angry stomach. This steered him toward the dire conclusion that he wasn't going to make it to Tundora on his remaining energy—he needed a snack to make up for all this lost sleep. Unfortunately, as he'd previously noted, the only legitimate necks around here belonged to druids; and since it just wouldn't be cool to run around chomping his new buddies, he had but two options.

The first was to fly to Bordym and chomp a dwarf, but the detour would cost him his grace period, and nobody in his right mind would want to rendezvous with someone like Frostwhisper without having made preparations beforehand. Among other things, he had to familiarize himself with Tundora and identify some good places to hide in the event that things went sour. This was not an optional objective—if he flew into this mess wearing a blindfold, he'd probably end up demonstrating how natural selection worked. He already had far too much risk on his plate to willingly embrace more of the same.

He was, however, caught between a rock and a hard place. There were no other towns in this part of the country, so the only alternative to Bordym was to chomp something else.

There was no *Vampirism for Idiots* handbook, so he had no way of knowing what would happen if he tried to drink the blood of an animal. Vampirism had been around for thousands of years, so it stood to reason that some enterprising and very desperate vampires *must* have pulled this stunt at some points in history. Unfortunately, the results had *not* been documented. Were he a negative person, he might have inferred from this lack of information that the experiment had killed the subjects, but it was *also* possible that they simply hadn't been able to find a publisher for their tales of success. Maybe animal blood was the key to vampiric health and happiness; maybe this information was being cruelly repressed by the Crown in order to prevent his kind from living out their days in peace.

Maybe you need to be measured for a tinfoil hat, the little voice in the back of his mind expressed its rather blunt opinion of that theory. *Think about it: mankind has been trying to destroy vampirism for three thousand years, without success. If they had another way to neutralize us, don't you think they'd have tried it by now?*

It was a fair point, so Rufino decided not to argue. He did, however, decide to take this plunge anyway, seeing as how he lacked a palatable alternative. It was widely theorized that certain animals had more in common with people than others, so perhaps he could positively influence his results by adhering to this train of thought. *Which animal, that I might find out here, will be the most compatible with halflings?*

Monkeys bore a striking resemblance to halflings, both in size and in character. This would have been the obvious choice if not for the small problem that there weren't any monkeys in Feybourne. Nyobi's climate was quite temperate for a northern-hemisphere country, but it would never be mistaken for one of those tropical paradises in which non-humanoid primates could be found. This country was full of bears, wolves, cougars, bison, and other very large animals that Rufino really didn't want to tangle with. In fact, the only mammals in these parts that *weren't* large enough to kick his ass were rodents—filthy, disease-ridden, disgusting rodents.

Bordym was starting to sound better and better. He didn't *know* that he'd need an escape route from Tundora, but he *did* know that chomping a rodent was going to suck no matter how he went about it. He needed to stop thinking about ideal scenarios and start concentrating on reaching his destination, period. This would all be for naught if he poisoned himself on animal blood and missed his rendezvous completely.

Satisfied with this reasoning, the little vampire took to the sky as soon as conditions permitted and pointed himself toward the not-so-distant dwarven town. Two minutes later, he realized he wasn't going to make it—his wings seemed to weigh about ten pounds each, and his energy level was barely sufficient to keep him off the ground. He needed blood and he needed it *now*, else he could kiss Kiralyn goodbye and her information along with her.

A handful of minutes later, he found himself back in a tree along the perimeter of Feybourne Forest, as far from the ground as he could manage. The two abandoned tree dens he'd slept in during this journey had probably been utilized by squirrels at some point in time, so now he needed to find one that was occupied. For all their flaws, squirrels were really cute, and he hoped this detail would somehow dampen the psychological trauma that he was about to endure. Rufino knew as well as anyone that a negative attitude was self-defeating, but he just didn't see a way to be optimistic about this.

His other half agreed, wholeheartedly and with gusto. *Wonderful mess you've gotten us into, dumbass,* it observed with its usual lack of tact. *We can either drink rodent blood or we can sit here and starve to death, and it's all because you let a hard-on cloud your judgment once again. Did we learn nothing from Megan?*

Rufino was definitely *not* in a mood to discuss Megan, and he doubted he ever would be. She was his only ex-girlfriend of significance, and she had, in fact, taught him a lot—she was the reason he knew how pointless it was to try to change someone who didn't want to change. For all her qualities—and there had been plenty of them—she was a self-absorbed, manipulative snob, and she would never be otherwise. Not counting vampirism, the four and a half years he'd wasted on that poisonous woman was the number one regret of his life. *If you know what's good for you,* he snarled at the increasingly aggravating nuisance inside his mind, *you'll drop this subject. Now.*

If you know what's good for you, the aggravating nuisance inside his mind retorted with vigour, *you'll listen to me for the first time in your miserable life. I realize Kiralyn isn't Megan, but from where I'm sitting, she might as well be because she's got you doing the same bloody thing: lying to yourself. Megan was never going to change, and Kiralyn—if she doesn't kill you—will never let you get out of the starting gate. Those are the cold, hard facts. Now, I happen to know you're an intelligent, objective guy for whom this stuff should be painfully obvious, so why...*

It is obvious, you bloody troll, he snarled back. *I know Kiralyn is dangerous to me, okay? I understand and accept that. What you aren't accepting is that our last six years together have sucked, and that I'm trying to save us from that miserable existence. If there's...*

She's got you chomping rodents, you idiot, came the emphatic reminder. *This will either kill us or create an army of undead squirrels, and so help me, I'm not sure which outcome sounds worse. You don't need blood; you need a tranquilizer dart right in the ki...*

You can go back to the safety of that trade cart if

you want, Rufino shot back with equal vitriol, *but this vampire has had enough of that pathetic excuse for a life. Yeah, I'm out on a limb, here, but do you remember what they tried to tell the guys with the boats who wanted to sail around the world? They said the world was flat, and that anyone who dared challenge this wisdom was gonna sail off the edge and die. But it didn't work out that way, did it?*

They got lucky, was the response. *You won't.*

The little vampire felt no need to respond, having seen the weakness of the response for what it was. He might need a bit of good fortune for this animal-blood experiment to turn out favourably, but after that he didn't believe luck would be much of a factor. It was completely within his power to demonstrate to Kiralyn that he was on her side, and it didn't sound like the druids were in a position to say no to some new friends right now. It was unlikely she'd ever feel for him as he did for her—his negative side was right about that—but he didn't require reciprocation in order to get the answers he sought. All he *really* needed was her cooperation, and that was surely within his grasp if he played his cards with an exceptional amount of skill. She couldn't be so unreasonable as to expect him to perform a service without *some* form of compensation. He realized his request would put her in an awkward position, but considering what she was asking *him* to do, he didn't believe she was in any position to complain about *awkwardness*.

His negative side had something to say again. *You're assuming she's going to abide by your concept of fair play,* it pointed out, *but she's using you to get out of playing fair with both the king and the guy she wants dead. What makes you think you'll fare any better?*

Again, it was a valid point, but there was one important distinction that needed to be made. *Those are her enemies,* he reminded himself. *I'm not her enemy.*

You aren't her enemy at the moment, his other half

made another important distinction. *This is an alliance of convenience; more so for her than for you. And while we're giving out history lessons about men with boats and whatnot, let's examine how most of the alliances of convenience throughout history have ended. Can you tell me?*

Rufino hesitated briefly. *Some of them ended in blood,* he gave the correct answer as he felt himself being pushed into a defensive position, *but several others blossomed into friendships that have endured to this day. Remember how Siddurna and Minta Cadra put their differences aside to fight against Nyobi seven hundred years ago? They've been friends ever since, an...*

They got lucky, it told him again, *you won't.*

***

There didn't seem to be any point in continuing this argument, so Rufino returned his attention to the task at hand. There *had* to be a squirrel in this tree somewhere. If not, he was going to be pissed, because if his luck was trending downward, it would only lend credence to the theory that he was doomed. Yes, things didn't look good right now, but when *had* they looked good in the last six years? He couldn't recall a single time. At best, he'd been alone in a dark tunnel with no end in sight. Now, at long last, there was a light at the end of that tunnel, and he was going to chase it no matter how much complaining he had to endure from his inner pessimist. Where could that negativity take him except back into the dark tunnel?

Nowhere.

Three minutes and several branches later, the increasingly desperate vampire finally found what he was looking for: a plump grey squirrel snoozing peacefully in an apartment just large enough to be comfortable. He stared at the furry rodent for a long moment, once again questioning the wisdom of what he was about to do before resigning himself to the fact that he'd chosen this path and now he had to live with it. If ever he found himself making a long-distance journey again, he vowed to stick to the established routes with some actual people on them. *No more roads less travelled, Rufino,* he etched into the stone of his long-term memory. *There's usually a reason people don't want to take them.*

What was done was done, though, and the moment of truth was upon him. *You worry too much,* he attempted to soothe himself. *Remember that brown stuff your parents had to shove down your throat when you were a kid? If you can survive that foul stuff, you can survive anything. Yo…*

That was lamb stew, his other half interrupted once more, *and yeah, it was gross, but it was made from ingredients that halflings have been eating for thousands of years. You ca…*

They didn't know the food was safe until they tried it, was the obvious retort, which just happened to tie in with the exploratory theme of this whole misadventure quite well. *For all you know, this'll taste like that whiskey dad was trying to age in the attic when I was four.*

It's more likely to taste like that roach you ate when you were five, the unwanted half of his mind piped up again, *but hey, we're dead already, so what do we have to lose? I'll watch from over here.*

Another word out of you, and you aren't going to watch at all, the little vampire snarled in annoyance, though how he was going to snuff out a part of his own mind, he hadn't a clue.

Rufino usually fed using his humanoid form, for two reasons: first and foremost, he could consume more whilst in his larger form, thus extending his time in between feedings. His precision flying also left something to be desired, so landing on a moving target was something he preferred not to do if he could help it. Since this particular target was not moving—and because he didn't want much of its blood anyway—he decided to remain in his flight form for the time being. He wasn't aware of his current altitude, but the fact that he couldn't see the ground was something of a hint that his wings may yet prove useful.

It then occurred to him that this could be a druid in animal form, which gave him a moment of pause. *Freakin' shape-shifters make everything so complicated.* In the end, though, he decided the odds were on his side and resumed his pre-chomp routine. If the worst-case scenario came to pass and this *did* turn out to be a druid, well, he could always plead insanity. Under the circumstances, such a plea would be impossible to refute.

A moment later, he was standing beside the sleeping squirrel. The worst part of all this was that if he didn't make it to Tundora, Kiralyn would undoubtedly assume he'd made a run for it. *Stupid vampire,* she'd tell herself, *I never should have taken him at his word.* She'd never know how much this had actually meant to him. If this squirrel-blood thing didn't work and he somehow found himself clinging to life, he decided his final act should be to try to escape the *Bog*. If he succeeded, his body might be found some day, and his fate could then be reported to the two or three people who still gave a damn. If Kiralyn happened to be among them, she could then remember him as an incompetent fool instead of a duplicitous coward.

He chomped the squirrel.

There was no time to put a finger on the taste—the rodent was awake and alert within milliseconds, and it was none too pleased with what was happening. Rufino could understand that, but he would probably never understand the action his prey decided to take: it jumped. They were inside a tree den with a low ceiling, he was more or less on top of his prey, and squirrels were excellent jumpers even when their strength *wasn't* being amplified by fear. He didn't need to be a halfling to realize this wasn't going to end well.

Sure enough, after one of the longest quarter-seconds of his life, Rufino was body slammed into the ceiling with enough crushing force to make a rugby professional proud. A split-second later, the squirrel hit the deck at top speed, its assailant still attached to its neck and in no condition to rectify the situation. The predator was a passenger now, and this wasn't likely to change until the squirrel either lost consciousness or ran out of energy. Not unless he could get his body to start obeying his commands again.

First things first, though—he needed to breathe. These could very well be the final breaths of his life, so he needed to make them memorable. It was difficult to cough and gag on the back of a rodent moving at the speed of sound, but after a few seconds of choking, he was able to clear a partial path between his mouth and his lungs. With his breathing more or less restored, he was able to compose himself and start thinking about how to extract himself from this ridiculous predicament. He still had some strength in his lower body, so perhaps he could use his claws to pry himself loose. All he had to do was…

…Panic. The squirrel, he now saw, was rapidly approaching the end of this branch. Rufino saw no indication that it intended to slow down any time soon, and he also didn't see anything it could possibly jump to. The time to abandon ship was upon him. With his abdominal muscles protesting every demand he made of them, he scrunched himself into the shape of a horseshoe and then used his legs for leverage as he attempted to free himself.

His effort was successful, but he wasn't out of trouble yet. The squirrel, having finally realized there was nowhere to go in this direction, came to an abrupt halt at the very tip of the branch; and Rufino—now detached from the efficient stopping power of his vehicle—kept going.

Right over the edge.

This shouldn't have been much cause for concern: he had wings, so why should he care if he was freefalling out of a tree? The answer, of course, was that his wings weren't working too well at the moment—certainly not well enough to keep him airborne, as a handful of weak flaps demonstrated beyond a shadow of doubt. He wasn't falling very fast, but he had absolutely no desire to find out if his bat form's terminal velocity was high enough to be fatal. He rolled onto his belly and started looking for something he could use to break his fall.

Sometime in the subsequent seconds, the cogs inside his head started spinning again. He didn't need to *fly*; he only needed to control his descent, and *that* was something even stunned wings should be able to handle. *Glide, you idiot. Glide!*

The six-year veteran of flight pointed his nose straight down and held his aching wings straight out. He had air beneath them almost immediately, so his next step was to tilt them slightly front-to-back in an effort to generate some lift. When he succeeded, he felt a rush of excitement as he realized that something was actually going his way for a change. *You see?* he told himself in triumph as he pulled out of his dive. *No swe…*

CRUNCH!

This latest episode of vampire versus tree trunk went as well as could be expected. Luck was on his side, though, because his limp form fell only three metres before the base of a very large branch broke his fall. He lay there for some time afterwards, gasping for air, groaning in misery, and choking down the blood still caught in his throat. It came as no surprise whatsoever that his mind decided to use this glorious opportunity to express a few more unwanted opinions. *Terrific idea, you idiot; now, instead of a snack, we need a body cast.*

Rufino conceded the point without argument.

***

With a great deal of pain in both his tiny frame and his digestive system, it was half an hour before the little vampire felt like moving again. It occurred to him during this time that his own death was imminent, but this realization wasn't as distressing as it should have been. Death could be damned seductive when it passed itself off as a release from physical or emotional suffering, and it was seducing him right now. Oh, and it certainly didn't help matters that his usually adversarial negative side had done a complete about-face and was now trying to come across as his best buddy. *It's not the easy way out when it's the only way out,* it was saying, sounding very reasonable as it did so. *We've learned what we can from this life. Let's move on.*

With a groan, Rufino finally sat up, coughing a couple of times as he did so. He had no broken bones that he knew of—it was a broken spirit that had him pinned down more than anything else. That was something he could fix, if only he could find it within himself to do so. Yes, it didn't appear that he'd still be alive by this time tomorrow, but it would only compound his failure to die without first escaping the *Bog.* It was bad enough that he'd let Kiralyn down—he didn't want to let himself down, too. *Not here,* he forced some determination back into his ailing spirit, *not like this.*

He took a deep breath and jumped out of the tree. He didn't dare flap his wings until they had some time to get used to the idea of working again, so he settled into a glide that he maintained until he was but ten feet off the ground. Then he tried his wings. They didn't work without a good deal of complaining, of course, but they'd recovered enough to get the job done at a most basic level. He wasn't breaking any speed records, but the fact that he was moving at all was a victory of significance. *Just get me out of this gods-forsaken swamp,* he willed himself forward, *that's all I ask.*

He flew northeast, for that was where the nearest boundary of the *Bog* could be found. Some of the pain in his body subsided as he settled into a rhythm, but there was nothing more he could do for his seriously depleted energy level. The only thing keeping him in the air right now was his emergency reserve, and he suspected this reserve was going to expire two or three seconds after he cleared the *Bog.*

It wouldn't be long before he found out.

***

His internal clock broke down at some point during his struggle, but eventually he crossed a small lake and found grassy plains on the other side. It was a minor triumph, but it was sufficient to put the sweet taste of victory on his tongue once again. Winning was not a miracle cure, but it *was* capable of breathing new life into an exhausted heap of flesh such as his. This wasn't to say that his predicament had improved dramatically, but he was now safely out of the *Bog of the Damned* and he was still airborne—something he would not have bet on a few hours ago.

So he kept going. His body didn't want to keep going, of course, but Rufino knew he wouldn't be able to get back into the air if he landed now. Momentum was easier to maintain than it was to generate—a concept he understood thanks to having stayed awake during physics class. With this in mind, he steered himself east, toward Bordym. He wasn't under any delusions that he'd actually reach the dwarven town—he was limping along at six or seven kilometres per hour whereas his sustainable cruise velocity was usually twice that—but Bordym was surrounded by rocky terrain that would almost certainly provide him with a luxurious cave in which to die. The closer he got to civilization, the less time it would take for his fate to be discovered and hopefully reported to his parents. He hadn't anticipated that closure for his folks would be his dying wish, but apparently it was. Hopefully his death would be easier for them to accept than his existence as a vampire would have been.

As expected, he didn't make it to Bordym—his body ran out of steam before he even made it out of the grasslands. He didn't know what time it was, but from the moon's position in the cloudless sky, he guesstimated it was around 03:30. That wasn't very late, but he was going nowhere on foot in this condition, so it was time to build what might be the most important dirt shelter of his life. He really, *really* didn't want to expire in one of these things, so this one had to be good enough to get a dying man through the day.

Thirty minutes of exhausted digging later, the little vampire shifted back into his bat form, crawled into his new shelter, and closed his eyes. He was afraid, which told him the allure of death had ultimately failed to win him over, but there was nothing more he could do to help himself. His life was in nature's hands now.

For a vampire, that was not a comforting thought.

***

When Rufino awoke the following evening, the sky above his shelter was that of dusk—he'd been asleep for sixteen hours. The sun was not yet below the horizon, so he stayed put until it was, and he used those minutes to perform an awkward self-diagnosis. He was still alive, obviously, and his muscles were still feeling the effects of their recent mistreatment, but he wouldn't be able to determine things like energy level or range of motion until he could climb out of this shelter and move around a bit.

When it was safe, he did just that, and what he discovered was encouraging. Though he was stiffer than a three-hundred-year-old elf, he felt little in the way of active pain. More importantly, he had enough energy now that he could no longer be categorized as a zombie. This wasn't to say that he felt *good*, because he was currently experiencing the vampiric equivalent of heartburn as well as some mild dizziness, but compared to the misery of yesterday, he felt considerably less dead. Did the credit for his improvement belong solely to these last sixteen hours of shut-eye, or was the squirrel's blood helping a bit as well?

It would be awesome to have an answer to this question—he hated to think he'd put himself through rodent hell when all he'd needed was to go back to sleep. He'd been desperate to avoid wasting time, though, and desperation could lead people to do some very strange things. Whether the squirrel's blood had helped him or not was debatable, but one thing was very clear: he was *not* going to be adopting a brand new diet any time soon.

Aside from that, his future was uncertain. A large part of him hadn't expected to make it this far, so there hadn't seemed like much of a reason to make plans. He needed a plan now, but before he could formulate one, he needed to establish whether or not he could fly. There wasn't a tree inside of five kilometres from which he could have jumped, but fortunately his bat form had been modelled after one of the few types of bats that did not need to jump from height in order to get airborne. He didn't know exactly what kind of bat he was supposed to be, but whoever had selected this bat form had done an excellent job of it. He was able to take off and crash as well as any bird whilst looking as awesome as any bat—it was the best of both worlds.

A moment later, he was ten feet off the ground, performing a variety of minor manoeuvers in an effort to generate feedback from his body. It was still not a happy body, but it was functioning reasonably well—far better than it had been seventeen hours ago. He also discovered he could perform a one-minute burst of speed without feeling drained by the effort, from which he concluded the energy he felt was real and not imagined. This raised some very interesting possibilities, one of which he decided to pursue.

He set a course and started to fly. He didn't make it twenty metres before he encountered some ferocious resistance from his inner doomsayer, but that was okay because he'd been expecting some backlash. It would have been unreasonable to expect otherwise—he had, after all, not chosen the conservative eastern course, which would have taken him to a town full of easy dwarven blood. He'd chosen a most ambitious course instead.

North. Toward Tundora.

You're nuts, was but a sample of the criticism, phrased as delicately as always, *completely stark-raving nuts. You've escaped the frying pan by the skin of your fangs, and all you want to do is jump right back in. I didn't realize insanity was a side effect of vam...*

Let's get one thing straight, "buddy," Rufino wasn't terribly interested in listening to any more whining, *I'm in charge here. From now on, if what you have to say isn't, "yes, sir," or, "you da man," you can keep it to yourself. This opportunity...*

This isn't an opportunity, his unwanted half didn't take long to violate the rules that had just been set out. *This is a way to expedite the process of dying. You need to be patient—now that our breakthrough has actually happened, who's to say there won't be another woman in a month or two who will have the same effect on us? One who* isn't *a notorious druid, perhaps?*

Rufino hesitated briefly—he was always a bit taken aback when his negative side tried to pass itself off as something else. Beneath the surface, however, it was still assuming he'd fail to get anything out of Kiralyn, so nothing had truly changed. *It took six years for the first opportunity to manifest,* he spelled it out slowly, *and I'm not spending the next six years hoping for a second chance. I'm taking this one, and if you don't like it, you may consider yourself at liberty to shut up and get lost. I...*

The only reason I'm here is because of your own doubts, you idiot. I'm a part of you, and you've had the power to silence me all along. That you can't do so now is a testament to the lunacy of these decisions you're making.

There was probably some truth to that, but the little vampire was no longer willing to discuss it. There was only one person who could settle this debate once and for all, and she'd be at the *Killer Cocktail* in just over twenty-five hours. He had approximately eleven hours of darkness in which to cover the ninety kilometres between here and there. Not only did he believe this was an achievable goal, but he felt strangely compelled to pursue it, for he wanted his recent struggles to actually be for something. It made no sense to pay for admission only to bail before the show actually started.

His grace period was gone, of course. He hated that, but it wasn't quite as bad as it sounded. If Kiralyn trusted him to make this journey on his own, then she'd probably let him out of her sight at least once or twice during the mission itself, if for no other reason than to get some sleep. *Nobody wants to catch a snooze with a vampire ten feet away, right?* Of course not, so he'd get his chance to explore the town. He just needed to make sure she didn't find out about it.

It was a mercifully uneventful night of travel—no wind, no rain, no dragons, no squirrels; nothing but grasslands and a few gently rolling hills. At one point, he thought he'd stumbled upon a small farming community, but it was abandoned and the overgrowth suggested it had been that way for some time. *Too bad.*

He maintained the best pace he could, though he was tiring more rapidly than normal—he would need to chomp a Tundoran as soon as he could get away with it.

The righteous druid-sorceress would likely object on general principles, but since he had nothing better to do, he spent his flight time preparing a couple of counters to any such objections. The most obvious counter was that she couldn't object to him having dinner any more than he could object to her eating whatever it was that she ate. This wasn't likely to solve anything and could easily lead into the sort of drawn-out argument that his people enjoyed so much. She was quick for a skyscraper—the term his people often used to describe tall people—but he doubted she possessed a halfling's passion for spirited debate. Redhead or not, it wouldn't be too difficult to crush her at a game of barely relevant discourse.

On the off chance that he didn't feel like arguing, he also developed a stronger counter—one which she was much more likely to accept without a fight. If a vampire chomped someone else *before* taking out her target, it would support the theory that the vampire was behaving normally and just happened to nail someone important. This would be more difficult to believe if the vampire took out the big shot on his first try. Nobody would be able to *prove* that it was a hit, of course, but when one person or a group of people just *happened* to benefit from a tragic "coincidence," the odds of them having something to do with it were pretty good. If Kiralyn had any brains at all, she should want to avoid attracting the attention of the tinfoil-hat crowd—they could be a real pain in the ass. Especially when they were right.

He reached Feybourne's perimeter at approximately 02:00, and by the time 05:00 rolled around, the treeline was leading him directly north. This was good, for it signified that he'd arrived at the very eastern edge of the forest, where Tundora could be found.

He'd run out of time this morning, though, so he dug himself another dirt shelter and settled in to wait out the day. He was tired, he was hungry, and he was still sore, but he was also excited—at long last, the finish line was just over the horizon. It was no longer in doubt that he would make it to that finish line, but would he make it in time? Sunset at this time of year took place at approximately 20:40; he was due at the *Cocktail* at 22:00, and there was still the small problem that he didn't know precisely where Tundora was. It could still be up to twenty kilometres away. Then, of course, he had to actually find the *Cocktail* after he found the town, which would gobble up more of the minutes that he no longer had.

He sighed to himself as he watched the sun light up the sky above him. He was so close to victory that he could taste it, but his work was far from over. *This* marathon had become a sprint to the finish.

Chapter Five
The Consummate Professional

18 July 1511N

Rufino seldom remembered his dreams, but the one he had that day was a cut above the rest. He'd been a mule, hefting heavy loads to and fro for his owner, who just happened to be Kiralyn. He was an exemplary mule—loyal, tireless and uncomplaining; unfortunately, he was also hungry. So after one particularly long day of work, he tootled over to his master and—because he was also a talking mule—said, "You know, it would sure be nice to have a bagel or two." He loved bagels, and he knew she made some every Friday morning, so a minor redistribution of wealth sounded perfectly reasonable to him.

Kiralyn had other ideas. She took a bagel, tied it to a string on the end of a stick, and attached the stick to his harness in such a way that the bagel could dangle right in front of his nose. He could both see and smell that scrumptious pastry as he toiled over the next few days, but it was always just out of his reach. Finally, near the end of another difficult day of labour, he developed an itch and went to relieve himself on a nearby fence. During the frenzied scratching that followed, his harness came loose, falling to the grass at his feet and permitting access to the bagel. At long last, he took his first bite, only to discover that his prize had gone stale during the time it had been dangling from that stick. But when he returned to Kiralyn to complain, she said she didn't care—that he should consider himself lucky he got the bagel at all.

There was a valuable lesson to be derived from this dream: d*on't let her string you along, Rufino. No bagels on* *sticks.* She would test him, he knew, but she wouldn't be doing so just for the fun of it. He believed this because the gods had bestowed upon him a sort of empathy that was unusual amongst his kind. Halflings were brilliant people, but they could also be more than a bit oblivious to the feelings of others. Rufino was not. When he stopped to *really* think things through, he could usually determine another person's feelings to an impressively small margin of error. So when he woke up an hour before dusk on the night of the rendezvous, he decided to pass the idle time by making an effort to understand where the druid-sorceress was coming from.

It was then that it first occurred to him that the fear between them was not just flowing in one direction. She'd admitted to mistrusting him, but something told him there was more to her feelings than she was letting on. He was obviously not a physical threat, but he could still do a lot of damage if he got it in his head to give the authorities a confession about their extralegal collaboration. Doing so would be suicide, but if she made him believe he was going to die anyway, he could very well decide that sticking it to her would be the best way to go. She obviously knew this—she had, after all, gone to great lengths in Borallis to persuade him that he'd never been in danger from her. He didn't buy that for a minute, but Kiralyn herself had said there was "always a reason" for a lie, and it seemed clear to him now that the reason for *this* one was that she was afraid of what he might do if she pushed him too far.

His competency was also an unknown quantity from where she was sitting. Even if he had the best intentions in the world, he could still turn out to be a bumbling, incompetent idiot who'd botch the operation and cost her people their only shot at this target. Many of the points he'd made back in Borallis had been correct, and perhaps the most correct point of all had been his claim that the druids wouldn't have asked an *unnatural* creature for help unless their need was urgent. They didn't have time to go find another undead beastie; they had to make do with the one they had. If this terrible risk of theirs turned into a resounding victory because of him, it went without saying that Kiralyn should be enormously relieved. *Maybe even a little grateful?*

However, as his internal pessimist had been correct to point out earlier, it would be folly to assume the two of them were thinking on the same wavelength. Setting aside the differences between men and women for a moment, Kiralyn was a half-elf, and that elven heritage could prove to be a considerable headache. Humans and elves were very different, both in physical characteristics and in how they approached life. Elves were long-lived people who were often highly conservative, valuing their culture and traditions above all else. If the woman was more elf than human, he'd be more likely to get his answers from banging his head against a wall than from trying to pry them out of her.

If she leaned more toward her human side, however, he had a chance. Compared to elves, humans were far more open-minded and willing to take risks—far more like halflings, in other words. It was easy to believe her human blood was dominant—she was way too tall to be much of an elf—but if she'd been raised by her elven parent, the blood thing wouldn't count for much. It was a well-established fact that if two identical twins were separated at birth and brought up in two completely different cultures, they'd become two completely different people. Experience played a far more significant role in the shaping of a person than did blood.

Fortunately, he was well equipped to handle challenging tasks. He was, after all, the consummate professional: suave, sophisticated, sexy, willing to compromise, and fiercely loyal to anyone who could give him important answers or fresh bagels. The key word here was "fresh"—he could find stale pastry in the trash outside any bakery in Nyobi, but it had been an eternity since he'd revelled in the orgasmic indulgence of some bagels that were hot out of the oven. Oh, what he wouldn't give to move his coffin into a bakery witho…

But he was getting sidetracked. What mattered was that Kiralyn's expectations of him were about to be obliterated. Now that he had some insight as to where she was coming from, he could tailor his approach to suit both of their needs. It wouldn't be difficult—she was afraid he was an idiot, but he was actually Rufino Endicott, Halfling Vampire Extraordinaire. For maybe the first time in her life, the druid-sorceress wasn't gonna know what hit her.

***

Now that the pep talk was over and done with, the Halfling Vampire Extraordinaire set his mind on the time trial before him. When the light in the sky told him sunset was imminent, he began a routine of stretching and breathing exercises so he'd be ready to go when conditions permitted. The breathing went smoothly, but the stretching did not. *Note to self,* he grumbled as he was repeatedly interfered with by the claustrophobic confines of his shelter, *dig bigger holes*. He was still able to stretch one wing at a time by rolling onto his side and reaching toward the opening, so his warmup was far from crippled—he just felt like a fool. It was a good thing nobody could see him.

What his exercises lacked in style, they made up for in effectiveness. Thirty seconds after sunset, he was northward bound, cutting through the air as though he'd been catapulted forth by a trebuchet. Somewhere just over that horizon was Tundora, and if ever there was a time for ludicrous velocity, this was it. Being late for the most important date of his life would really mess with his aura of competence.

Breakneck speed, for him, was about twenty kilometres per hour. There was no way he'd be able to sustain that speed for a full hour if Tundora was indeed still twenty kilometres away, but he did think he could cover that distance in *seventy* minutes, which would leave him ten minutes with which to find the *Cocktail* and spruce himself up a bit. He'd have given the rest of his hair for fifteen more minutes of search time, but fortunately, his need to spruce was as minimal as ever. He was the only guy he knew of who could go on a four-hundred-kilometre journey, scare off dozens of gigantic snakes, stare down a bird of prey, wrestle a ferocious animal, and come away from it all looking great.

Though his interest in wordplay was nowhere near as strong as he'd suggested to Kiralyn, he did sometimes think about penning an autobiography. It seemed destined to become a best seller, for his ability to cheat death was the stuff of legends. Unfortunately, there were two significant barriers standing between him and a lifetime supply of royalty payments. For starters, he would definitely need an agent, and that agent would need to know his big secret. Rufino wasn't comfortable with that, and his agent wouldn't be comfortable with that, either—it was a crime to protect a vampire from the hunters. Even if he *could* find someone who was willing to play cat and mouse with the authorities on his behalf, there was no guarantee that he could actually commit his thoughts to paper—even letting him get within spitting distance of a bottle of ink was a recipe for disaster. Pencils had gotten him through school well enough, but one simply did *not* submit a great manuscript in pencil, lest he invite an overzealous editor to fiddle around with things.

If things go well with Kiralyn, maybe I should broach the subject. The sorceress-spy would probably charge an arm and a leg for her elite services, but she already knew his secret and she obviously wasn't scared of the authorities. If she was any good with a pen, he could make them both rich.

Rufino's mad dash for the finish line was going on forty-five minutes when, at long last, his hard work was rewarded. There were three farms—two vegetable and one dairy—ahead of him now, and just beyond the farms he saw hundreds of widely dispersed lights that could only belong to Tundora. The fatigue in his badly mistreated body now temporarily forgotten, he drove forward with single-minded determination and managed to reach the city ten minutes later. At the last minute, he also clawed for some altitude—in the absence of a map, a view from a hundred feet was a tourist's best friend.

Tundora was one of several cities that supported the nation's budding manufacturing industry, and as such it was a fairly decent size, sporting a population of approximately twenty thousand. The city's shape was that of a bullet pointed directly at the forest—imagery that had undoubtedly done zilch to endear the place to its druidic neighbours. Setting aside the imagery for a moment, it was immediately apparent that the layout of the town was both simple and logical: the western part of town— the head of the bullet—was the industrial sector, the centre of town was commercial, and the eastern part was residential. This simplified his search for the *Cocktail* tremendously.

Rufino made for the centre of town, but he wasn't out of the woods just yet. This was a pretty decent-sized town with a pretty decent-sized commercial district—the *Killer Cocktail* could be any one of the hundreds of buildings he had to choose from. What kind of spy would set up a rendezvous without providing a bloody address?

He immediately wished he hadn't asked himself that question, because there was a very obvious answer: *one who doesn't expect the other person to show up.*

He dove to about thirty feet and started buzzing some buildings. He soon learned that he was above Ventura

Street, and that he was in the wrong part of town—he passed a shoe store, a tailor, a barber shop, a place called *Auspicious Alchemy,* a hardware store, and several other places that weren't even close to being taverns. He made a quick note of the alchemist's shop and moved on.

At the next semi-major intersection, Rufino turned east onto Spartan Avenue, which, unfortunately, was appropriately named. Half of the shops were vacant, and the ones that were occupied didn't look all that reputable: pawn shops, sex shops, and the like. He then turned north onto Hacksaw Street, and he *did* find a small bar, but it wasn't the *Cocktail.* Still, he took this as a positive sign, though he hadn't the faintest idea why. Maybe he was just desperate for something to feel good about.

Several turns later, the little vampire found himself above Artery Avenue, which appeared to be a major route. He followed it west for a few minutes and found that he was definitely getting warmer—there were restaurants and a couple of inns, though Tundora was hardly a tourist hotspot so Rufino figured there wouldn't be many places for visitors to hole up. At the intersection of Artery and Main Street, he passed a building that claimed to be City Hall, though it didn't look any different from the dozens of single-floor shops he'd inspected already. Either they didn't hold their politicians in high esteem around here, or the mayor was trying to blend in.

Across from City Hall was a police station, so Rufino took that as his signal to move on. The next block was full of law offices, so the courthouse was probably nearby, but it didn't appear to be on this particular street. He also saw a library and a medical laboratory, the latter of which could be extremely useful if he wasn't able to catch a meal in the next few hours. A vampire won no style points for swiping blood samples from a lab, but Rufino's struggle to survive was not a contest to be graded or judged. As long as nobody saw him, it was all good.

It was beginning to dawn on him that Artery Avenue wasn't going to pan out, so he took a right-hand turn at Oak Street and followed it north for a few blocks. There were more people on the sidewalks of Oak Street than there had been anywhere else in town, so Rufino took this as another positive sign. *Something* was still open nearby, but if it wasn't the *Killer Cocktail,* he was going to have to swallow his pride and ask someone for directions before he ran out of time. It was about five minutes until 22:00, and he didn't want to give Kiralyn an opportunity to interpret the word "deadline" literally.

Rufino saw a couple of people leave a building at the northeast corner of the next intersection, so he landed in a narrow service alley between two buildings and reverted to his natural form. Whatever that building up the street was, he promised himself as he started up the eastern side of Oak Street at a brisk jog, it was about to become his personal Tourist Information Centre. So what if they took offense to his interest in a rival business? He didn't have time for wounded egos—if they were so upset that Kiralyn had chosen the *Cocktail* over their own grubby establishment, they should do something about it. *Extend Happy Hour,* an idea sprang to mind and he approached the intersection, *that's the first publicity stunt everyo...*

He skidded to a halt at the southeast corner of the intersection of Oak Street and Plantation Avenue. His train of thought did likewise. There, across the avenue from where he stood, was a smallish building with very distinctive saloon doors at the main entrance. Above the doors—clearly visible thanks to the nearby streetlamps—was a prominent sign that read, in calligraphic writing: *The Killer Cocktail.*

He stood there staring at his finish line for the better part of a minute. Its task now complete, his body was beginning to let go of whatever it was that had sustained him until now, and he was suddenly feeling very tired once again. But though his condition mirrored that of an improperly hydrated marathon runner, the flame of accomplishment now burned bright inside his dead heart. The first challenge was behind him now, and he'd kicked its ass. The *Bog of the Damned* had been no match for the Vampire of Destiny. If Kiralyn was expecting a no-show—and she probably was—she was going to be in for a shock. It was too bad he didn't have an easel and canvas in his back pocket, because the look of stunned disbelief that was going to be on her face would make for a terrific painting.

He crossed the street and approached the saloon doors. As he drew closer, he noticed a small red-and-white sign posted on the right door that declared, in no uncertain terms, No Druids Allowed. However, there was no sign forbidding undead patronage, so the little vampire considered himself welcome and pushed his way through the entrance.

The *Cocktail* had a reputation for being one of the finer establishments in this part of the country. That wasn't saying a whole lot, but Rufino's first impression of the place was a good one. It was very bright—the little vampire had seldom seen so many burning candles in a single room. Perhaps the unusual saloon doors weren't just for show—maybe they were also for ventilation.

To his immediate right was a small sitting area. A bit further up the east wall was the bar itself. From a design standpoint, it was nothing special—semi-circular with dyed wood, probably local product—but it was impressively large, featuring no fewer than sixteen stools and lots of standing room. Twelve of the stools were currently occupied, and the bartender—a raven-haired human woman in her twenties—appeared to be plenty busy. A menu was displayed prominently on a chalkboard that hung above the bartender's access to the storage area. The selection paled in comparison to the *Squid*, but it was decent, though Rufino didn't see anything he was particularly interested in.

What this country needs, he told himself, *is a vampire bar. It would be so awesome to walk into a tavern after a rough night and be able to order an O-negative on the rocks.*

To his left, separated from the rest of the establishment by some fake palm trees, was a small casino. Though it featured only four card tables and a handful of other games, Rufino was willing to give this corner of the *Cocktail* plenty of credit for its ambiance. Between the fake vegetation, the exotic fish in the large tank at the southwest corner of the building, the golden-sandy-coloured floor, and the floor-to-ceiling wall painting of an ocean as seen from a beach, the casino did a very adequate job of passing itself off as an exotic locale. If Rufino got his hands on some gold during his stay in town, he'd have to come back here and clean out some amateurs.

This was no time to be thinking about cards, though. He ran his eyes over the booths and tables at the back of the building, but it didn't appear as though Kiralyn had arrived yet. *Probably scared off by that sign they have out front.* He then scanned his surroundings for a clock, eventually finding one on the wall behind him, above the saloon doors. It displayed 21:56. *Damn,* he smiled to himself, *I'm good.*

He ducked into the men's room in the back-right corner of the building and spent the next few minutes preening—a professional needed to look good, after all. Fortunately, he did—after washing his face, straightening his hair and brushing a bit of dirt off his clothes, he was as ready as he was going to get. It would have been nice if he had some fancier duds to support his new image, but unless he went shopping in Galensdorf, he'd have more luck finding a tap-dancing troll than he would in finding an off-the-rack suit in his size. In spite of what had taken place out in the *Bog*, he knew it would still be some time before he'd be ready to go home, so there would be no suits for Rufino any time soon.

He decided to wait for Kiralyn just inside the front entrance. It was a fairly chilly night for the middle of summer, which probably meant some foul weather was on the way, but that was fine. Anyone who'd lived in Nyobi for thirty years had seen his share of strange weather, so it had long since stopped bothering him. Besides, a storm system of a different sort was due to arrive at this tavern in about two minutes, at which point Rufino's life as he knew it would never be the same again. When he recalled his Tundoran misadventure a year from now, he doubted he'd even remember that he'd felt a little cold at the time.

***

22:00 arrived.

Kiralyn did not.

Rufino wasn't the most patient person in the world—something that could be said of all halflings, really. By 22:05 he was pacing between the intersection and the *Cocktail's* entrance, stewing in silence over the druid-sorceress's tardiness. *She*'d been the one to decide on 22:00, so where in the hells was she? The notion that she'd forgotten about this meeting was absurd, as was the notion that he'd been victimized by an incredible practical joke. Frostwhisper didn't strike him as the type to engage in nonsense—especially not with a vampire—so he was forced to conclude that she'd simply been delayed for some reason. *Figures.*

Five whole minutes of disgruntled pacing later, the little vampire decided he'd had enough. He pushed his way back through the saloon doors and started looking for something to do. Unfortunately, the five silver coins in his pocket weren't going to get him anywhere, so his only real option was to watch the card games taking place in the casino. The playing tables were over three feet tall, but for once this wasn't going to be a problem because there was a nice counter under the fake palm trees upon which he could sit.

The counter sat almost five feet off the ground, but halflings had an easier time with pull-ups than most races—it was one of the few physical activities in which his paltry forty-two-pound body weight could be considered an advantage. A few seconds and one slightly-out-of-practice muscle-up later, he was seated comfortably on the counter, facing the nearest of the card tables. One of the players had been watching him climb onto the counter, but the man—a very thin, balding middle-aged man in a white dress shirt with thin blue stripes—seemed to lose interest as soon as it was clear that Rufino wasn't going to slip and hurt himself. *No free show tonight, pal.*

Rufino's attention then shifted from the disappointed man to the table at which he was playing. There were six men—one dwarf and five humans—playing what appeared to be Seven-Card Stud High-Low, a game in which terrible hands could be almost as lucrative as great ones. It had never been one of Rufino's preferred variants of poker, but he would say this for high-low games: they saw a lot of action, particularly at micro-stakes tables as this one appeared to be.

Indeed, the chips were flying, even in situations when it was obviously unreasonable to continue. Rufino had a newfound appreciation for insanity, for it was what had gotten him all the way here, but that didn't mean he was going to apply the trait to his card game in the foreseeable future. He came from a place where every man and woman claimed to be a better card player than everyone else, and the only way to shut them up was to assert some dominance on the field of battle. Galensdorf was a *ridiculously* competitive place when it came to cards, and in fact it had once been the site of the most prestigious card tournament in the entire country. Halflings seldom wandered far from home, so although the Galensdorf tournament had never been able to offer the richest purses, it *did* give the wannabes something no other tournament could: a shot at the evil midgets.

Rufino had never won at the big tournament, but he did have one particularly agonizing second-place finish to his credit in the discipline of Omaha poker. He didn't know what was worse—that he'd lost the decisive hand despite being an eighty-percent favourite going into the final card, or that the winner had been his now-ex-girlfriend, Megan.

The tournament still existed, but because of the kobold threat, only a handful of non-halflings still attended on an annual basis. Just over twenty years ago, a displaced tribe of kobolds—three-foot-tall reptilian bipeds—had gotten it into their empty heads to claim Galensdorf for themselves, and they'd been attacking it at random intervals ever since. Kobolds weren't the best fighters by *any* stretch of the imagination, but even a blind man hit the bulls-eye every now and then, and hundreds of halflings had been killed defending their home over the years. Until the kobold situation could be resolved, casual tourists wanted nothing to do with the battlefield that was Galensdorf, and Rufino couldn't honestly blame them. He only wondered what was important enough to compel the stupid kobolds to keep coming after being defeated in battle so many times.

He'd been pondering that question for a few minutes when something bumped into his leg. Hoping Kiralyn might finally be here, he returned his attention to the present; but instead of an exotic sorceress, he saw the hairy dwarf from the poker game standing before him. "Hey, li'l buddy," the ginger-bearded dwarf greeted him in the heavily accented Common that was a hallmark of his race. "You look bored."

The dwarf's willingness to talk to him was no surprise—their two vertically challenged races had long since decided to stick together. What *was* surprising was that the dwarf had left his seat with plenty of chips still at the table. "I am bored," the halfling admitted easily. "I'm supposed to meet someone here, but she's running late."

"You wanna sit in for me?"

That wasn't what Rufino had expected to hear. "Excuse me?"

The dwarf pointed toward the saloon doors. "I gotta step out for a few, an' if I leave the building, I forfeit my seat unless I got a buddy to hold it for me. Whaddya say?"

It sounded like there was a wait list for this table, which gave the little vampire some leverage. "I'll do it," he decided, "in exchange for a small bottle of peach cider."

The dwarf didn't appear to be thrilled by this development, so Rufino decided to nudge things along with a sob story. "The lady doesn't like it when I gamble," he explained, concealing his relationship with the mystery woman on purpose so as to preserve whatever story Kiralyn intended to use. "If she walks in here and sees me playing poker, a bottle of her favourite might just be the difference between a minor headache and a massive one."

The dwarf bought it. "Hah!" he exclaimed jovially. "Ye got a deal. Take a seat and I'll get yer drink. Peach cider, ye say?"

"Yes," Rufino confirmed as he hopped off the counter.

"Who in the hells drinks that?"

It was a valid question coming from a dwarf—they liked their liquor strong enough to fell an ogre. "She's a skyscraper," Rufino explained, once again being careful to avoid specifics because he didn't know if Kiralyn would be posing as a half-elf or a full human. "Who knows why they do anything they do?"

"True, that," the dwarf agreed as he started toward the bar. "I be right back with yer drink." Before he got there, though, Rufino was certain he heard the words, "If ye can call it that," coming from his partner's general direction. That was to be expected, though, for alcoholism was so thoroughly ingrained in dwarven culture that it was probably difficult for them to understand that getting hammered and passing out on a tavern floor was *not* everyone's idea of a good time.

Rufino tootled over to the vacant chair at the low-stakes table. Every last player, including the dealer, watched the newcomer climb onto the chair and try to sit down, only to decide that he couldn't sit because the chair was too low. Rufino then stood up on his chair, which elicited a strange wince from the man in the striped dress shirt but good humour from everyone else. One of them—with a mostly empty bottle of rum in the cup-holder in front of him—decided to break the ice. "Need a booshter sheat?"

Rufino would have written the man off immediately had he not fallen for Kiralyn's drunk routine a week ago. Misrepresentation, he reminded himself, was very much a part of poker, and he'd be a fool to take these guys at face value. "I don't know how much you overheard," the little vampire addressed the dealer whilst ignoring the drunk who thought he was clever, "but I'll be sitting in for my vertically challenged pal over there until he gets back from whatever it is he needs to do. None of these chips belong to me, but he did say it's fine if I play some hands on his behalf."

"Of course it's fine," someone else—a muscular young man in a brown vest over a dirty white T-shirt—snorted. "Who *wouldn't* want to get some of that halfling luck working in his favour?"

That would have been a fair question if not for the mistaken contention that halflings needed luck. *Mad skills all day, baby.* "I haven't played in a while," he eased his way into the hustle, "because the lady doesn't like gambling. I…"

"Oh, horseshit," the young man declared, though the grin on his face lacked the severity of his profane tongue. "You've been sneakin' games behind her back. Admit it."

Rufino shrugged. "It would be pointless to deny it considering what I'm doing right now." He turned back to the dealer and put on an expression of irritation. "We gonna play, or are we gonna sit here dissecting my personal life until the dwarf gets back?"

"It's your big blind," was the dealer's curt response.

What he was saying was that the game couldn't go on until the "big blind" made a forced bet to get the next hand started. Rufino rolled his eyes as he tossed a couple of chips into the fray. "'Course it is."

***

Rufino didn't play the first hand, which helped endear him to the table a little bit. The dwarf delivered the bottle of peach cider, as promised, and then took off through the saloon doors at a brisk jog. Briefly, Rufino wondered what was so important, but in the end he didn't really care—he only hoped the man returned before Kiralyn deigned to show up. She wouldn't understand the fellowship that existed between dwarves and halflings.

His second, third and fourth hands all sucked, too; and after folding the fourth hand, Rufino checked the clock near the entrance. *22:45—you've got to be kidding me. A druid shouldn't need a clock to know what time it is—she should be able to use the sky, just as I do.*

He was starting to get very frustrated, and also a little worried that Kiralyn might not be coming at all. So when the fifth hand saw him dealt Ace-two-three of the same suit—positively *divine* starting cards in a high-low game—he decided to take his increasingly bad mood out on the other players. The fixed-limit betting structure of the game took a lot of the mind games out of betting, which was a big part of why Rufino usually played something else, but in this case it didn't make much difference because when one had a hand like this he wanted all the action he could get.

The other players stayed in for a few streets—rounds—before bowing out, except for one. The man in the striped dress shirt was still in, and Rufino couldn't figure out why. His visible cards were garbage, and even if his hidden cards gave him a disguised monster, at best he'd only win half the pot because he didn't have enough small cards to qualify for the low pot. Rufino, with the Ace-two-three-four-five straight he ended up making, was guaranteed to win the low pot and also stood a respectable chance of winning the high pot, too.

Fixed-limit games had a bet ceiling—a point at which the previous bet could only be called, not raised. The little vampire was aware that, if the pattern of re-raising held true, he was going to be the one making the final bet, at which point he would be called and would be forced to show his cards. If the caller realized he'd lost, it was his right to throw away his own cards without showing them to anyone. Rufino, however, was very interested in seeing those cards—he wanted to verify his read on the man—so just before hitting the bet limit in the final round of play, he threw a cog in the works by calling his opponent's bet instead of raising it.

The man glowered at him for a moment before slowly revealing his hidden cards. His hand was every bit as terrible as Rufino had suspected: a pair of sixes, which in a six-handed, seven-card game was, for all intents and purposes, worthless. Rufino revealed his wheel—a common nickname for an Ace-to-five straight—and the dealer responded by pushing the entire pot, minus the casino's cut, toward the victorious but very confused vampire. Maybe he should have left it at that, but the halfling thirst for knowledge was still very much a part of him, and he found himself unable to hold his peace. "What in the hells was that?"

The enigma in the nice shirt was aware that the halfling was speaking to him, but he didn't seem to understand why. "I beg your pardon?" he demanded in a soft voice.

Rufino pointed at the centre of the table, where the man's miserable hand had defiled the entire game with its existence. "I'm wondering what was going through your mind when you played that hand," he spelled it out for the guy. "I can't figure it out, so I have to ask."

It was usually considered self-defeating to give lessons to an opponent who still had money on the table, but since Rufino wasn't going to see a copper of that money anyway, he had no reason to care. "I was hoping you were only after the low pot," the other claimed with a shrug.

"So you raised what you *hoped* was a split pot as high as it would go, increasing the casino's cut in the event of a split, and counting on your pair of sixes to measure up to the myriad of straights and flushes and trips or two-pair combos I could have had." Rufino nodded slowly as a conclusion came to him. "Are you really this bad, or are you losing on purpose?"

It wasn't likely that someone would tank a game on purpose, he knew, but sometimes it took a ridiculous suggestion to explain an absurd occurrence. No rational player would have played a hand like that under these circumstances, *especially* not against a halfling. The stick-thin man clearly understood basic poker theory because of a comment he'd made about Rufino's table image ten minutes ago, so things just weren't adding up.

The man folded his arms across his chest and suddenly looked very annoyed. "You're a lippy one," he observed quite severely, "aren't you?"

He obviously didn't know it, but he'd just described the entire halfling race. "My people are famous for our uncensored opinions," the little vampire retorted with pride. "You didn't answer my question."

The man then leaned back in his chair, though his arms remained crossed. "You obviously played the hand better than I did. Now, a question for you: does your attitude grow in relation to your chip stack?"

One of the others at the table snickered under his breath. For his part, Rufino opened his mouth, though it took a short moment before he was able to decide on an appropriate retort. "In case you've forgotten, this isn't my stack, so I don't care if I win or lose." That was a lie, of course—halflings always wanted to win—but it sounded good under the circumstances. "I was simply wondering what was going through your mind when you made that play."

"So you could tell me what I did wrong, no doubt," the man replied with some degree of accuracy. He then unfolded his arms and stood up from his seat, which told Rufino the situation was about to escalate. "Listen: I know I suck at this game—I lose almost every time I play. I also know there's a lot you could probably teach me about optimal play, but it just so happens there's something I can teach *you* about this particular table."

Rufino was silent, so the man continued. "This table has a maximum buy-in of five gold, sir," he explained, though the *sir* was anything but polite. "It's meant to be a place where casual players and beginners can have some fun without having to worry about losing more than a bit of drinking money. It is *not* a place for an elitist tool to dish out condescending lessons after putting others down for poor play."

The man was pissed, but that was fine. Rufino's date was almost an hour late, so he was pissed, too. "Dude," he snapped as the stresses of his journey finally caught up to him, "I don't friggin' care if you feel slighted by my criticism. I don't want to be here. I'm playing a game I don't want to play, for a dwarf I don't even know, while I wait for a woman who wouldn't know punctuality if it slapped her in the face. Once the dwarf comes back from wherever the hell he's gone, I will be *more* than happy to leave. In the meantime, I feel compelled to point out that although your poker game could be described as a philanthropic endeavour, these losses are *not*, in fact, tax-deductible. The Cr…"

"What's it to you?" one of the others at the table spoke up as the man in the shirt sat back down. "If he wants to spew, isn't that his business?"

The little vampire stared daggers at the insignificant man who'd dared to interrupt his rant. "Poker is about more than just money," he told the other. "It's also about competition, and for one such as me who values the competitive aspect of the game above all else, my fun gets neutered every time I cross paths with a player who doesn't give a shit. There's no sense of accomplishment in winning by default."

"I knew he was lying about not wanting to win," the muscular man spoke up again, as if he expected someone to give him a medal.

With perfect timing, the ginger-haired dwarf—now sweaty and gasping for breath—barrelled through the saloon doors. "'Bout bloody time," Rufino voiced his thoughts as he reached another finish line. "I'm outta here."

He grabbed his bottle of cider and turned to jump off his seat, but before he could do so, he was stopped by an intriguing comment from the man in the striped shirt. "Oh, you're outta here, all right." The man then snapped his fingers for no apparent reason. Rufino stared into the man's eyes, looking for some clue as to what was going on, but for once the man's face was betraying nothing.

The enormous slab of muscle that arrived at the man's side an instant later, however, explained a lot. It was a tuxedo-sporting, grey-skinned, seven-foot-tall male half-orc—undoubtedly a bodyguard, since orcs weren't hired for their brains. That made the man in the shirt a VIP of some sort, but the little vampire was beyond caring about such things—his week had already been so craptacular that an altercation with a VIP would just be the cherry on a sundae. "Nice orc, pal," Rufino remarked sarcastically, "but if you think he scares me, you've got another thing coming. I…"

"Grunk," the man in the shirt looked up at the orc, "escort this gentleman from the premises." He then returned his attention to the gentleman in question. "I'm afraid you've worn out your welcome."

Who does this clown think he is? "I'm not leaving until the woman I'm supposed to meet shows up," he made his position known. "I have powerful friends, so if yo…"

Nobody was listening. "Toss the bum," the seemingly important man issued revised instructions to his pet behemoth.

The sweaty dwarf and the hulking orc reached Rufino's chair in perfect unison. "What in blazes be goin' on, here?" the former demanded.

"Let's just say," the man in the shirt replied, now sounding insufferably smug, "it's a good thing you returned when you did, because this seat was about to be given to someone else."

Rufino wanted to regale the dwarf with his own version of the story, but he was silenced as Grunk grabbed a handful of his clothes and hoisted him into the air. The bottle of cider was then ripped from Rufino's grasp before he could even think about using it as a weapon. Every last person in the tavern was watching the scene in the casino by now, and from his suddenly elevated perspective, Rufino could see that many of them seemed to be entertained by what they saw. In a moment of dark, humiliated fury, he wondered how *entertained* they'd be if he shifted into his bat form and went on a chomping spree. "You can't do this!" Rufino protested instead, his composure now all but gone as the bodyguard started striding toward the side door. "I'll have the owner throw you out! I'll get the *police* on your ass, you miserable…"

"The police won't do anything," the man called back at him, now from thirty feet away, "and the owner is quite satisfied with this resolution."

"Hah!" Rufino cried, his mouth moving of its own accord. "You wait and see! I'll…"

Then his mind caught up to his mouth. "You…?"

The half-orc paused just shy of the exit, giving his master one last chance to gloat. "My house," the man declared with a grin, "my rules, the most important of which is to exercise a certain level of civility." He lifted his right hand to wave at the suddenly speechless vampire. "Bye."

At that, Grunk—not a bodyguard, but a bouncer—threw open the side door and chucked Rufino out into the night.

Chapter Six
Ground Rules

Rufino crash-landed in the middle of Oak Street, bouncing once before sliding to a halt. He lay still for a few moments thereafter, fighting against both the pain in his body and the fury in his heart. There were regulations, he knew, prohibiting owners and employees from playing at their own casinos, so either the *Cocktail's* owner was ignoring the regulations or his casino was unlicensed. Though unlicensed casinos were technically illegal, they often managed to escape the notice of the authorities, and it didn't take a genius to figure out how. *So I take my frustrations out on an opponent and it turns out to be the one guy in the whole bloody building who can kick me out. If that isn't a perfect summation of my week, I don't know wha...*

A glimmer of refracted light was his only warning—Kiralyn's bottle of cider was ten feet in the air and one short moment away from smashing onto the packed dirt road beside him. Instinct overrode conscious thought as he rolled onto his side, reaching out as far as he could in a desperate effort to save the fruit of his labour from destruction. He did succeed in catching the bottle, but he hyperextended his left shoulder in doing so, which was just another perfect summation of his week as far as he was concerned. Now he was going to have to add an ice pack to his Tundoran shopping list. *Great.*

He needed to get off the street. It was only 23:00, so there could still be a few carts out there, and this was probably going to be the busiest road in the city for as long as he was sitting on it. Before he could get back to his feet, however, a shadow fell over him as a human form approached. Rufino would have looked up to see who it was, but he didn't need to—given the unbelievably awkward timing, this shadow could only belong to one person.

He was right. "You certainly have a way with people," a familiar female voice commented.

Rufino sighed, his embarrassment temporarily drowning out his pain. "You asked me to meet you at the *Killer Cocktail*," he tried his best to sound like everything was going according to plan. "You said nothing about inside or outside."

"True," Kiralyn Frostwhisper conceded easily, "but this isn't quite what I had in mind."

Rufino hauled himself to his feet and brushed the dirt off his trousers. "Yeah, well, you being an hour late isn't quite what *I* had in mind, either." He turned to face her and held up the bottle as a peace offering. "For you."

She hesitated a second, then accepted the bottle. She was as beautiful as he remembered, but now that he knew who she really was, it should be simple enough to avoid falling into *that* particular trap. Until she demonstrated that she was no longer a threat to him, all he needed to do to protect himself was to pretend he was looking at Grunk every time he looked at her. *That stupid orc is going to be good for something after all.*

Grunkalyn's clothes hadn't changed a whole lot—her blouse was red instead of green, and her black pants looked even more expensive than her last pair. She was also in one-inch heels now instead of flats, which was an affront to his halfling sensitivities. Why in blazes would a woman who was already six feet tall feel the need to be *taller*? "How's the weather up there?" he made his feelings known.

She'd been inspecting the label on her new bottle, but his question was enough to grab her attention. "Pardon me?" she asked, sounding a bit confused.

The offended halfling pointed accusingly at her footwear. "Your shoes," he spelled it out for her. "What gives?"

She looked down at her feet for a moment. "What do you mean, what gives?" she still wasn't getting it. "Surely you have heeled shoes in Galensdorf."

Rufino nodded and smiled rather sardonically. "Those women are three feet tall," he pointed out, "not six."

The sorceress led them over to the sidewalk and turned south, keeping her pace slow enough that he had no trouble keeping up. "This might blow your halfling mind," she told him after a moment, "but I wore these shoes tonight because they're stylish and comfortable and *I like them*. The fact that I'm one inch closer to becoming a human lightning rod is incidental."

Her response was somewhat disarming—the irritation in her voice had been expected, but the self-deprecating humour had not. "I'm sorry," Rufino decided to back off for a bit. "My people see four-six to five feet as being the ideal range. It's difficult for us to imagine wanting to be taller than that."

She shrugged. "Perspective is everything, Rufino. Do you want to know what my nickname was when last I visited an orcish settlement?"

"What?"

She smiled. "They called me, 'little girl'."

That didn't sound particularly healthy. "Did they know who they were dealing with?"

She took a moment to assess their surroundings. "They did," she eventually replied, though her voice was significantly lower.

"Are they still alive?"

"Of course," she murmured whilst simultaneously raising her right index finger to her lips. She obviously had little interest in continuing this line of conversation.

That was fine, because Rufino didn't give a damn about the orcs anyway. "Okay," he changed the subject, "if you don't wanna talk about that, would you mind telling me why you kept me waiting in there for a whole bloody hour before…"

She stopped dead in her tracks, prompting him to do the same. "Take the hint and stuff it," she growled through clenched teeth. "We can talk about work once we're indoors."

Slightly taken aback by his companion's severity, Rufino decided to conduct his own visual scan of their surroundings. Aside from a very talkative human couple on the other side of the street, he didn't see anyone. "We do appear to have some privacy," he pointed out.

She sighed through her nose and folded her arms across her chest. "If I told you," she said in a quiet voice, "that until a moment ago, I was following three separate conversations taking place inside the *Cocktail,* would you believe me?"

The little vampire glanced back at the tavern, which was now about seventy metres away. He couldn't hear anything. Kiralyn's half-elven ears were obviously more sensitive than his own, but he'd never known how big the elven advantage really was. This seemed like as good a time as any to find out. "Yeah, right," he attempted to bait her.

She went for it. "There's a man at the bar who thinks the bartender shorted him on change," she described without hesitation, "a married couple is concerned about their babysitter's lack of experience, and there's also a noisy dwarf going on about his 'little buddy' being mistreated. I assume he means you?"

It was nice to know the dwarf remembered him. It was also nice to have some solid information: Kiralyn's ears could pick a conversation out of a crowd from half a block away, and she was only *half*-elven. With this knowledge in hand, there was only one reasonable course of action: *I'm never going to an elven city again.* "Yes, that was me," Rufino admitted with some reluctance. "The dwarf needed someone to hold his seat for him at a poker table, and I needed a way to get that bottle for you, so we hooked up."

"And then you insulted the owner?"

The little troublemaker shrugged. "I wouldn't call him an owner," he corrected her, "so much as I'd call him a power-hungry dictator presiding over a tiny fiefdom. He's breaking the law with his unlicensed casino, yet somehow *I'm* the one who got tossed."

Kiralyn stifled a laugh. "Good for you," she heaped some unexpected praise upon him. "Getting kicked out of the *Cocktail* is a badge of honour among druids."

Perhaps there was more to that sign on the door than was outwardly apparent. "Really?"

She nodded. "I've been kicked out twice," she boasted, "once for performing an improvised anti-industry ballad on karaoke night, and once for correctly accusing the bartender of watering down the drinks. On the Cocktail Ejection Leaderboard, however, I'm not even in the top ten."

"The Cocktail Ejection Leaderboard?" he repeated stupidly. If she was pulling his leg, she was doing her usual masterful job of it.

"Don't sound so surprised," she admonished him mildly. "Druids need to have fun too, you know."

Rufino didn't know what to say to that, so he turned as if to start walking again. He didn't make it one step, though, before she stuck a leg out to impede his progress. "Are you finished, then?" she asked.

He looked back up at her, making no effort to hide his confusion. "What difference does it make?" he demanded. "If someone is listening, he's heard th…"

She cut him off with a shake of her head. “We are currently standing inside an invisible bubble that prevents sound waves from entering or leaving,” she explained matter-of-factly. “This bubble is not going to follow us down the street, though, so we’re not going anywhere until you’ve exhausted your supply of incriminating inquiries.”

It did seem odd that he couldn’t hear *anything* from the *Cocktail* at this range, so he attempted to verify Kiralyn’s claim by taking a few steps back toward Plantation Avenue. During one of those steps, he went from hearing nothing at all to hearing everything as usual, which confirmed what the druid-sorceress was telling him. Unfortunately, this presented a new problem. He was hardly an authority when it came to magic, but his understanding was that spellcasters needed to use words and arm gestures in order to cast spells. These things helped focus the mind, or so he’d been taught.

Now, it *was* possible that he wasn’t remembering correctly—he’d just flown four hundred or more kilometres and his mind was in no better condition than his body. But unless he’d blacked out for a few seconds *and* failed to notice it, the druidess had cast her bubble without using words *or* gestures. That was bad. If this stealth-casting trick of hers also worked on, say, a lightning bolt, then it was within her ability to kill him before he even knew what was happening. *Still happy you signed up for this, dumbass?*

He turned around. Kiralyn was saying something again, but he wasn’t much of a lip-reader, so he took a half-step back into her bubble. “…Detectable for forty-eight hours,” she was explaining, “but only by those who know *exactly* what to look for. Since we’re in Tundora and not Strelas or Sylvany, we should be fine. That is, of course, assuming you’re quite finished telling the universe what we’re doing here?”

The little vampire didn’t like the sound of that. “I didn’t…”

"I know you didn't mean it," she cut him off smoothly, "but I'm obviously going to have to give you a crash course in discretion before the mission can proceed. It's a wonder you've survived for so long without it."

That wasn't exactly fair. "I can be plenty discreet," he objected with a sneer. "It's just so *difficult* to curb my enthusiasm when you're around."

To her credit, she seemed to realize he was fishing for a reaction, because she went out of her way to deny him one. "Try harder," was her only response, delivered in a cold and expressionless voice.

A voice that was too cold and expressionless for his taste. Patience was a finite resource, and it seemed clear that her supply of it wasn't going to last much longer. The time to smile and nod was upon him. "I can shut up," he told her, "for as long as I have to. Make no mistake, though: once we reach safety, I *am* going to be back on your case about why you were so late."

"Did that make you angry?" she challenged.

He shook his head. "Not angry," he corrected her, "but I *was* afraid you weren't coming, and if not for my frayed nerves, I doubt I would have bothered with the argument that led to my new ranking on your Leaderboard. I just want to know what was so bloody important."

Her expression softened. "Well, fortunately for you," she informed him, "my delay did pertain to this specific operation, which means I'll actually be able to tell you."

Rufino rolled his eyes. "Don't I feel privileged," he remarked with all the sarcasm at his disposal. "Let's get moving, then."

They'd been walking for fifteen minutes—and had just turned east onto Alder Avenue—before Rufino found his voice again. "Don't you want your drink?" he asked after it occurred to him that she had yet to open it.

"I do," she replied, "but it'll have to wait until we're inside."

"How come?"

"I don't drink from bottles."

Rufino didn't understand. "Why not?"

"It's not how I was raised," she said simply.

Then, without warning, she took an abrupt left turn into a dark alley between an accountant's office and a general store. Rufino stayed close, not knowing what was going on but recognizing that she did want him to follow her lead. Hopefully his inquiry about the drink hadn't set her off again.

The sorceress-spy spent the next minute combing the alley for signs of humanoid life, even going so far as to open a garbage can to see if anyone was inside. When she was finally satisfied that they had some privacy, she set her bottle on the ground on its side, then turned to face her miniature henchman. "We're almost there," she told him. "Follow me."

Before he could think to ask where they were going, Kiralyn's humanoid body morphed itself into the elegant form of a snowy owl. He'd known all along that druids were shape-shifters—and very capable ones at that—but her transformation was unsettling all the same. Aside from the fact that he had some personal issues with birds of prey, the question of which Kiralyn was the real one was complicated enough without a bunch of animal forms being thrown into the mix. His poor halfling brain could only handle so much weirdness.

As if on cue, his bizarre-o-meter went completely off the scale when Kiralyn wrapped her flight form's talons around the narrow end of the bottle and then took off with it. For the second time in as many hours, he lamented his lack of an easel and canvas—an owl with an appetite for cider was one of those once-in-a-lifetime sights that absolutely *needed* to be captured on paper. He had no way of capturing anything right now, though, so he shifted into his own flight form and followed her into the sky. Her awkward but apparently precious cargo prevented her from staying aloft at his paltry cruise velocity, but there was no need for them to fly in formation—her white-with-brown plumage was highly visible, even at night.

So visible, in fact, that he began to wonder why a spy would use such a poorly hidden form. It was possible she had more than one flight form to choose from, but the quality of her flying told him this snowy owl form of hers had some serious mileage on it. He'd have to broach the subject some time—maybe druids didn't get to choose the animals they could emulate. *Or maybe she just likes snowy owls.*

There was a three-storey hotel just a short block away. It was a wooden building, of course—like Samradyn, this entire city seemed to be made of wood—but it was immediately obvious that this place was a *lot* nicer than the inns he'd buzzed on Artery Avenue. There was a working fountain near the front entrance, which strongly suggested the building's suites had running water as well. Rufino wouldn't have expected to find a luxury like that in an out-of-the-way town like this, but he wouldn't have expected a charming and beautiful schoolteacher to be Kiralyn Frostwhisper in disguise, either. *Not calling 'em too well this week, are you?*

On the far side of the fountain was a parking lot for wagons—of which there were twelve—and to the east of the building was a stable for the horses. To the north of the building was a huge garden—complete with sculptures and even a small hedge maze—and just beyond the garden was a park that extended all the way north to the next avenue. The park featured a couple of duck ponds and plenty of trees, so Rufino could certainly understand why a druid would favour this hotel over the others he'd seen. What he didn't understand was how she was paying for these upscale rooms of hers—he'd never seen anything to indicate that druids had significant financial resources.

Kiralyn had obviously found a way around the money problem, though, because she dove to rooftop level as soon as she was above the garden. She then flew to the far end of the building and through an open window into the corner suite. From a security standpoint, the selection of the corner suite made sense: with no suite above or on one side, the number of potential eavesdroppers was cut in half. The top-floor suite was not absolutely ideal, but since both of them could fly, the inconvenience would be minor.

Rufino steered himself through the appropriate window, being careful not to crash into the nice chandelier on the other side. Except for the narrow hallway near the door, the room was covered in a fluffy white carpet that was probably an unbelievable pain in the ass to keep clean. The last thing he wanted was to invite the wrath of the cleaning crews, so he put off landing and shifting until he was standing on the hardwood floor near the entrance. He then removed his shoes and deposited them on the rack inside the coat closet, noticing as he did so that the closet contained a small handbag. The fact that Kiralyn's handbag was by itself told him she was indeed staying somewhere else. That was good news—he still needed to load up on supplies at the alchemy shop, and doing so behind her back should now be a relatively simple task.

He tootled back into the main room. The queen-size bed was to his right, the large double-pane window with soft white curtains was dead ahead, and a standing mirror was tucked into the corner on his far left. A landscape painting of Mount Nozebli—the tallest peak in Nyobi and fourth-tallest in the world—dominated the left wall, and a work desk sat beneath it, tucked into the near corner. Upon that desk rested a silver candelabra, a stack of paper, and… a fountain pen. *Oh no.*

He ripped his attention away from the weapon of mass destruction and took in the rest of the suite. The ensuite bathroom—beside the bed and behind the hallway—did appear to have running water, but it lacked a bathtub due to size constraints. In the tub's place was an upright, semi-transparent glass box that the little vampire assumed was a shower stall, but since he'd never seen one before, he couldn't be certain. He also didn't understand why anyone would prefer an artificial waterfall over a warm bath, but whatever. Tall people were weird.

There was also a door between the hallway and the desk that led into a room behind the coat closet, but that door was presently shut so Rufino didn't know exactly what was behind it. *Probably a reading room,* he decided. *I'll check it out later.*

While he'd been familiarizing himself with the suite, Kiralyn had closed the window behind them. The woman was decidedly paranoid for someone who wasn't undead. "This will be your suite," she confirmed what he'd already figured out. "As you've probably already noticed, the window faces north, so the sun shouldn't give you any trouble."

He put his right hand over his dead heart. "Your concern for my welfare is touching," he remarked with a very heavy dose of sarcasm.

It came without warning: a short puff of wind, sufficient to knock him onto his butt but not enough to do any damage. The fluffy carpet cushioned his landing quite nicely, and by the time he realized what had actually happened, the druid-sorceress was speaking again. "Before you get up," she said, "we need to get something straight."

He shuddered involuntarily—when it came to women, "we need to get something straight" was only slightly better than the dreaded "we need to talk." "Hey, wait," he raised a hand to stall her, "I…"

"Relax," she instructed coolly. "You're not in any danger, but you do need to be paying attention to what I'm about to say because the success of the mission is depending on it."

The little vampire blinked a few times before deciding to remain silent. For her part, Kiralyn took a seat at the foot of the bed before speaking again. "From now until the end of the operation," she told him, "you are to treat everyone except me as a potential member of the secret police. You are not to discuss this operation with *anyone* except me, and you are not even to discuss it with me unless we are inside this reasonably soundproof room. Do you understand?"

Rufino nodded, at which point Kiralyn seemed to relax a little. "Now, as far as anyone else is concerned, the red-haired girl and the green-haired halfling are on their way out of town, never to return. When I booked these suites, I did so as a raven-haired noblewoman named Veronica Pentaghast—you'll meet her tomorrow evening."

He nodded, though he was somewhat disturbed by her choice of words. *You'll meet her tomorrow evening,* she'd said. This Pentaghast chick was just Kiralyn in disguise, yet the sorceress-spy had spoken of her as if she was a completely different woman. This could be the biggest case of Multiple Personality Disorder the world had ever seen. "I can't wait."

She stood up. "Lady Veronica is extremely wealthy and does not go *anywhere* without one of her servants," she explained as she walked past him toward the coat closet. "You will be posing as her servant," she picked up her handbag and started rummaging through it, "and you're going to need to look the part."

Before he could ask what she meant by this, she found what she was looking for and tossed it into his lap. It was a hairpiece—a brown one that came very close to matching his long-lost natural hair colour. "I think I'm offended," he grumbled on general principles.

He wasn't all that upset, though, and they both knew it. "I hate to interfere with abstract artistic expression," she replied only somewhat sarcastically, "but sooner or later, the locals will speak to the real Veronica Pentaghast and discover that I wasn't her. When that happens, would you rather they remember an unremarkable brown-haired halfling servant or a flamboyant green-haired one?"

That was some darned good thinking. "What about my clothes?" he asked. "Someone might realize I'm wea…"

"Relax," she instructed him as she stepped back into the middle of the room, her handbag now slung over her left shoulder. "I *have* done this sort of undercover work before, you know. I'll have a halfling-sized hooded robe for you to wear over your clothes by dusk tomorrow. Nobody will see them."

That was interesting. And potentially useful. "Where are you getting one of those?" he inquired. "Halfling clothes are tough to come by outside of Galensdorf."

"I'm sure they are," she replied easily, "but as luck would have it, there *is* a halfling among our ranks, and he's been made aware of our unexpected need."

So much for the secret halfling clothing store that could have solved all my problems. "Anyone I know?"

She shook her head. "I doubt it—he's eighty years old and has been a druid for most of them."

He remained silent, so she went on, but not before posting her hands on her hips. "Now, you may not like this next rule, but I'm afraid I'm going to have to insist that you not bite anyone. I don't want people to know there's a vampire in town until our work here is complete."

She was right—he didn't like that rule. "Well, what in blazes am I supposed to do until then?" he protested, finally standing up again as he did so. "If I don't get some blood *really* soon, I'm going to be in big trouble."

As usual, the druid-sorceress was one step ahead of him. "Fortunately for you," she began as she started rummaging around inside her purse again, "you're working with someone who is very capable of setting her misgivings aside for the sake of a mission."

She then pulled a vial of dark-red liquid from her purse and handed it down to him. For a moment he just stood there, staring at the vial in a sort of stunned stupor. He hadn't been expecting a free meal; in fact, a part of him had believed Kiralyn would kill him before she'd actively support his unnatural blood dependency. This was one very intriguing druid. "Thank you," he offered his gratitude as he accepted the vial. "Do you mind? I'm famished."

She extended a hand, as if to push him away. "In the hallway, please," she told him in a voice that suggested she'd like nothing more than to leave Tundora right now. "I would die of old age before they'd get a blood stain out of this carpet."

That was probably true, so he took her advice and sauntered back into the hallway. Once he had solid hardwood beneath his feet, he popped the cap off his vial and downed its precious contents in one eager gulp. He would have expected her to prank him with male B-positive or something equally vile, but what he actually found inside his mouth was human female O-negative, his favourite. Not only that, but there was an exotic background taste that he'd encountered a few times before but had never known what it was. *The product of a mixed heritage, perhaps?*

Smacking his lips in approval, he resealed the vial and tracked down his benefactor. Unsurprisingly, Kiralyn had holed up in the room behind the coat closet, which just happened to be on the other side of a *very* opaque wall. It was, in fact, a library, and she was pretending to scrutinize the books on the shelves, but Rufino was certain she was just trying to get out of watching him be a vampire. He could understand that—six years ago, at the beginning of his unlife, he'd been squeamish about this whole blood thing too. He'd gotten used to it, though, so hopefully she'd be able to do the same. "Very nice," he remarked from just outside the entrance to the library. "Was that yours?"

After a brief moment, the druidess turned away from the books and made a face that fell somewhere between diplomatic and completely disgusted. "Wouldn't you like to know?" she replied with raised eyebrows as she stepped past him back into the main room.

Her sudden shift from forthcoming to secretive told Rufino he'd called the blood thing correctly, but in the interest of fostering goodwill, he decided not to press the issue. He had more important things to worry about. "Okay, so we're a noblewoman and her servant," he steered the conversation back toward business, "but you haven't yet told me what we're actually going to *do* with these spiffy new identities."

Kiralyn crouched and picked up her bottle of cider, which told him she intended to leave soon. "The Pentaghasts own fifty-one percent of the Sawin' Logs Lumber Company," she explained before turning back to face him, "which operates out of Tundora and a few other cities. Tomorrow night they're going to get a surprise visit from Lady Veronica, who doesn't know a darned thing about logging but is very determined to learn how her future inheritance is being spent. Our target will not be on site tomorrow evening, so there won't be anyone who can actually answer the questions that Veronica will be asking. This will make them nervous, and I'll use their anxiety to make a few inquiries about our target without raising any suspicions. We need to know more about his routine before we can identify when he'll be vulnerable."

She offered no more. “And then…?” Rufino prompted.

“Then,” she sighed, “we’ll make up the rest as we go along.”

Rufino hesitated a moment until he was certain he’d heard correctly. “We’ll make up the rest as we go along?” he snorted. “What kind of a plan is that?”

“One that lacks the appropriate perspective,” Kiralyn explained as if she’d known the question was coming. “This is uncharted water for my people, Rufino, so I’m going to be counting on you to help me determine how you can pull this off without getting caught.”

“So I’m indispensable, hey?” the little vampire beamed. “Can’t live without me?”

Kiralyn covered her face with her palm and shook her head slowly. She seemed to do that a lot. “This seems like an excellent time to discuss my pay,” he broke the awkward silence with an even more awkward statement.

She knocked him back onto his butt with another puff of wind, but this time he was waiting for it and went down with a big grin on his face. When he decided to cackle with glee and rub his hands together in anticipation, she decided in turn that she’d had enough for one evening. “Get some rest,” she advised him. “I’ll be back just before sunset.”

The blood-haired druid turned and started to leave. “Kira,” Rufino called after her, “one more thing.”

She didn’t turn around, but she did stop walking. “This better be good,” she growled in a voice that told him she wasn’t kidding.

He had nothing to fear, though, because this *was* good. “On my way here,” he explained, “I stumbled across the half-eaten body of a human knight in the middle of the *Bog of the Damned.*”

Kiralyn slipped her hands into her pockets, then leaned back against the wall in the hallway and turned her head to face him. "A troll wouldn't leave a body half-eaten," she told him. "They have three stomachs."

"I know," the little vampire agreed, "so I figured something was wrong and took a closer look. The body—what was left of it, anyway—had been burnt to a crisp."

Kiralyn's expression was now thoughtful instead of irritated, but she wasn't sold on this just yet. "So the troll took a bite," she surmised, "realized the nutritional value had been burned away, and left the other half untouched."

Rufino nodded. "The man was murdered."

"Murder victims get dumped in the *Bog* all the time, Rufino," the druid explained softly. "There's no better place in Nyobi for disposing of evidence. Why do you believe this man was a knight?"

"Some undecorated steel armour was dumped with him," he explained.

"That doesn't necessarily mean he was a knight," she suggested. "Fakes do pop up from time to time."

That was probably true, but it was also irrelevant. "There's more to the story than the man's identity, Kira," he went on grimly. "It wasn't a normal fire that killed him. As you probably know, we cremate our dead in Galensdorf, so I know *exactly* what charred flesh is supposed to smell like, and this stuff wasn't even close. I think he was killed by demon's fire, and I…"

"Describe the smell," she instructed him.

"Pretty unforgettable," he told her. "It was like a decomposed corpse crossed with a few loaves of moldy bread. I've never bumped into demon's fire before, though, so I'm not actually certain that's what the smell was. I was hoping you could tell me."

She turned away from him and stared directly at the doors of the coat closet for a few moments. Every second that passed told him he was right, so when she finally spoke again, her words came as no real surprise. "Sounds like demon's fire," she murmured out loud, "but it doesn't prove that you're remembering things correctly."

Rufino had known this would be a difficult sell, but it was nevertheless difficult to listen to such a suggestion without getting upset. "No, it doesn't," he agreed in a neutral voice and expression, "but since I'd expect you to kill me for lying about such a forbidden topic, it would seem like an awful lot of risk for little to no gain."

Kiralyn took a few steps back into the main room and then dropped to one knee for the purpose of re-establishing eye contact. "Rufino," she spoke softly, "if I killed people for lying to me, half of Nyobi's nobility would be dead by now. May I ask you something?"

The little vampire blinked twice before nodding. "Of course."

"It still sounds like you believe I'm looking for an excuse to kill you," she told him. "If that's really the case, why did you come here?"

"I already told you," he reminded her, "back in Borallis. Don't you remember?"

She let out a slow sigh. "You said you had some feelings for me, but that you didn't understand why."

Rufino nodded. "Are you a little more willing to believe me now that I've passed on my opportunity to run away?"

"You have earned some trust," she told him. "Not enough for me to believe every word you say, but I do believe what you've told me just now about the body."

Rufino blinked a couple more times in surprise. "You do?"

Kiralyn nodded. "Knight-Lieutenant Gregor Sutcliffe has been missing for two weeks. There's no way you could have known that because the information hasn't been made public, which gives me reason to believe that you did actually find something. Ca…"

"I was approximately six hundred metres south of the treeline," the little informant was all too pleased to be a step ahead of her for once, "and roughly ten to twelve kilometres from the western edge of the *Bog.* Is this as bad as I think it is?"

She hesitated, but only briefly, and her expression didn't change. "It's too soon to tell," she explained softly. "I'm hoping it's not actually demon's fire, but we won't know for sure until one of us has a look at it. If it *is* demon's fire, it's probably just another rogue warlock, and he'll be dealt with before he can do too much damage. They can't just summon demons at will—they need to enslave them, too, and that's easier said than done. Most warlocks can only control one demon at a time."

"What about Krexin Vath?" Rufino asked.

Kiralyn shrugged. "There have been warlocks who could control more than one demon at a time," she admitted, "but they're rare; and if you've heard of Krexin, you probably know what happened to him in the end."

Rufino nodded. "He summoned a succubus. She seduced him into releasing her from slavery, and then she killed him in his sleep." He pinched his lower lip and looked thoughtfully at the floor. "Considering how many people were out for his head at that point, he probably got off easy."

"Indeed," the druid-sorceress agreed in a soft and somewhat distant voice. "A quick and painless death was way too good for him. My people had an agreement with both the royal family and several of the more powerful churches to let the families of the victims decide his fate if he was somehow taken alive. Unfortunately, I wasn't able to get the job done."

The way she'd said that made it sound very personal to her. "You hunted Vath?"

She stood back up to her full height. "I hunted him," she told him. "I was on his trail for a year and a half, but he was aware of me, too. On February twelfth of 1508N, I was following up on a lead in the Docks District of Port Hesper when I was approached by an urchin bearing a handwritten message addressed to me by name. It provided an address, a deadline that was in thirty minutes time, and a promise that two hostages from the city guard were going to die if I didn't show. It was Vath, and he wanted to force a confrontation with me before I could summon help."

On one hand, what she was telling him sounded pretty unbelievable. On the other hand, her agenda thus far had been to *avoid* scaring the crap out of him, so she had nothing to gain from telling this story. "What happened?"

She stepped over to the bed and sat back down. "I didn't really have a choice," she went on, "so I walked into his sanctum and gave him the battle he wanted. I'll spare you the details, but in the end I had to make a choice: I could capture Vath as a demon killed the two hostages, or I could save the hostages as Vath escaped. What would you have done?"

He hadn't been expecting the question, but it was a pretty easy one. "Hostages," he said.

She lifted an eyebrow. "You sound very certain of that."

"I am."

The druid-sorceress almost smiled. "I was, too, when I saved those hostages. I was certain I'd get another shot at Vath. Unfortunately," she paused for a second, "I didn't."

Rufino wasn't sure he understood where her regret was coming from. "He's dead, though," he felt compelled to point out. "Isn't that what matters?"

"The world is certainly better off without him," she agreed, "but for my people, Krexin Vath was a missed opportunity. If we'd managed to deliver him to the king and queen for trial, it would have done wonders for our relationship with them. We could have been in a position to help when the queen was assassinated and the king started losing his marbles; instead, we're the same old outcasts we've always been, and things don't look like they'll be improving any time soon." She stood up again and smirked in a knowing sort of way. "That decision I made with the hostages doesn't sound so simple anymore, does it?"

Rufino folded his arms across his chest. "Actually," he decided to argue, "in spite of everything you just told me, this one still sounds pretty easy." He lowered his arms to his sides. "If you sacrifice innocents to achieve your goals; if you become your enemy to defeat your enemy, then you've only replaced one monster with another."

Kiralyn stared at him for a moment, then got back to her feet and favoured him with a nod. "There are a few arch-druids who could stand to hear those words. Anyway, try not to worry about the body in the swamp. I'll get someone to find the remains at the earliest opportunity, and then we'll track down whoever's responsible."

"Then gift wrap him and present him to the king?"

She shrugged. "That's not my call," she told him, "but it couldn't hurt."

The druidess then turned toward the door. "Good night, Rufino. I'll be back at 19:45."

"I'll expect you at 20:30," he murmured.

She ignored his barb and reached for the door's handle, only to pull her hand away at the last second. "Whoops," she murmured to herself as she turned around and made for the window.

At first, he didn't know what she was getting at; but when she pushed open the window, he remembered her description of her cover identity. "The hair?" he inquired mildly.

"The hair," she admitted rather sheepishly.

"Why not use an invisibility spell?" he suggested. He assumed she had one, because every mage in every book ever written did.

"Those leave evidence, like that bubble outside," she explained with a smirk. "This doesn't."

Two seconds later, she was in her snowy owl form; two seconds after that, she was through the window and gone; two seconds after *that,* Rufino realized he never had gotten her to explain why she'd been so late this evening. After what they'd discussed, however, he couldn't fault himself for allowing such an insignificant gripe to slip his mind. He had no way of knowing with absolute certainty that she'd been telling the truth about Vath, but he did recall hearing rumours of a Crown investigation in the Docks District of Port Hesper a few years ago. The authorities closed two city blocks for an entire week without bothering to tell anyone why, so it was obvious that something very serious had happened.

Rufino was too tired to waste his energy on another unsolvable puzzle, though, and he was *way* too tired to sack the alchemy shop tonight. All he could think about was the large, inviting bed not ten feet in front of him, and how long it had been since he'd slept on something in his humanoid form. He smothered all but one of the chandelier's flames using the extinguisher, then stripped down to his underwear and climbed onto the mattress. As expected, it was very comfortable—so comfortable, in fact, that it kept him awake for hours just thinking about how comfortable it was. Beds were among the things he'd taken for granted in his earlier life.

He wasn't going to make that mistake again.

Chapter Seven
Bonding

19 July 1511N

Rufino's beauty sleep was interrupted three times that day: once by children in the park; once by a cleaning crew knocking on the door to his suite; and at approximately 19:25, an argument between two men broke out in the unit below his that even a few layers of soundproofing couldn't dampen fully. At this point, he gave up—Kiralyn was due to return in about twenty minutes, and he had enough energy anyway, so he decided now was a good time to catch up on one or two things. He still needed some quality time with an ice pack, for one, and he also had a strange desire to look at the sun again. In the week since fate had decided to throw the druid-sorceress at him, what remained of his human nature had been making its presence known in ways he couldn't have ignored even if he'd wanted to. This sudden desire to see the sun again was but one more manifestation of that long-buried humanity.

Buried, he admitted to himself, *but never forgotten.*

Sungazing was not *completely* out of the question. Direct exposure would kill him, of course, but during his first month as a vampire, he'd made the *very* accidental discovery that windows protected him from the sun as effectively as did walls. He hadn't taken advantage of this loophole in the vampiric rulebook very often out of fear that the windows might break, but he didn't *want* to live in constant fear of death anymore. He didn't *want* to spend the majority of his time thinking about the million different ways he could die on any given day of the week. Sure, the window *could* break with him standing behind it, but it was also *possible* that the whole building could be flattened by some monster earthquake five minutes from now. He could dig himself a bunker somewhere and wear clothes made of thick foam under a suit of plate armour, but he'd never get around the fact that he was going to die sooner or later.

Though a vampire's plight was pretty unique, they were hardly the only people with lower-than-average life expectancies. Many soldiers died before their time, too; but when a soldier fell, he was typically remembered not for the circumstances of his death, but for the strength of his life. Nobody could say the same for Rufino right now, but he had the power to change that. He had the power to see the roses on the bush instead of the thorns. It wouldn't be easy to so drastically adjust his outlook, but it could very well be worth the trouble.

He dressed himself and also tried on the handsome brown toupee Kiralyn had left with him. It looked good—it was almost like turning the clock back to about two hours before the barber had wreaked havoc upon his head. In a way, Rufino felt as though he was coming full circle: if the green hair symbolized the end of his old life, this brown hairpiece might symbolize the beginning of a new one. There were tales of a mythological creature called a phoenix whose mortal remains gave birth to a brand new life. That was precisely what he needed: not a real death, because that would suck, but a *symbolic* death from which a new and improved Rufino could be unleashed upon the world.

What you need, the other half of him spoke up again, *is a strait jacket. You are not a phoenix, and wishes don't make poppies. It's not too late to run away and sa...*

Oh, go back to your bunker, you insufferable little troll, the vampire-phoenix snorted in defiance. *I'm in charge now.*

There was no response, which gave some more credence to the theory that Rufino had the power to shut out his own negativity if his will was strong enough. He could totally get used to this.

Now looking presentable, he pulled the door to his room open and stepped out into the hallway. There was a door directly opposite his own, and a window to his left through which he could see out to the east. To his right was a long, straight hallway, ending in another window that would have been perfect for sungazing if not for one thing: the sun had just disappeared behind the enormous redwoods of Feybourne. *Of course*, he hung his shoulders in disappointment. *You've gotta be a good deal farther away from the forest than this before you can actually see anything. What was I thinking?*

You weren't thinking, Mr. Negativity spoke up again. *You've been in la-la land since Borallis, and it's blinding you to the cold, hard facts.*

That was probably an exaggeration, but his other half was still right about one thing: distraction was bad to begin with, and distraction around Kiralyn was a lot worse. Long-term goals were multiple-step processes, and step one of his process was to survive long enough to see step two. The sorceress had been patient with him thus far, but her intentions were no clearer to him now than they had been a few days ago. Until he knew for certain what she had in mind, he needed to watch her like a hawk for *anything* that might help him figure out where things stood.

In the meantime, he decided not to head downstairs for an ice pack. Hairpiece or no, he was still wearing the same clothes as before, and he didn't want to give anyone a chance to realize that the green-haired halfling from the *Cocktail* was still in town. He'd wait for Kiralyn to show up with his new duds before he went downstairs for some ice, or perhaps he'd ask her to zap some up for him. He had, after all, sustained this injury whilst saving her much-appreciated bottle of cider from destruction—surely that was worth an ice cube or two.

He re-entered his suite, closed the door behind him, and removed his shoes. This seemed like as good a time as any to familiarize himself with the parts of the suite that weren't the bed. Kiralyn wouldn't have left behind anything he could use as a weapon—except perhaps the fountain pen—but what he desired right now was information. A map would be grand, but even a book of Tundoran history could be useful if it was descriptive enough. He didn't know how long he had to find a suitable hiding place, but something told him he needed one as soon as possible. Was that *something* fear, or was it common sense?

Is there a difference if you're a vampire?

To his surprise, someone had left a large map of Tundora on top of the desk. He doubted it came standard with the room, so he assumed Kiralyn wanted him to learn the lay of the land for some reason. If she knew how close he'd come to chickening out of this little adventure, she probably wouldn't be giving him the tools he needed to plot an escape route, but what she didn't know wouldn't hurt her.

Maybe a map wasn't all she'd left for him. She'd neglected to mention anything except the hairpiece, but they'd been talking about some pretty heavy stuff at the time, so it might have slipped her mind. Sure enough, he found a small pouch inside the top drawer that contained thirty gold coins and a few silvers. Rufino Endicott could not be bought for such a paltry sum, but he was grateful to have some spending money—he might need some more cider if he intended to stay out of Kiralyn's doghouse.

The little vampire spent the next ten minutes going over the map with a fine-toothed comb. He took particular note of the two highways leading out of town—one to the south, toward Bordym, and one to the east, toward Strelas. Oddly enough, there was no road leading to the north, but after consulting with an atlas from the library, he realized there *wasn't* anything to the north of Tundora for about seventy kilometres or so.

More to the point, what was up there was mostly dwarven, and Tundora existed to serve human interests. Though the human monarchy technically controlled all of the land within Nyobi's borders, they seemed quite content to let the dwarves govern themselves in exchange for a percentage of the tax revenues. Because the dwarves were not paying normal taxes, they weren't entitled to resources from the human parts of the country, but they didn't care because they *did* control most of Nyobi's mining operations and could therefore trade ore for whatever they needed. The arrangement was probably a bit better for the dwarves than it was for the humans in a strictly economic sense, but since dwarves accounted for almost twenty percent of the country's population, the humans probably figured it was worth a small loss to keep such a large group happy.

Rufino returned the atlas to its place in the library, made certain the door to the suite was unlocked, then climbed back onto the bed. Kiralyn would be here in ten minutes to one hour, at which point he'd once again be required to push his brain to the limit in an attempt to separate fact from fiction. If she was plotting against him, the signs would be subtle, but he didn't believe even *she* would be able to hide her intentions from him completely. Sooner or later, she would tell him something useful—his job was to make sure he was awake and alert when it happened.

Not fear. Prudence.

***

Maybe twenty minutes later, the awaited knock on his door finally came. *Ten minutes late—she's improving.* He wanted to give her the impression that he was still waking up, so he invited the druid-sorceress to open the door herself with a very groggy-sounding call of, "It's open." He then buried his face in one of the pillows, as though it would take a tray of fresh pastry to get him out of bed. Maybe he'd get lucky.

He heard the door open and shut, followed shortly thereafter by the sound of heeled shoes walking toward him along the wooden floor of the hallway. When he could no longer hear that recurring sound, he figured she'd reached the carpeted main room and could now see him. "Nice bed," he murmured into his pillow, "I think I'll stay here a while longer."

He could practically hear her roll her eyes. "Early bird gets the worm," she told him.

"But this early bird doesn't *want* a worm," Rufino spelled it out for her as he rolled onto his back and started to open his eyes. "*This* bird wants an apple and cinnamon ba…aaaah."

His jaw hung slack, refusing to move, and his eyes would never be the same again. The casual clothes she'd sported in Borallis and last night were long gone, replaced by a dress so mind-blowingly ludicrous that to even call it a ballroom gown was to do it a grave disservice. The fabric was black, and it was also quite insignificant because of the dozens of modestly sized diamonds—and several not-so-modest ones—that had been sewn onto the torso. There was no obvious pattern in how they'd been placed, but Rufino's mind was currently far too *distracted* to care about patterns. "For the love of the gods," he blurted out as soon as he found his voice, "are those *real*?"

She posted her right hand on her hip and lifted her eyebrows. "I'm going to assume you're referring to the stones," she told him in a voice that managed to be both irritated and amused at the same time.

He grimaced—indeed, the question hadn't sounded all that great the way he'd worded it. "Of course," he pleaded innocent, "I…"

"What do you mean, 'of course'?"

As awkward questions went, that one would have scored about a nine point four out of ten if not for his gut feeling that she was just messing with him. "Give me a break," he snorted as confidently as he could. "In case you've forgotten, lady, you're a druid—*unnatural* alterations to your body would probably get you kicked out of Feybourne faster than if you turned out to be a big-industry sympathizer. I'm surprised they even let you paint your nails."

The druidess smirked, and as she did so, the game she was playing came to an end. "Depends on the paint," she told him. "I have to admit, I'm impressed—most men don't recover so quickly when they see me wearing this thing."

He could believe that—the dress was completely out of this world, but so too was the woman who wore it, and the garment had been fitted accordingly. The dress was snug enough to show the world how perfectly flat her tummy was, and the V-neckline—albeit a conservative one—showed *just* enough cleavage to make him forget all about the diamonds. Oh, and the black hair she currently had on was pretty magnificent, too. "You're going to walk onto a work site wearing a dress that was designed for dancing with a prince?"

She nodded. "Veronica Pentaghast is the quintessential spoiled rich girl—hers is the wealthiest family in Meridian, and her father is one of those parents who can't say 'no' whenever his only daughter wants something. As a result, she has absolutely no appreciation for the finer things in life, and walking onto a work site wearing something like this is exactly the sort of thing she might do."

"Uh huh," the little vampire murmured as he finally took in the accessories. She wore a single ring—on the ring finger of her left hand—featuring what appeared to be a sapphire. It wasn't an enormous stone, but the deep blue colour was absolutely stunning *and* it was perfectly matched by the stones in her two drop earrings. Last, but certainly not least, was a three-strand necklace of pearls that had probably come from somewhere in the deep blue depths of those sapphires. The total value on display here had to be equivalent to that of a pretty nice house, but one accessory was conspicuously absent. "All that jewellery," he pointed accusingly at her left wrist, "but no *watch*?" He had no intention of letting her off the hook for being a combined seventy minutes late for the past two meetings—in Galensdorf, the penalty for tardiness was some pretty merciless teasing.

She heaved an exaggerated sigh and leaned against the short wall between the hallway and the door to the bathroom. "If you simply *must* know, I was late last night because I made an unscheduled stop at the central records building in Strelas," she paused just long enough to point a finger at him in return, "where I was looking up *your* file."

That was interesting, if it was true. "I wasn't aware you had access to that sort of information."

"I don't," she smiled sweetly, "hence the delay."

Fortunately, there was a very simple way of verifying the truthfulness of her story. If he was lucky, he might even be able to learn something that he'd been wondering about for years. "What did you find?"

She shrugged casually. "I found the record of a halfling male named Rufino Endicott, born to Thomas and Sabrina on the ninth of October 1479N in the village of Galensdorf. He was reported missing from the city of Strelas on the twenty-fifth of July 1505N, and was described to the police as three-two with blue eyes and a short green mohawk haircut." She paused just long enough to smirk. "If you're not Rufino Endicott, that's one of the best disguises I've ever seen."

Rufino hopped out of bed and made a conscious effort to ignore her little jab. "Am I still listed as missing," he asked of her, "or have they written me off?"

The druid-spy stood up straight. "You're still listed as missing," she informed him, "and in case you're wondering, the law in Nyobi is that a missing person can be declared dead in absentia after four years. Someone is obviously still holding out hope of finding you."

The missing halfling nodded his understanding. "Half of Galensdorf is probably still holding out hope," he told her as he walked past her into the centre of the room. "It isn't the halfling way to give up, but they don't want to see me again *nearly* as much as they think they do."

Kiralyn turned toward him and leaned against the wall again. "Don't you think that's their decision?"

He turned to face her and put on his very best frown. "Surely you're not implying they'd be *happy* to see me in this condition," he attempted to steer her clear of making such a misguided claim. "Better that they believe I'm dead."

There was a brief hesitation before she spoke again. "Unfortunately, we have reason to believe they *don't* believe you're dead," she reminded him. "I'll be the first to admit that I don't know a whole lot about the halfling psyche, but has it occurred to you that learning the truth might be easier on them than not knowing anything at all?"

He shook his head adamantly. "Your own people have described my condition as, and I quote, 'a fate worse than death.' How do you su…"

"Forget my people. How would *you* describe it?"

Rufino blinked a few times, uncertain how to respond. He obviously had an opinion on the matter, but he'd never been asked to put it into words before. "I wasn't aware that I was addressing Doctor Frostwhisper."

"You're not," she corrected him effortlessly. "I'm just someone who knows from experience that there are two sides to every story. I've never heard a vampire's perspective before, so I'm interested in hearing it now if you're willing to tell me."

He wasn't sure if she actually wanted to know or if she was merely killing time until sunset, but he didn't see that he had anything to lose by indulging her. "Have you ever been in a hedge maze?"

"Of course."

"Ever been in one *before* you could turn yourself into a bird and cheat your way out of it?" Rufino demanded with a gentle sneer.

She nodded. "Like you, I didn't possess a flight form until my mid-twenties."

That might have been a lie. "It's fairly well known, Kira," he told her, "that druids learn their animal forms during adolescence."

"Quite true," she admitted, "but I didn't join up until I was twenty-three."

That might also have been a lie, but something told him it wasn't—if she'd been born a druid, Nyobi would have heard her name long before it actually had. "What were you before then?"

"Oh, just a student," the suddenly modest druid said with a sigh, "a student who learned a bit too much."

Rufino estimated that was about eleven point four percent of the whole truth. "If you think I wa…"

"You were speaking of a hedge maze?"

Her meaning was clear: she had no intention of discussing her background in greater detail. He suspected she came from somewhere in the nobility—higher education was expensive—but getting her to admit as much would be like getting a dwarf to go on a diet. "Being a vampire is like being stuck in an enormous booby-trapped hedge maze," he explained. "You know there's an exit somewhere, but after hitting a hundred dead ends, it starts to feel like you're going in circles."

Kiralyn tilted her head to one side. "If I may," she began, "what does your vision of success look like? What's waiting for you at the end of your hedge maze?"

That was an easy one. "I know it's impossible to undo what's been done to me," he told her, "but I still believe it's possible to live a fulfilling life as what I am. Success, for me, looks like a safe home, a ridiculously comfortable coffin, a couple of generous female blood donors, an open-minded friend or two, and some way of making myself useful."

She pushed off the wall and took a seat at the foot of the bed. "What you describe *is* theoretically possible," she told him.

It sounded like there was a lot more on her mind than just that. "But…?"

"But," she went on with a sigh, "to the best of my knowledge, it's never been achieved. You're not just fighting your own nature; you're also fighting the tendency of others to fear what they don't understand. I know how the latter feels, and I don't envy your struggle."

"Do you fear me?"

Her response was to smile, which surprised him. "I'm not easily frightened, Rufino. I've been bitten by a spider the size of your hand, I've tended to a wounded and very aggravated troll that was forty times my size, I've eaten orcish cooking, I've done battle against demons, and I drank half of your Arcane Explosion despite not having the faintest idea what it actually was. That being said, the rumours of ice water flowing through my veins are somewhat exaggerated—there *is* one thing that scares the hell out of me, and it's…"

He could see where this was going. "Human nature," he cut her off with confidence.

She nodded, which made him feel quite proud of himself. "Human nature," she agreed. "What mankind is capable of and what I actually see in society around me are two completely different things."

"Is that why you dumped higher education to go live in a tree?"

She nodded again, and she didn't seem the least bit embarrassed by it. "Druids are all about sustainability, and if there is to be a long-term future for humanity, it is going to have to learn how to effectively manage the world's resources. Which brings me to Martin Scirocco."

Rufino slipped his hands into his pockets. "He's the dude you want dead?"

Kiralyn sighed. "We don't *want* him dead," she reminded him, "we simply don't see that we have any other option. Scirocco is the head foreman of Sawin' Logs here in Tundora, and he thinks only in terms of profit margins and performance bonuses—the ecological consequences mean nothing to him."

The little vampire scratched his noggin thoughtfully. "You dropped the words 'sustainable logging' back in Borallis. How, exactly, do your people define that?"

"First, some background," she told him. "Do you know the story of Meridian Wood?"

He nodded. "It was a forest directly to the northeast of Meridian; one that was wiped out three hundred years ago by over-logging."

"Correct," she nodded. "What you may not know is that, at the current rate of consumption, Feybourne will meet Meridian Wood's fate in approximately eighty years. Also worth mentioning is that the rate of consumption increases several times per year, so in reality Feybourne doesn't even have that long. Our best guess is sixty years."

Rufino held his hands up in front of him. "What makes you think they'll destroy the only remaining forest in Nyobi?"

She lifted an eyebrow. "If a demolition crew showed up at the doorstep of your hypothetical house, would you believe they only intended to destroy half of it?"

He didn't answer, so she took the invitation to continue speaking. "Our belief that Feybourne is in grave danger is not solely predicated on what happened to Meridian Wood. Other countries—Siddurna being a nearby example—have been completely deforested, and what we're seeing here in Nyobi is the same song and dance that the global druidic community has seen dozens of times before. When industrialists see quick profit, few of them stop to think of the cost. What is the cost, you may ask? Here's but one example: *Fifty species* went extinct when Meridian Wood was destroyed. The trees can be replanted, but those species are gone forever."

Rufino started pacing around the room. "By my understanding, the word 'sustainable', in this context, means that the harvesting of trees shall not exceed the rate at which the forest expands. What I don't understand is how simply cutting back on logging is supposed to prevent animal deaths?"

Kiralyn stood up again. "Our guidelines don't completely prevent deaths," she admitted, "but if the work is spread out so as to not cause severe damage to any one habitat, and if baby birds and non-flying animals are rescued from the trees before they're brought down, deaths can be reduced by ninety-eight percent and extinctions can be eliminated altogether. My people accept that logging is a fact of life—our mission isn't to stop it, only to minimize the damage as much as we can within the bounds of reason."

The little vampire would have paled if he could have. "Who in blazes would want to climb one of your trees?" he demanded. "I spent a day in a tree in the *Bog of the Damned* on my way here, and those fifteen hours probably took ten years off my life."

She smirked knowingly. “Yes, those pythons can be rather large,” she agreed, “but you’ll be pleased to know that they only inhabit two small areas of Feybourne, so they’re easy enough to avoid. As for wanting to rescue small animals and babies from enormous redwoods for a living, I can tell you that Kinneman Lumber—one of the companies that *does* follow our guidelines—employs four men for that very purpose, and I would invite you to ask any one of those men how they feel about their work.”

He wondered how she expected him to accomplish that, being as allergic to sunlight as he was. “Is that company profitable?” he asked instead.

“Yes,” Kiralyn replied. “After everything was paid for last year, the Kinnemans made about two million gold. The Pentaghasts made about fifteen times that, but it was blood money and sooner or later they will have to answer for that.”

Rufino turned and tried to point west, toward the forest, but he aggravated his sore shoulder in doing so and grimaced involuntarily. “What’s wrong?” the druid asked of him.

He looked back at her, his face still betraying his physical discomfort. “I hyperextended my left shoulder when I saved your bottle of cider from Oak Street last night,” he explained. “How was it, by the way?”

“I’ll tell you when I drink it,” she replied. “I’m saving it for tonight because I’m *really* not looking forward to walking into that camp and pretending to be their empty-headed heiress.” She paused just long enough to point at his shoulder. “Why didn’t you say something? I can make you some ice as easily as this: *Ch’ulu tormu krosas*.”

Right on cue, a small block of ice appeared in her outstretched palm. She then turned and walked into the bathroom, reappearing a moment later with the block in one hand and a towel in the other. She handed the two objects to him and then returned to her seat at the foot of the bed as he wrapped the ice and applied it to his shoulder. "Thank you," he expressed his appreciation.

Kiralyn did not speak in the moment that followed, which gave Rufino time to work up the courage to ask about her magical abilities. "How did you cast those spells last night without using words?" There was so little that he knew about magic, but he'd always wanted to learn more.

"Do you know the difference between a wizard and a sorcerer?" she asked him without even a moment's hesitation.

Rufino blinked a couple of times in confusion. "There's a difference?"

"I'll take that as a no," the sorceress snorted gently. "Wizards are scholars. They have no more innate magical talent than you do, but through years of study, they eventually learn how to use arcane magic in a rather awkward fashion. Speech and hand gestures are used to keep a wizard's mind properly focused. *Sorcerers*, on the other hand, are born with the ability to harness the arcane. Casting a spell comes as easily to us as does moving an arm or a leg."

She seemed to notice the puzzled expression on her student's face, because she stopped to think for a second before switching gears. "Tell me," she said, "when you became a vampire, how did you know how to shape-shift into a bat?"

"I…" Rufino hesitated, "I don't know. I just knew."

"Right," Kiralyn agreed, "you just knew. Just as a dog knows how to wag its tail, or a spider knows how to spin a web, or a dragon knows how to breathe fire, you know how to become a bat. A sorcerer just knows how to use magic. And because sorcerers don't need to use the focusing techniques of a wizard, we can cast spells without using words and often without using hand gestures either."

"Then why did you use words just now?" Rufino asked, thinking he'd possibly caught an inconsistency in her story.

But as it turned out, he hadn't. "That was a nature spell," Kiralyn replied. "Nature spells are more like prayers and blessings in that the actual power comes from somewhere else—from a deity if you're a priest or a paladin, or from the earth if you're a druid or a shaman."

"I see," Rufino murmured. "So you use words while casting a nature spell to, like, *tell* the land what you want done, and then *it* does the rest?"

The druid nodded. "That's accurate."

"So anyone could be a nature spellcaster?"

"It's not that simple," Kiralyn shook her head. "Unless you've dedicated your life to your cause, you will have very little power—the strength of a divine or nature spellcaster is determined by the strength of his or her devotion. Furthermore, even a powerful priest or druid can be rendered powerless if, at *any* time, he strays from his chosen path. Or from the path that's been chosen for him, depending on how you look at it."

The little vampire was a bit taken aback. "Why are you telling me all of this?"

Kiralyn blinked a few times in rapid succession. "I do recall you asking about this just a few seconds ago."

"Well, yeah," he shrugged a bit sheepishly, "but aren't you supposed to be mistrustful of me, or something?"

"I'm not worried that you'll spontaneously learn how to turn me into a frog, if that's what you're asking. Magic doesn't work like that. As to why I'm free with this information," she added, her voice dropping to what could best be described as a soft growl, "I reckon that knowing a thing or two about what I'm capable of should keep you from trying something stupid. 'A gram of prevention is worth a kilogram of cure', or so goes the saying."

Rufino sighed. “Do you see hidden blades everywhere you go?” he asked dejectedly.

It was her turn to shrug, though hers was considerably more confident than his. “I’m simply being cautious,” she explained, “which I think is perfectly justified under the circumstances. You have earned some trust, as I said last night, but you and I are in a situation for which there is no precedent. I don’t have any way of knowing what’s going to happen next, and frankly, neither do you. In a more honest moment, I think you’d admit that you’re also feeling apprehensive about this collaboration.”

She’d read him so well that he wondered if he had a page number stamped to his forehead. “I’ve been having doubts ever since I left Borallis,” he admitted, knowing he wouldn’t fool her if he tried to claim otherwise, “but I do *want* to be able to trust you.”

The druid nodded solemnly. “I want to be able to trust you, too, but I won’t have that luxury until Martin Scirocco is put to rest.”

The euphemism was not entirely unexpected, but Rufino was having an increasingly difficult time faulting her for it. In most cultures, *murder* was a term used to describe a premeditated killing in cold blood; but the more he thought about this situation, the more he realized this blood wasn’t all that cold. Nyobian citizens had the right to use all necessary force to defend their homes against threatening intruders, which just happened to be what the druids were doing. Feybourne Forest wasn’t *officially* recognized as being the incredibly eccentric home of the druids, but that’s what it was, and whether the plan for Scirocco was a crime or a duty depended solely upon a person’s perspective. *Why is nothing ever simple?* “They’ll just replace him, you know,” he spoke up.

Kiralyn nodded again. “A valid point, but there’s someone you should meet before we discuss the matter in depth. He’ll be at the Sawin’ Logs compound when we arrive." She pointed toward the hallway. "Your disguise is in the bag beside the shoe rack, along with an envelope containing some forged financial documents. Sunset this evening will take place at precisely 20:36, so I've arranged for a horse and carriage to meet us downstairs at 20:40. It's worth repeating that I expect you to remain in-character for the *entire* duration of this masquerade."

"So how do I be a convincing servant?" he asked with an expression of bewilderment on his face. "We barely know what those are in Galensdorf."

She stood up and walked past him. "Your duties will be to stand a half-step behind me, off to my left," she explained as she pulled one of the desk's drawers open, "and to give me the envelope when I ask for it. You will address me as 'mistress' or 'my lady'; anything else would be inappropriate and might be noticed. I also want you to pay close attention to what's being discussed, because I will want to compare notes with you when we return here."

That sounds simple enough, he decided as she lit the candelabra on the desk. He hated the idea of having to keep his mouth shut for more than five minutes, but what he had before him was a golden opportunity to watch Kiralyn Frostwhisper fool some targets as she might also be fooling him, and he intended to make the most of it. She was continuing to treat him reasonably well, but she was also continuing to deny him a way of *confirming* that she was, in fact, treating him well. Women could be tricky to read sometimes—even for him—but *this* was just ridiculous. "How long will th… good god."

She was lighting the chandelier now. The tips of the candles were about seven and a half feet off the ground, but Kiralyn could reach them *without* having to stand on something and *without* having to use any tools. She wasn't even straining herself. "What?" she demanded in a slightly exasperated tone, almost as if she knew what was coming.

Whaddya mean "what?" If you were any taller, you could pluck the moon out of the sky. "Can't you at least *pretend* to need the damned reach tool for that?"

She shook her head slowly and resumed the process of lighting the candles. "If you want to work with me, you're going to have to get used to the fact that I'm… how did you put it in Borallis?"

He was no longer paying attention, though, because something was starting to make sense in the back of his mind after his unspoken mention of the moon. "…If you want some friendly advice," she was blathering on, "comparing a lady to a mountain giant isn't the best way to get on her good side, even if she *is* almost four times your size. Now, *I* can forgive you for being an outspoken little rhinoceros, but…"

The slander was an irritating distraction, but when he took another look at her dress, he suddenly understood what he was looking at: *bright points against a black backdrop*. "The diamonds on your dress," he interrupted as he pointed at her tummy. "They're stars, aren't they?"

"Excuse me?"

It was a challenge, to be sure, but he'd dealt with her enough by now to know that she might only be challenging him to prove his assertion. "The diamonds are the stars and the black fabric is space," he explained what he was now seeing.

"Is that so?" she murmured as she lit the final candle.

He smiled and folded his arms across his chest. "Yes, it's so," he told her with confidence. "I can see Pira'scutala, the constellation of a young dragon, near your left hip."

Kiralyn blew out the match, but she didn't discard it right away. "In fact," she told him, "the placement of these stones is an accurate model of the Urtona Vitri star cluster as it appears in our sky. All five of the cluster's constellations are featured."

The little vampire clasped his hands behind his back and grinned up at her. "The words 'heavenly body' do spring to mind," he remarked somewhat boorishly but very intentionally. "Now, before you frog me for saying so, I should probably inform you that were I not an 'outspoken little rhinoceros', it's very unlikely those words would have managed to dribble out of my mouth."

Her palm was going for her face again, but this time she paused in mid-gesture and simply glowered down at him for a long moment. He held his big grin for the entire fifteen seconds that it took for her to come up with a response, but when it finally came, it was most certainly *not* the response he was expecting. "Someone should run ahead to the Sawin' Logs compound," she suggested as she lowered her palm back to her side, "and have them evacuate."

He wasn't sure what she was getting at. "Why?"

Kiralyn cocked an eyebrow. "They're about to be paid a visit by a mountain giant and a rhinoceros," she explained her reasoning. "An evacuation would be prudent."

That made Rufino's day. Sure, her joke probably wasn't the hardcore flirting that it would have been from a halfling woman, but he'd been expecting sarcasm or hostility and she hadn't given it to him. She hadn't exactly backed down, either, but in referring to herself as the mountain giant, she was demonstrating a willingness to consider his perspective. That *had* to be a good sign.

It had to be.

Chapter Eight
The Giant and the Rhino

The taxi ride from the inn to the compound was uneventful—the driver had taken one look at "Lady Veronica's" dress and seen the potential for a gargantuan tip, so he was on his very best behaviour. It was somewhat entertaining to listen to the man's pitiful attempts to emulate the dialect of a noble, but in all honesty, Rufino's own version of "noblespeak" was no better. That was why he never used it.

Three blocks west of Oak Street was where the commercial district gave way to the industrial district, and they travelled six blocks further west—and four to the north—before they arrived at their destination. The Sawin' Logs compound was located at One Industrial Way, which was a factually accurate address if not a particularly imaginative one. One could tell a lot about a town from how its residents named their streets, and Rufino had enough information by now to conclude that the people of Tundora were boring as hell.

A packed-dirt driveway led to a small cluster of buildings a few hundred metres away, but the cab driver stopped at the hole in the fence. "This is as far as I'm permitted to go," he explained unhappily. No doubt he was afraid for the well-being of his tip.

"This is acceptable," Kiralyn told him as she stepped down from the mostly enclosed carriage. "I require you to sit here and wait for me to return. My business should not take more than forty minutes."

That was a long time for a taxi to wait. "Yes Ma'am, I can do that," he would have agreed to anything at that point. "However, there is a waiting charge of ten gold per fif..."

"You will be handsomely compensated," her interruption might have been rude if not for the promise of gold. "Don't worry."

If the huge smile on the man's face was any indication, his only "worry" right now was that he might wake up. Playing chauffeur for an ultra-wealthy heiress while at the same time being paid to sit around reading a book was pretty much taxi heaven. "My humble carriage awaits your return, Lady Veronica."

Yes, she'd told the taxi driver her name, and that was just the tip of the iceberg—she'd also told the hotel staff and just about everyone else who'd gotten within earshot. The real Veronica had to have one ginormous ego for Kiralyn to be dropping the name every ten seconds. Rufino had no choice but to keep this particular complaint to himself for the time being, but he was *definitely* going to make fun of her when next they had some privacy. *Hello, I'm Veronica Pentaghast. That's Penta-ghast. P-E-N-T... by the gods, shut up.*

They were fifty metres along the service road when Kiralyn broke the silence between them. "Just a friendly reminder," she murmured through barely moving lips, "no smart remarks. You're not in Galensdorf anymore."

"I will be the model of restraint," the little vampire assured her. "You won't even know I'm here."

She snorted with considerable amusement. "I'll believe *that* when I see it."

Rufino smiled in return, though he knew she couldn't see it from her position a half-step in front of him. "How many times do I have to surprise you before you realize I'm not a fluke?"

She didn't slow down, but she did twist her upper body enough to allow for some eye contact between them. "At least once more," she milked the bagel on a stick for all it was worth. "Now hush—someone's coming."

Indeed there was a man coming toward them from the direction of the buildings up ahead. He was young and muscular, dressed in dirty brown overalls and shin-high work boots. The man's hair colour was a mystery—hidden as it was beneath his bright yellow hard hat—but his height was as plain as day, and Rufino could already tell that Kiralyn had a good four inches on the guy even without her heels. It would be interesting to see if she'd rely on her acting skills to neutralize this man or if she'd simply brute force the encounter.

He was about to find out. "Woah there," the man called out as he approached, "this is a restr…"

"I am Lady Veronica Pentaghast," Kiralyn interrupted confidently, her voice once again becoming as unbearably snooty as one would expect of an upper noble, "daughter of Lord Reginald Pentaghast, the majority owner of this enterprise. I will come and go as I please."

The labourer seemed to be having some difficulty wrapping his mind around what he was hearing. "Um," he hesitated, skidding to a halt a couple of metres away. "Wha…"

"Are you the man in charge?" "Veronica" demanded. Kiralyn Frostwhisper was undoubtedly aware that this very unfortunate man wasn't a supervisor or a foreman, but it was the sort of question that a sheltered noble with little real-world experience might be expected to ask.

"No," the man admitted, "I…"

"Then who is?"

"Uh," he thought for a second, "Earl, I guess…"

Kiralyn folded her arms across her chest, being careful as she did so to avoid disturbing the diamonds. "Take me to him," she spoke as though she expected her commands to be obeyed without question.

The labourer didn't seem too pleased about being treated like a servant, but he obviously had absolutely no desire to get himself fired by upsetting someone important. "Follow me," he said, "and watch your step."

He led the pair to the Sawin' Logs "town square," which turned out to be approximately three hundred metres from the front fence. There was still a decent amount of light in the sky, but the braziers in and around the compound had been burning for what looked like a while now. Rufino was fairly certain he wouldn't be attacking Scirocco anywhere on this property, but he made a mental note of each brazier's location anyway. He also started counting how many men were still on site at this time of night, and he didn't like what he was seeing: between the labourers and the men who transported the wood from here to Strelas, there were twenty-five men hanging around the square right now. Every last one of them was aware of Kiralyn's approach, too, which pissed Rufino off no end. *If I hear even one whistle,* he told himself, *someone's gonna get smacked.*

The square consisted of a first-aid hut, a waiting area for the transporters, a changing area for the labourers, and an office. Unsurprisingly, their escort led them into the office. Though it was the largest building in the square, it was still pretty small, consisting of only three rooms: the mess hall, which took up most of the space; a small refresher station to the left of the entrance; and the supervisor's office itself to their right. Several loggers were seated in the well-lit eating area, and Rufino could see the startled awe in their expressions as they feasted their eyes upon the noblewoman. Her dress was designed to be noticed, and it was never going to fail at its objective in a place like this. He just hoped Kiralyn knew what she was doing.

Without ceremony, the labourer led the druid and the vampire to the supervisor's office and triple-knocked on the open door. "Earl," he called into the room, "you have a visitor."

Earl, a middle-aged man with curly brown hair and a beard that was probably a work in progress, looked up from his paperwork without bothering to conceal his irritation. "Who…"

His tirade was cut short when he noticed Kiralyn. "Well I'll be darned," he said instead as he stood up from his desk, "this is unexpected."

"Of course it is," Kiralyn hissed at him. "I'm more likely to see the real picture when I neglect to announce my plans in advance."

The foreman was less easily run over than their original host. "And you are…?"

Part of Rufino was just dying to know how the men in here would react if the druid-sorceress dropped her real name right now. "I am Lady Veronica Pentaghast," Kiralyn denied her servant the pleasure of watching a mad scramble out the front door, "daughter of Lord Reginald Pentaghast, the majority owner of this enterprise." She tapped Rufino on the shoulder and said, "Show him the papers."

Rufino took two steps forward and dutifully slid the envelope onto the foreman's desk. Supposedly the forgeries were very good, but the faux servant doubted the man would take more than a cursory glance at them. He was correct—the foreman scrutinized the paperwork for only a moment before returning his eyes to the noblewoman. "I also need to see your I.D. card," he informed her, sounding less than thrilled about having to confront an owner but recognizing that he had no choice. "I have no wish to come across as disbelieving, my lady, but I'm not at liberty to discuss company business with unverified persons."

"A fine policy, if I do say so," Kiralyn told him as she reached into her purse and withdrew what had to be a forged Pentaghast I.D. card. "I would not be happy if our competition managed to breach our security."

It must have been a good forgery, because Earl fell for it hook, line and sinker. Briefly, Rufino wondered if this

I.D. card was the reason he and Kiralyn hadn't made the trip from Borallis to Tundora together. "I am pleased you have chosen to visit us this evening, my lady," Earl said as he handed the card back to its owner. Unlike the taxi driver, this man was addressing the noblewoman as protocol demanded of a man of his station, which suggested he was reasonably well educated. "How may we be of service?"

"As I implied," she reminded him, "I wish to see my family's money at work. Please give me a tour of the operation."

"It would be my pleasure," the foreman's sycophantic onslaught was relentless. "But for your own safety, I must insist that you put on a hard hat." He gestured toward Rufino. "Your servant, too."

"I assure you," Kiralyn argued, "he doesn't need one. His head is hard enough as it is."

You'll hear about that one later, Kira, the little vampire promised himself as he bit his tongue hard enough to hurt.

The logger joined his hidden enemy in having a laugh at Rufino's expense. "Be that as it may, my lady," he said, "I'm afraid I'm not at liberty to make exceptions to this rule, either."

"If you insist," Kiralyn acquiesced with what sounded like a great deal of irritation. Rufino couldn't help but be impressed with her ability to so completely immerse herself in whichever disguise the situation called for. The schoolteacher from Samradyn and the heiress from Meridian had absolutely nothing in common, but she'd played the former role to perfection and she was doing likewise with this one, too. Her belief in the druidic cause had to be *very* strong, because a woman with her skills could make a staggering amount of money on the open market.

Foreman Earl led his guests to the changing area, which doubled as an equipment shed. He asked them to wait outside whilst he located a pair of suitable hats, then he disappeared through the door. Rufino had been expecting to pass the time in silence, but Kiralyn surprised him. “This won’t take long,” she murmured down to him. “I want to get out of here.”

He simply nodded, realizing that Kiralyn was still in-character. If anyone had overheard, it would be assumed that she was simply a stuck-up noblewoman who felt uncomfortable on a work site, not a druid-sorceress who wanted nothing more than to shut the place down for good. He wanted to put a hand on her shoulder in a show of solidarity, but since all he could reach was her butt, he decided not to do anything. A very prudent decision, if he did say so himself.

Earl reappeared a moment later carrying two hats, one slightly larger than the other. “We don’t have any halfling employees,” he explained as he presented both hats to Lady Veronica, “so this is the best I can do. I’m sorry.”

Kiralyn handed the smaller of the two hats down to Rufino, but even the smallest hat for a human was still too large for a halfling. The brim of the hat came down to the little vampire’s nose, leaving him unable to see past the first few metres in front of him. “I’ve never felt safer in my life,” he quipped with the sincerity of a used wagon salesman.

The man laughed again. “For what it’s worth,” he offered as he led them toward the west end of the square, “all of our dangerous work ceases at sunset. The only reason you still need those hats is because sometimes a bunch of druids get it in their heads to drop rocks on us from above.”

“How often does *that* happen?” Kiralyn asked in expertly feigned surprise.

Rufino could no longer see above the man’s boots, so his ability to read body language was severely handicapped. “Once or twice a month,” the foreman replied quite casually. "There aren't enough druids to harass all of the logging operations around Feybourne, so they have to cycle if they want to bother everyone. You'd think they'd have better things to do, but…"

For a moment, nobody said anything. "So," Kiralyn spoke into the silence, "what do you do in the evenings, if not cut down trees?"

The larger humans started walking, so Rufino hustled after them despite not having the faintest idea where they were going. "Only a handful of the men are fallers—the ones who actually bring down the trees," Earl explained. "Most of the men process fallen trunks for shipping and prepare the terrain for the next trees to be felled. You wouldn't guess it from their size, but redwoods are fairly fragile, so if they land on rough terrain, they'll more than likely suffer damage."

"You were a faller, I assume?" Kiralyn asked.

Rufino was certain she already knew the answer, so it came as absolutely no surprise when the foreman admitted it. "Yes, my lady," he told her. "I got my start with Sawin' Logs as a simple lumberjack twenty-five years ago. Three years later, I was noticed for my work ethic and trained to be a faller, and after nineteen years in that role, I was advanced to the role of second-shift foreman. I've often heard it said that there are no opportunities for advancement in this industry, but I feel it would be more accurate to make the distinction that there are no opportunities for the lazy. *Every* industry, including ours, will do what it can to retain a hard-working man."

"Would it consider a hard-working woman?"

Rufino highly doubted the druid-sorceress gave a damn whether a logger was a man or a woman, but he already knew it was a part of her character to ask a few stupid questions, so he assumed this was but one more. And speaking of stupid, he was getting *really* sick of not being able to see anything, so the time to do something about it was upon him. The hard hat had a couple of straps on the inside that could be tightened or loosened as necessary, so he tipped his hat back and positioned the front strap across his forehead to keep the bloody thing from falling off. He accomplished this feat just in time to see the foreman nod in response to the heiress's somewhat awkward inquiry. "I know I, personally, wouldn't say no to a woman who's physically capable of doing the work, my lady," he explained. "However, it's been my observation that the women who *are* tough enough for logging have more lucrative opportunities elsewhere. Police departments, for example, are always looking for women."

Kiralyn looked really funny in her opulent dress and hard hat, but now was definitely *not* the time to start laughing. Unfortunately, it seemed as though he was going to need a distraction to keep himself from doing so, so he tugged on her dress until she looked down at him. "What is it?" she demanded.

"I have a question," the little vampire spoke up, "if I may."

She nodded, which surprised him. "You may, as long as it's relevant."

"Yes, mistress," he assured her before looking over at Earl. "Sir, I'm aware that the Tundoran branch of Sawin' Logs has the lowest employee-turnover rate of any of the sites, and that it has achieved this distinction only recently. I was wondering if you could describe for us, please, the measures you and the other foremen have taken to achieve this."

"I would like to know this as well," Kiralyn spoke up.

Earl smiled. "I'm afraid I can't take much of the credit for the turnover rate, my lady," he explained. "Things took a turn for the better in this camp when Martin became our head foreman four years ago. He's made several changes, but the most significant one was the introduction of the second shift three years ago. We used to have a single shift working up to twelve hours per day, but now we have an early shift and a late shift. Martin's reasoning for this move was that bringing in fresh arms and legs after seven hours would increase our productivity, but it's also had the benefit of giving the men more time for other pursuits. Happier men are less likely to quit."

"Would not some of the men be upset over the lost wages?" Veronica asked.

The foreman shook his head. "With Lord Pentaghast's approval, Martin took two steps to ensure that our men can earn as much as before: he introduced performance bonuses and the optional weekend shifts. We used to shut down for the weekends, but now we operate seven days per week with smaller volunteer shifts on the weekends. Nobody is allowed to work both of the volunteer shifts as per the queen's regulations, so most of the men who want an extra day are able to get one."

"Well, it is difficult to argue with results," Kiralyn sounded happy, though Rufino knew she was anything but, "and the productivity of this site, when measured against its peers, is very impressive."

Earl nodded once again. "We have it good here in Tundora, my lady," he explained. "Having a home nearby is a luxury that most of the men in our field don't have."

"It is a luxury that your Martin has figured out how to work to our advantage," the phony heiress thought out loud. "I would like to meet with him to discuss the finer details of the operation."

"He's actually doing the evening shift tomorrow," was Earl's response, "so if you want to come back at arou…"

"I do not wish to return at night," Kiralyn interrupted.

"Okay," the foreman accepted. "Well, the day after tomorrow is his day off, but on the following day he'll be back to his regular morning shift. I can set up an appointment for you, if you wish."

"Thank you," Kiralyn responded politely, "but I cannot afford to wait that long. Would you give me directions to his house so that I may converse with him on his day off?"

"I'm sure he'll be very pleased to meet you, my lady," Earl assured her, "but on his days off, he's more easily found at the *Killer Cocktail* tavern on Plantation Avenue than at his actual home."

The conversation between Veronica and Earl continued for another ten minutes, but Rufino was no longer listening. The last piece of information—that Scirocco would be at the *Cocktail* two days from now—started the wheels turning inside Rufino's devious little mind. By the time their tour was over, he'd formulated a plan that he intended to present to his partner in crime.

The hit wasn't a go yet, though. If the druid-sorceress couldn't give him a tangible reason to believe things were going to improve once Martin Scirocco was removed, then he was going to call the whole thing off. No one was going to talk him into taking a man's life only to watch the next head foreman follow in his predecessor's footsteps. This task was difficult to swallow as it was, even given Scirocco's complete disregard for non-humanoid life.

He wasn't looking forward to confronting Frostwhisper about this, but he had no way out of it. This was important.

***

The taxi ride back to their inn—the *Duchess*—was a quiet one. Kiralyn's expression was perfectly neutral, but for once he knew exactly what was simmering beneath her tranquil exterior. *It can't have been easy for her to hold onto her temper in a place like that.*

She paid the taxi driver a hundred gold—twice as much as she'd owed—which sent him on his way in a state of euphoria. She then led Rufino into the lobby, where she broke the silence between them with an unexpectedly considerate question. "Do you need some more ice?"

His shoulder was still sore, so he nodded. "Yes, please."

The druidess turned to their right and approached the front desk. "My servant requires an ice pack," she requested of the woman behind the desk. Rufino did notice her failure to say "please," but for all he knew, such behaviour was common in the upper nobility.

Veronica's lack of manners made no difference—in the dress she was wearing, she could have demanded the deed to the place and they'd have given it to her. Forty-five seconds later, Rufino had his ice pack and they were on their way up the stairs to the third floor.

Kiralyn didn't speak again until they were safely inside Rufino's corner suite. When she did finally lose the persona, her mood was every bit as foul as he'd expected. "You see, now, what we're up against," she brooded, as much to herself as to her vampire. "What we call the destruction of our ecosystem, they call a *job well done*."

Rufino made a conscious decision to remain silent. *The more steam she blows off now,* he reasoned, *the less she'll have left to blow off at me.*

There would be no more venting, though—Kiralyn simply took a seat at the desk and rested her forehead upon the smooth surface of it, almost as if she intended to go to sleep. She didn't, though, and after three minutes of silence, the little vampire decided he'd waited long enough. "Sorry I asked that question at the compound," he told her, "bu…"

"No need to be sorry," she cut him off. "You earned a passing grade."

"…If you'd let me finish," he persisted, "I aske that question because it was the only way to stop mysel from splitting a gut over the sight of you in a half-million gold dress and a hard hat." He knew it was reasonably safe to tease her about this, and hopefully some humour would be therapeutic. "If your objective was to make ridiculous look exquisite or vice versa, you've set a standard today that may never be beat."

Kiralyn was silent for about five seconds before she started to laugh a little. "You know what else was funny?" she eventually snorted as she sat back up. "When you put on *your* hard hat, I was afraid it was going to swallow you whole."

He could listen to height jokes all night long if it kept her from frogging a certain someone. "It's a good thing he gave me a small hat," he agreed, "because a big one *would* have eaten me alive."

She stood up, and it was clear from her expression that she was trying really hard to keep her laughter contained. "I've been doing this sort of thing for five years now," she told him, "and I take pride in my ability to read people. Do you want to know what Earl was thinking when he looked up and saw the two of us?"

Rufino rather loved that question—there were so many smartass answers to choose from. "A woman and a halfling?" He then lowered his voice to mimic the man they'd met. "Quick, where did I put the application forms?!"

Kiralyn probably didn't lose control of herself very often, but she did right then, and she spent the next minute laughing so hard that Rufino was certain she was going to pull a muscle. Sure enough, when she finally calmed down, she placed her left hand over her diamond-adorned abdomen and started rubbing it very carefully. He tried to lend her the ice pack, but that only got her laughing again for another thirty seconds or so. He'd always thought that a n's laughter was a pleasing sound, but when it was ıg from the woman of his craziest dreams, it sounded ıat much sweeter.

Unfortunately, he felt it necessary to declare his now, lest he think about what he was about to do and ıis nerve. "Kiralyn," he gurgled, "we need to talk."

Just like that, her laughter ceased. A part of him lered if women feared those words as much as men but somehow he doubted it. "Are you about to give me bad news?" she asked.

The little vampire clasped his hands behind his back took a deep breath. "That remains to be seen. I don't k I can do this without some sort of assurance that ıng Scirocco will actually result in change for the er."

Naturally, she didn't seem too happy to hear this. Having an attack of conscience, are you?"

He nodded.

The druidess folded her arms across her chest, as she typically did when her mood was deteriorating. "And your attack is strong enough that you've decided you're better off risking a confrontation with me?"

Rufino wanted to put some attitude into his response, but a weak acknowledgement was all he could manage in his frightened state. *Maybe this wasn't such a good idea.*

Kiralyn took a few steps forward until she was looming over him with her very intimidating six-foot frame. When he found the nerve to look up at her face, though, he found not a promise of impending doom, but rather a glimmer of approval. "Someone else had that very concern about this mission. Do you want to know who it was?"

The answer was obvious enough that he decided not to wait for her to tell him. "You."

She nodded. “During this mission’s conception,” she told him, “six weeks before you and I crossed paths, I went to my arch-druid with a very similar question: how can we be certain the next head foreman will be any better than Martin Scirocco?” She took a couple of steps around him and once again took her seat at the foot of the bed. “I’ll tell you what he told me: do you remember how far above quota the Tundoran operation is at the moment?”

That was one of the first figures he’d noticed. “It said forty percent,” he replied.

She leaned back slightly and used her arms for support. “Let’s see if you were paying attention when you went over those papers. Do you remember at which point extra productivity is no longer rewarded with larger performance bonuses?”

The little vampire shook his head.

She nodded toward the hallway, where he’d left the envelope and its documents. “I’ll leave the documents with you so that you may verify what I’m about to tell you.” Her offer was not necessary, since he already knew she wasn’t going to lie about anything that was so easy to check. “The performance bonuses have a ceiling of fifteen percent above quota, which means the men are producing the extra twenty-five percent for free.”

Rufino winced. “Something tells me they’re not at all happy about this.”

The sorceress shook her head slowly. “They’re not,” she confirmed. “In fact, their vaunted turnover rate is projected to take a serious turn for the worse in the coming months.”

“You don’t want that?”

She shook her head again. “Martin Scirocco is the key—he’s the reason the Tundoran operation is forty percent above quota while the rest of the Sawin’ Logs branches are struggling to achieve theirs. The man is a single-minded bulldog—full of ambition and business sense, but completely devoid of ethics or compassion. We believe this productivity push is his bid to become president of the company when the position becomes available in two years, but that's just an educated guess."

Rufino scratched his neck to buy himself some time to think. "Earl is the one you wanted me to meet tonight, right?"

"Correct," Kiralyn nodded. "The foreman of the morning shift recently moved to Siddurna in order to reconcile with his estranged wife, so Earl Mantikan will be elevated to head foreman once Scirocco is removed."

Rufino broke eye contact to stare at the carpet between his feet and hers. "The man seemed quite competent to me," he voiced his biggest concern. "How do you know he won't try to match his predecessor's numbers?"

She shook her head. "Mr. Mantikan spoke highly of Mr. Scirocco to me because it's what a subordinate is supposed to do, but we have inside information that he's been arguing against pushing the men harder than they're being paid for. We are certain that Earl, as head foreman, will settle for fifteen percent above quota if it means avoiding a worker revolt."

"What if the bonus system is expanded?"

"Lord Pentaghast has already declined to expand the system once," she explained without hesitation. "His argument was that quality suffers if the men try to go too fast, and we've seen no indication that he intends to change his mind."

The more they discussed this, the more the little vampire hated it. A big part of him had been hoping Kiralyn would give him an excuse to call the whole thing off, but the evidence did strongly suggest that bumping off Scirocco would do the world some good. "I need some context," he voiced his remaining concern. "How many animal lives will be saved if this outfit's productivity drops from 140 percent to 115 percent?"

"It's difficult to determine exactly how many animals are killed by displacement," she explained, "but we estimate that this action will save twelve thousand avian and mammalian lives per year, and that's *without* counting all of the unhatched eggs in abandoned nests. If you count those—and I do—you're looking at double that number."

That was a sickening figure. To the Sawin' Logs people, it was a simple statistic; but to Rufino, it was a symptom of a much larger problem. It wasn't just birds and squirrels being butchered by the thousands in the name of profit, it was other humans, too. Rufino could think of several examples of recent wars fought over resources, with many tens of thousands of casualties. It was frequently claimed that the resources were "necessary" in order to preserve the quality of life of the invader's populace, but he wasn't so certain they were. If there was one thing he could say for his six years as a vampire, it was that he'd learned a *lot* about what was important and what wasn't. "I hope you realize," he spoke up, "that Scirocco isn't your true enemy. Nyobi is a highly materialistic society, and as long as the Nyobian compulsion to acquire everything under the sun exists, there will be companies like Sawin' Logs trying to cash in on it."

The druidess did indeed know that. "I never said this mission would defeat materialism overnight," she spoke. "In fact, I expect to spend the rest of my life fighting against greed in one form or another. I am prepared to do so, though, because my heart and my brain are both telling me that this is the most important battle I could ever fight."

There was only one question that still needed to be asked. "Is it not hypocritical of you to complain about materialism whilst wearing the dress you're currently wearing?"

She looked down at the diamond starscape on her tummy and chest. "I've been in conflict over this dress ever since it was given to me," she admitted. "On one hand, it's a work of art the likes of which I've seldom seen before. On the other hand," she looked him in the eyes, "this dress does indeed represent the very thing I'm sworn to fight, so I can't justify wearing it unless I need to impersonate someone like Veronica."

"Are you sure you don't like it *just* a little?" he pressed. "I mean…"

She may as well have been reading his mind. "I do not need a million-gold dress in order to look good, Rufino."

Truer words were never spoken. "I have a plan for Scirocco," Rufino changed the subject before he found himself up a creek without a paddle, "and it'll look like a perfect accident. The catch is that I'm going to need your help to set it up."

She stood up and took a couple of strides to gaze out the window. As she did so, Rufino was certain he heard her run herself through a breathing exercise. "I'm listening," she eventually invited him to continue.

"Earl said Scirocco spends a lot of time at the *Killer Cocktail* on his days off, and that he has a day off coming up on the day after tomorrow," he recalled. "I'm assuming he's single based on how he spends his free time—can you confirm this?"

"He is divorced, with an adult son who lives in Strelas."

"Okay, we can use that," Rufino was still talking to her back. "Two days from now, he'll go to the *Cocktail* for a drink or three," he paused dramatically, "and he'll meet *you* in one of your many disguises. Whether you go as Veronica or someone else doesn't really matter—all I need you to do is to keep him there until after sunset. Then I can chomp him on his way home and nothing will appear out of the ordinary."

He deliberately omitted his plan for actually killing the target in the hope that Kiralyn would notice the hole and suggest a way to fill it. It was important that he learn whether druids were cruel or merciful at times like these.

The sorceress-spy turned around to face him again. "I can do that," she nodded after a moment, "but you'll need to do more than just bite his neck—you'd be giving him that twelve-hour window in which to find a healer." She bit her lower lip thoughtfully. "He should lose consciousness for up to fifteen minutes after you bite him, so if you…"

"Where do you get 'fifteen minutes' from?" Rufino demanded with interest. "My food wakes up after three or four minutes."

Kiralyn seemed a bit perturbed by this. "Fifteen minutes is the established figure," she told him in a voice that was far less confident than the words implied. "It's been verified thousands of times throughout recorded history."

The little vampire shook his head emphatically. "Unconsciousness lasts three minutes when I chomp a large human, four minutes when I chomp an elf or a small human, and it may not happen at all when I chomp a dwarf," he explained. "This has been verified dozens of times throughout my *personal* history. You may have a druidic encyclopedia's worth of knowledge, Kira, but when it comes to vampire bites, *I'm* the expert around here."

She shrugged. "Whether you have fifteen minutes or four minutes is irrelevant because, either way, if you sever his jugular vein during or just after the attack, he'll be dead before he can wake up. I know severed jugulars are messy, but since you're too small to break a human's neck, I don't see that we have any other choice. It is critically important to us that he not suffer."

Rufino nodded, deciding as he did so that Kiralyn had passed her latest test. "I'm also gonna need to know what this guy looks like. If I'm not absolutely *certain* I'm chomping the right guy, I'm not gonna do it."

Kiralyn looked up, possibly toward the front door at the other end of the room. "Hmmm," she fished around for the most appropriate descriptive words, "average height, average build, brown hair, brown eyes…"

"I don't care about his *eye colour* when I'm thirty feet in the air, Kira," Rufino interrupted her with a snort.

"I'm doing the best I can," Kiralyn growled in response as she glared back down at him. "Would you rather I tell you he's so physically indistinctive that he could lose himself in a crowd of three people?"

"Tell me something *useful*," he insisted. "What does he wear? How is his hair cut? Does he have a limp? Any facial hair?"

Kiralyn shook her head. "I don't have most of those answers, but I do believe there's a way around this problem. You intend to stake out the *Cocktail* on the night of the hit, correct?"

"Correct."

"All I need to do, then," she told him, "is to exit the *Cocktail* at the same time as he does. That way you'll only need to spot me in order to mark him."

Rufino wasn't yet convinced. "Are you certain you can arrange this?"

Kiralyn found the question quite amusing. "Not only am I certain I can hold his attention for as long as I please," she said with a snort as she stepped past him into the short hallway, "but *Veronica* might even be able to get him to walk home on his hands."

Maybe she could, but there was still one small problem. "My eyes aren't that great in my bat form, Kira," he informed her, "so maybe yo…"

"Can your bat form see colours?" She cut him off.

Rufino nodded.

"Then I'll simply wear the full-length red dress I brought with me," she made a quick and decisive adjustment to the plan. "You'd need to be unconscious to miss it, even at night."

Now his head would be filled with fantasies of Kiralyn in a sexy red dress for the rest of the night. *Great.* "Won't it be uncomfortable for you to wear an attention-grabbing colour like red in a place like a logger bar?"

Kiralyn hesitated a moment. "I'll hate every second of it," she eventually admitted with a sigh, "but the success of the mission is more important than my *discomfort*."

Rufino stuffed his hands into his pockets and looked down at the soft white carpet between them. "Do you tell yourself the same thing when you're working with me?"

He kept his head down, expecting a downright brutal or at least a very sarcastic response. But when she dropped to her knees before him and placed a hand on his shoulder, he realized the woman was about to defy his expectations once again. "A week and a half ago," she told him, "this wasn't even a serious mission—this was a theoretical long shot that I didn't think would ever get off the ground. In fact, I personally told my arch-druid that it would take a minor miracle for this plan to actually achieve a positive result." She tilted her head ever so slightly to one side. "That positive result is now only two days away, and we have you to thank for it. I'm not going to go so far as to call you a 'miracle,' out of concern that you might get a swelled head and start fitting into those hard hats." She had to stifle a giggle. "I will say, though, that if someone had told me when I walked into the *Squid* that I was about to meet a vampire who was both able and willing to pull this off, I wouldn't have believed it."

She was right to be concerned about his cranium—it was definitely beginning to expand. "So I'm a miracle worker, hey?" he took the key word and ran with it.

"I just sa…"

"I know what you *said*," he positively beamed as he stepped away from the hand on his shoulder, "and I also know what you *meant*. I assure you, baby, this bat has more going for him than just mad skills. You must have noticed this sculpted hunk of miniature man by now, but wha…"

Still in a kneeling position, she raised a palm to her face and shook her head slowly. "What have I done?" she murmured into her palm.

"…What you don't know is how great a pair we could be. I can make your heart flutter with my poetry; I ca…"

"*If sweaty brutes are not your style, why not hang out with me a while?*" she attempted to deter him with a reminder of his most recent poem. An instant classic it was not.

But it simply wasn't that easy to stop a halfling's mouth once it got going. "…I can seduce your stomach with my cooking, I ca…"

"Yes, I noticed that in your file," she interrupted him again as she stood up. "I've been wondering about something."

That shut him up long enough for her to speak. "In a town with an average IQ of 140, you opened a restaurant called *Good Eats*?"

Rufino grinned. "I co-opened it, actually, with my best friend. He wanted to call it *Good Food*, but fortunately I was there to talk some sense into him."

"Thank goodness for small favours."

Her sarcasm had come out to play now, but for once he still felt completely in control of the conversation. "Oh, sure," he admitted, "it was within our creative capacity to call the place something epic, like *The Galensdorfian Great Hall*, but we halflings have little use for pomp and pageantry. We decided on *Good Eats* because when a tired halfling finishes his work in the fields, he doesn't *want* a dainty little serving of food that's been arranged to resemble a smiley face—he wants all the fish and vegetables he can pile onto his plate. He wants *good eatin'*, and we were all too happy to oblige."

He hesitated a moment, for he'd just thought of something to ask. "Was there anything in my file about the business? I haven't heard a peep in six years."

She shook her head. "There was nothing else in the file, but if I ever go to Galensdorf, I'll see if it's still there. I could go for a big plate of fish and vegetables right now."

The little entrepreneur brightened up again. "You see?" he insisted. "*Good Eats* is a name that appeals to your base instincts. Just *thinking* about it made you hungry. I…"

"Pretending to be a Pentaghast is what made me hungry, Rufino," Kiralyn corrected him gently as she stepped into the hallway. "On that note, good night—I'll return tomorrow after sunset so we can fine tune our plan."

She picked up her purse and reached for the door, but Rufino stopped her before she could open it. "I know what you just did, you know."

The druid-sorceress paused and looked back at him. "Excuse me?"

He folded his arms across his chest and smiled knowingly. "You distracted me to shut me up," he accused her. "It's an oft-used technique where I come from."

She paused for a brief moment before giving him one last smirk for the night. "I always knew your people were clever."

Seconds later, she was gone.

One short moment after that, post-Kiralyn letdown started to set in. Though he was still far from willing to claim that he was in love with the woman herself, he *was* most certainly in love with his dream of a brighter future. He was certain she was a significant part of that future, though the role she would actually play in it was still as clear as mud. Would she be friend or foe? Would a friendly relationship be strictly professional, or would she eventually allow herself to be wooed by his overwhelming charm? Another night had gone by in which he'd learned little, and this lack of progress was becoming very frustrating. His dead heart and his instincts were still telling him to trust her, but… *arrrghhh.*

Fortunately, he didn't have to think about this right now. Kiralyn was unlikely to return whilst he might still be in a mood to babble, so there would never be a better time for his little junket to the alchemy shop. He didn't remember exactly which street *Auspicious Alchemy* was on, but it was a fairly distinctive building, so he didn't believe he'd have any trouble locating it again. There had been a small, round black chimney on the roof of the building—the only one of its kind on the entire street. Not only was that chimney a landmark he could spot from a block away in favourable moonlight, but it was probably going to be his access point as well. Hopefully there wouldn't be anything too disgusting at the bottom of it.

He waited five minutes, just to be certain Kiralyn wasn't going to return. Then, after depositing his ice in the shower stall and locking the front door, the little vampire pushed open the window, assumed his bat form, and took to the skies.

Chapter Nine
Falling Into Place

It was an excellent night for some shoplifting—the light from the moon was being obscured by clouds, and the temperature was dropping quickly enough to encourage people to go inside. Under other circumstances, the latter detail might not have been significant; but though Rufino could almost always enter a building through its chimney, he was *not* always capable of exiting via that same point. It all depended on the chimney, and something told him that an alchemist's chimney was going to be a particularly demanding one.

He was right. It took him only ten minutes to find *Auspicious Alchemy* again, but tackling the point of entry was going to be considerably more troublesome. He couldn't see it, but there was definitely a cauldron in the room below him, and that cauldron definitely had something in it—something that smelled *really* foul. To make matters worse, the inside of the chimney was smooth and cylindrical—about eight inches in diameter—which was a festering pile of manure in every conceivable way. He couldn't fly in such a small area, and the smooth surface gave him nothing to hook onto with his claws; his only option was to jump in, spread his wings to slow his descent, and then find a way *not* to land in anything nasty. *Just another day in the life of Rufino Endicott.*

Staring at the obstacle wasn't going to make it disappear, though, so he manoeuvred himself into position and took the plunge before he could talk himself out of it. His first instinct was to flap his outstretched wings, but a hummingbat he was not—he could maintain a hover for a few seconds when he needed to, but going straight up or straight down was beyond even his stupendous ability. He knew he wasn't about to land in anything hot because he'd be able to see a glow if there'd been a fire recently, but that wasn't a whole lotta comfort. This was obviously a ceiling chimney, but…

In mid-thought, he fell out of the chimney's claustrophobic confines, but the room he now found himself in was completely dark. Fortunately, a dark room was no match for a crafty bat such as him. He emitted a couple of exploratory clicks, and his brain used their echoes to construct a three-dimensional image of his surroundings, from which he determined that the cauldron was about four feet directly beneath him. *What a surprise.*

His wings started flapping of their own accord, not wanting a surprise bath any more than the rest of him did. In his mad scramble to avoid the cauldron, however, he bumbled his sightless way into a collision with something on one of the workbenches. The mystery object fell over onto its side and proceeded to roll off the workbench before he could do anything to stop it. Rufino wasn't certain what it was, at first, but a very telling *SMASH-tinkle-tinkle* sound gave him all the information he needed. *The Great Flash Powder Heist* was only five seconds old, and already it had become *The Not-So-Great Flash Powder Heist*. What was done was done, though, so he set down on the workbench beneath him and clicked several more times in order to paint a more accurate picture of his surroundings.

The floor layout was a perfect square, and Rufino could make out two doorknobs positioned diagonally across from each other. Workbenches covered every inch of the room's perimeter that wasn't occupied by the doorways, and shelves had been installed three feet above the benches to provide some additional storage space. The rather large cauldron was, of course, in the centre of the room, directly below the chimney. Echolocation couldn't tell him what was in the bloody thing, but from the almost-unbearable smell, he decided it had to be either cologne or some sort of medicine. He wasn't very familiar with Tundoran culture, but in Galensdorf it was widely believed that the most vile and revolting medicine was also the most *effective* medicine because it gave people some extra incentive to get better. It wasn't much of a stretch to believe that the humanoid brain—an immensely powerful thing—could accelerate the recovery process when its only alternative was to quaff some vile halfling cough syrup for another week or two.

Several dozen vials and beakers had been left on the workbenches, not counting the one that now lay shattered on the floor. Rufino could make out the shapes of the containers just fine, but his echolocation was not capable of determining what the labels on the containers said, or even if there were any labels at all. Rufino didn't intend to swipe anything except what he'd come here for, but it would have been awesome to know which containers were dangerous as he snooped around for his prize—getting blown up whilst looting the alchemy shop would be bad form, indeed.

There didn't appear to be any flash powder capsules in this workshop at the moment, but they had definitely been created in here. Flash powder could only be created in dark rooms like this one—if the stuff was exposed to *any* form of non-magical light, it would become unstable and explode. The tiny glass capsules in which the powder was sold protected the stuff from exposure—not unlike how windows protected vampires from the sun—but when a fragile capsule broke in a well-lit area or even a poorly lit one, the powder went boom. Unlike most other explosive devices, however, this "explosion" was naught more than a momentary flash of blinding light and a very loud pop. There was very little in the way of chemical expansion, which meant there was no shrapnel, and the disorienting effects wore off in about a minute. When the objective was merely to escape and not to harm, flash powder was arguably the best tool for the job.

Unfortunately, it appeared that he'd have to venture into the merchandising area in order to obtain his loot. He'd wanted to avoid doing so because the merchandising area was where the risk of detection was greatest, but since he couldn't escape through the chimney, he would have to take this chance sooner or later anyway. He'd just have to be smart about it.

To Rufino's relief, the door between the workshop and the merchandising area opened without a creak. He pulled it open about two inches, then shifted into his bat form and squeezed himself through the opening, his eyes and ears on alert status. Fortunately, the owner hadn't decided to work late; unfortunately, there was a big freakin' window at the front of the store and a big freakin' streetlamp just beyond that, so the room was still fairly well lit. This solved his problem with the labels, but it also meant that even his bat form might be visible from the sidewalk outside, which was *not* a trade he would have made willingly.

To his right was a seven-foot-tall shelving unit behind the sales counter. Straight ahead were two large shelving units against the north wall of the building. Approximately thirty-five feet away was the east wall, which featured the main entrance and the not-quite panoramic window he'd been cursing at a moment ago. The south wall featured two small double-hung windows flanked by bookcases that had been drafted into the role of displaying potions and salves. In the middle of the room were four pyramid-shaped display units that featured the "deals of the week," none of which happened to be flash powder. If this place didn't have what he needed, the little vampire would have to leave a *very* scathing note on the counter before he left.

There was a cardboard box of moderate size resting on top of the sales counter, so Rufino flew up to it and landed on the rim with great skill and agility. Unfortunately, the box contained small, circular containers labelled as "face powder." His complexion was in no need of improvement, so he hopped off the corner of the box and started scanning the shelves behind the counter.

The selection was an eclectic one, to say the least. *Elixir of water-breathing, no; elixir of invisibility, no; elixir of great stamina, no need; flask of anti-aging, no.* The next item was sunblock, which was worth a snort of derision—it would have to be about a hundred times stronger than it was before it would do him any good. *Elixir of fearlessness, no need; elixir of great strength, maybe... love potion?!*

That was very interesting. He was reasonably confident that Kiralyn would warm up to him eventually, but he'd be lying if he said he didn't want to expedite matters a little. Unfortunately, there was no getting past the fact that this wasn't the solution he was looking for. The potion was probably naught more than a colourfully labelled aphrodisiac, and even *thinking* about stuff like this would probably make Kiralyn angry, which could in turn get him frogged. If the frogging lasted only for an hour or two, it *might* be worth it—for curiosity's sake—but for all he knew, she was capable of making the spell last for days. *No thanks. Where's the bloody flash powder? Don't tell me this is the one alchemist in the world who doesn't like to make things go boom.*

He then noticed that there were some more boxes under the sales counter, which seemed like a logical place to store goods that could potentially be used to escape without paying. Rufino hopped off the counter, shifted into his humanoid form, then turned around and inspected the contents of the closest box. It contained smoke grenades, which told him he was getting warmer. The next box was empty, but it had been labelled *stink bombs,* which might explain the cauldron of crap he'd almost landed in a few minutes ago. The little vampire couldn't imagine a purpose for such devices beyond law enforcement or shenanigans, but apparently the things weren't illegal here in Tundora. They had been in Galensdorf, and with good reason—leaving devices of mass mischief within reach of halfling children was not a good idea.

The third box—smaller than the first two—was not labelled, but when he pulled it out and looked inside, he saw dozens of tiny glass capsules full of grey powder. *Bingo.* Rufino grabbed two of the flash powder capsules, then replaced the box and set his mind on the next challenge: how was he going to get out of here undetected?

With the front door and chimney eliminated from consideration, there were only two legitimate options: the south windows—which led into a small alley between this shop and its neighbour—and the second door he'd "seen" back in the workshop. The second door probably only led into a refresher or a storeroom, but he owed it to himself to verify this assumption before he gave up on a potential escape route. A back door would be really nice right now.

Naturally, there was no back exit—the second door out of the workshop led only to a dead-end storeroom. That left the windows. He couldn't reach the locking mechanisms for those windows on his own, but help was available in the form of a wooden stool sitting behind the sales counter. He'd have to use his humanoid form to move it into position, of course, but doing so seemed the lesser of two evils compared to walking out the front door.

He returned to the merchandising area, closing both the storeroom and workshop doors behind him so as to erase the evidence of his presence. Even with the shattered vial in the workshop, there was a reasonably good chance the proprietor would never realize he'd been broken into. He'd have to know *exactly* how many flash powder capsules were supposed to be in that box in order to realize that two of them were missing, and even *then* he might assume he'd simply miscounted when last he'd done inventory. After all, who in the hells would go to the trouble of breaking into a store only to take naught but a tiny amount of inexpensive flash powder? *Nobody at all. Except me.*

The little vampire slipped the capsules into his breast pocket, then grabbed the stool with both hands and lifted it about six inches into the air. It didn't weigh much, but it was somewhat top-heavy, so it was a bit of an awkward journey to the nearest of the two side windows. He made it without incident, though, at which point he threw a cautious look toward the front of the store before climbing onto the stool. He didn't want to be in this compromised position any longer than necessary, so as soon as he was in position, he released the lock on the window and gave it a very brief assessment. This window pushed out instead of sliding up, so with an awkward lunge and some brutish halfling strength, he *pushed* as hard as he could.

The window gave way far more easily than anticipated, which left him in danger of falling face-first into the alley beyond. He was able to use his midsection to steady himself, but not before one of the flash powder capsules managed to escape the confines of his breast pocket. It was only a four-and-a-half-foot drop, and the alley wasn't nearly as well-lit as the store; but as Rufino watched the capsule fall toward the packed dirt outside, time seemed to pass in slow motion. He could see, with clarity, every single rotation the tiny glass container made, and what *should* have been a one-second drop seemed to take four or five. At the last possible instant, he winced and closed his eyes, which turned out to be a very fortunate thing.

POW!

With words too profane to be mentioned running through his mind, the little vampire fell back into the shop, grabbed the stool, and returned it to its original position behind the sales counter with all the panicked haste he could muster. He then shifted into his bat form, flew out the window like a peregrine falcon with its tail feathers on fire, and quickly ascended to an altitude of fifty feet to assess his surroundings. He needn't have bothered—none of these commercial buildings had any second-floor apartments, and none of them were currently open for business, so nobody had any reason to be here. He'd gotten lucky. This time.

A moment later, after the adrenaline had worked its way out of his system, he returned to the alley beside the alchemy shop and shifted back into his humanoid form. He couldn't quite reach the open window from where he stood, but a quick search of the alley produced a broken broomstick that was more than long enough to help him push the window shut. He couldn't lock it from out here, of course, but he didn't think it would matter. Even if the proprietor *did* realize his shop had been broken into, nobody would ever realize a halfling vampire was the bastard who'd done it—not even Kiralyn, which was the most important thing. He had his flash powder and she didn't know it, which gave him a fighting chance.

Hopefully he wouldn't need it.

***

He returned to his suite via the window he'd left open, noticing as he did so that the door was still locked and everything was where he'd left it. This wasn't *absolute proof* that Kiralyn hadn't been in here, but… *oh, shut up,* he snarled to himself once he saw the trap he was falling into. *You're being paranoid again.* Changing one's approach to life wasn't as easy as it sounded.

Mercifully, his other half remained silent this time, which left the little vampire with some time to kill—time that he didn't want to spend by himself in this suite. Banned from the *Cocktail* he may be, but perhaps the *Duchess*'s staff could recommend an alternative. Maybe Tundora had a *legitimate* casino, or a late-night theatre, or even a restaurant that wasn't terrible. One might infer from his old title of head chef that he was picky and impossible to please, but in actual fact he appreciated just about any food as long as it wasn't undercooked, overcooked, too spicy, too bland, harder than stone, too mushy, or unpronounceable.

He put on his hairpiece and robe, retrieved his key from beside the bed and his coin pouch from the desk, and then stepped into the hallway outside his door. He'd been down this hallway a few times now, but this was the first time he'd actually stopped to take a good look at it, and what he saw was impressive. The lighting was perfect—not too bright, not too dim. The walls were beige and decorated with landscapes and a few portraits, the carpet was light brown with a three-foot-wide burgundy stripe running down the middle, and the doors were a darker brown with just the slightest hint of red. The small six-point chandeliers were pale gold—though they were probably just painted—and when Rufino reached the wide half-landing staircase at the centre of the building, he noticed that the wooden balustrades were made of the same material as the doors. *I'll say this for Kiralyn: she sure knows how to pick a hotel.*

Halflings normally hated human staircases, but this one wasn't so bad—he counted ten steps down to the landing and ten more down to the second floor. He was in the lobby thirty seconds later. The main entrance was directly ahead, about sixty feet away; the service desk was ahead to his left, complemented by a sitting area ahead to his right; and to each of his near sides was a corridor leading to first-floor suites. His nose told him there was a kitchen down one of those corridors, but he couldn't see it from where he stood.

There were two women behind the service desk now, whereas before there had been a man and a woman. The brunette in the blue dress who'd procured the ice pack for him earlier saw him coming, and she didn't even wait for him to reach the desk before seizing the initiative. "Do you need more ice, sir?"

He *really* didn't want the hotel staff to start thinking of him as Mr. Ice Pack. "Maybe later," he deflected her suggestion, noticing as he did so that the woman had quite a bodacious neck. In fact, she had a lot more going for her than just her neck, but he simply wasn't looking at her the same way he looked at Kiralyn. "I'm just looking for a drink and I came to ask for directions to the local watering holes, please."

"Certainly," she smiled in a way that was more than simply polite. "The two closest taverns are *The Pit Stop*, which is one block to the east, and *The Gravity Well,* which is one block beyond that. You may also wish to consider *Paulson's Refuge*, which is just across the street. It's a restaurant, but it does have a small bar."

The restaurant sounded good—maybe he'd even sample the cooking and offer some unsolicited but very excellent advice. "Thank you," he expressed his gratitude as he turned to leave.

"May I ask you a question?"

That stopped him dead in his tracks, though it was hardly the first time he'd been in this position. *Here we go again.* "Sure," he agreed as he turned back to face the woman.

What followed was not the proposition he'd been expecting. "What's it like working for Lady Veronica?" she asked instead.

The phony servant blinked a couple of times before returning his mind to the moment. "The cardinal rule in my line of work," he replied carefully, "is to never answer that question."

The woman giggled. "That bad, huh?"

Rufino shrugged. "I'm not at liberty to discuss the details of my employment," he told her. "I'm sorry."

He turned and made for the front entrance at the highest speed he could manage whilst still appearing relatively casual. Halfway through the door, however, he heard the woman say something to her companion behind the desk. "He's cute," she said.

The C-word. Again. Oh, sure, some other cultures took it as flattery, but when a human used the word to describe a halfling, it never seemed to come across as complimentary. Teddy bears were *cute*, too, and halflings did *not* appreciate being compared to stuffed animals even if it did sometimes get them laid. When one wanted to describe a halfling, the words "handsome" or "beautiful" could be used without offense, and of course "sexy" worked on just about everyone. Whenever he pleaded his case to a human woman, though, her first thought was usually, "aww, that's so cute."

Positive attitude or no, sometimes life just wasn't fair.

***

The woman's information was good, even if her language left much to be desired—*Paulson's Refuge* was visible from the moment he stepped outside. It wasn't very busy at this late hour, but the door was still propped open and the petite ginger-haired hostess was still wide awake and full of bubbly enthusiasm. He appreciated her existence—after spending the past two evenings with a woman who was over six feet tall in heels, it was *extremely* refreshing to meet someone who was only four-eleven. He asked for a stool at the small bar and he got one, along with a menu; an introduction to the bartender, Lionel; and several recommendations as to their best dishes. He didn't get her address with an invitation to come over later, but elsewise it was a pretty good first impression.

The restaurant's prices were very reasonable, and they also had a children's menu that just happened to be perfectly suited for halflings. It wasn't every day that a patron ordered his meal from both the children's menu and the alcohol menu, but fortunately there were several ways of telling the difference between an adult halfling and a human four-year-old. Rufino didn't have facial hair—he'd also shaved that off as part of the green-hair dare—and he certainly didn't have breasts, but halflings of both sexes had disproportionately large heads and extremities when compared to their human counterparts. Fortunately, this was common knowledge, so he seldom got asked for the I.D. card that he no longer possessed.

He ordered a salmon fillet with some peas and carrots, along with a bottle of blackberry-flavoured vodka. Whilst waiting for his food, he decided to chat up the bartender—a stick-thin man who was about five-six. In fact, all of the staff here seemed to be shorter than average, which certainly made their halfling customer feel welcome.

The two men conversed for the next fifteen minutes, during which time the little vampire learned a bit about the history of Tundora. It hadn't existed until thirty years ago—he knew that—but he hadn't known that from an infrastructural standpoint, it was one of the most modern cities in the country. The entire town had plumbing, and the administrative buildings also had electricity—within two or three years, it was expected that the entire town would be "on the grid," whatever that meant. He also learned that the town had initially been built with the approval of the druids, but that relations with them had gone downhill ever since Sawin' Logs Lumber Co. had moved into town.

It was at this point that his food arrived. The cut of fish was probably a little too big for him, but since he didn't actually *need* any of it, he decided not to complain.

That being said, the fillet was delicious and the vegetables were vegetables, so he intended to give credit where credit was due before he left for the night.

Lionel didn't give him that much time. "How is it?"

Rufino finished chewing his current mouthful and then nodded in approval. "It's good," he told the other, "and I used to be a chef, so I know quality when I taste it."

The bartender smiled and rested his arms on the counter. "I'll be sure to give Gwen the good review. So whaddya do these days, if not cook?"

The old chef finished another mouthful. "Actually," he said between his last two bites, "I now work for the Pentaghasts—the majority owners of the same Sawin' Logs Company we were discussing a moment ago."

The man paled quite noticeably. "Well, shit," he wore the expression of a man who'd come to a gunfight armed with a spatula, "I…"

Rufino didn't want to watch him squirm. "Relax," he instructed the other calmly but decisively. "I'm a servant, not a spy—I'm only here for some good food and some good conversation. But while we're on the subject," he added, for something had just come to mind, "I'd be interested in knowing if the Tundoran citizens feel the same way about the loggers as I do."

"How do you feel about them?"

Rufino shrugged, though beneath his somewhat loose-fitting robe, the gesture was barely visible. "The foreman we met was a well-mannered fellow," he described to the other, "but the labourers were pretty crude—all they did was stare at my mistress." He neglected to mention the million-gold dress since doing so would probably destroy the case he was trying to make. "It would be nice if they'd at least *try* to act like they've seen a lady before."

The barkeep rested his arms on the counter again and dropped his voice to a conspiratorial whisper. "We don't like them, either," he said as Rufino took a sip of his vodka. "The Eager Beaver guys aren't so bad," he went on in reference to Tundora's other logging company, "but the Sawin' Logs guys have a lot of free time on their hands and they like to spend it partying. The last three years have been great for the taverns and an absolute nightmare for everyone else. You want to hear an example?"

Rufino nodded, his mouth now full of vegetables.

Lionel stood up straight again. "Two months ago," he said in what was still a fairly quiet voice, "my old friend, Edal, came into town on his weekly supply run. He doesn't have a horse or a mule to pull his small wagon, so he has to do it himself, and he can't pull that thing very fast anymore."

"Where does your friend live, if not in Tundora?"

The man pointed to the north with his right index finger. "There's an old civil war catacomb three kilometres to the north of town. Edal's the keeper, and he also lives there because he, quote, 'doesn't want to spend any more time in Tundora than necessary', unquote."

Rufino finished chewing some more food. "Is your friend a hermit, then?" he asked in an effort to conceal his true thoughts. *An underground graveyard, you say?*

Lionel shook his head. "Actually, he was the city's bookkeeper until seven years ago," he explained. "What happened to him then is not my story to tell, but I do still consider him a friend. Anyway, where was I?"

"Your friend came into town two months ago," he reminded the other.

"Right," the other man nodded. "You know how spectators line the streets during a bicycle race? Six drunken Sawin' Logs guys did the same to Edal—cheering him on from both sides of the street, warning that the 'second-place cart' was catching up and that he needed to go faster. Two more of their guys then held some tape—a finish line—across the street at the end of the block. Edal tried to ignore it, but when he was about to reach the tape, one of the original six guys came sprinting up the street to 'win the race' himself. If they'd left it at this, it would have been bad enough, but they proceeded to boo the 'second-place finisher'; hurl insults like, 'too slow, old man'; and throw some street trash at him. This went on for two or three more minutes before they finally got bored and moved on."

Rufino didn't say anything, so Lionel kept going—clearly he was quite passionate about the subject. "I've told you this specific story because it happened to my friend," he explained, "but there are *hundreds* of incidents to choose from, ranging from harassment and indecent exposure to robbery and assault. This is *not* what the original residents of Tundora had in mind when we built this place, and we would be eternally grateful if you could somehow persuade your bosses that their lumberjacks are in dire need of some civility training."

The little vampire set his cutlery down on the plate and wiped his mouth with a cloth. "I can bring this to the attention of my mistress," he told the barkeep. "She'll be meeting with the head foreman before we leave town, so they'll have an opportunity to discuss the matter."

"Do you think they'll actually do something about it?"

The man was right to be suspicious—this was never going to end in disciplinary action. Just not for the reason he thought. "Probably not," Rufino admitted as he took another sip of vodka. "I'm not at liberty to discuss how my masters do business, but I can tell you this: if you want to see change, I recommend you gather about fifty like-minded individuals and then take your complaints directly to the head foreman. The Tundoran employees are his responsibility, and he won't be able to ignore their misdeeds if you and your unsatisfied friends start making his life miserable."

Lionel rested his arms against the counter again and looked straight into Rufino's eyes. "I appreciate your honesty. I've been holding out hope that this wouldn't come to a protest, but perhaps there's no other way."

"All too often, the loudest voices are the only ones that get heard," Rufino reminded the other.

The man lifted his eyebrows. "A servant-sociologist?"

Rufino smiled. "As much as I'd like to believe Lady Veronica keeps me around for my muscle, she doesn't. My value to her is in my understanding of some more advanced business and social concepts." He took a brief look around, but there were only a handful of other patrons and none of them were within thirty feet. "I would very much appreciate it if you'd neglect to mention my role in the upcoming protest."

Lionel shrugged. "It's been on the table for months," he spoke somewhat sadly. "All you've done is to help me see the necessity of it." He slapped an identical bottle of blackberry-flavoured vodka onto the counter beside the original. "Consider yourself forgotten, and consider this a token of my gratitude."

The little vampire, struck by inspiration as though it had been a bolt of lightning, pushed the second bottle back toward the bartender. "To tell you the truth, Lionel, vodka's a little strong for halflings. Do you have a peach cider, by chance? It's my favourite."

To his surprise, the small bar did have peach cider, which he gratefully accepted on Kiralyn's behalf. If she'd wanted a bottle with which to wash away the misery of tonight's fact-finding mission, surely it would be in his own best interests to offer her another one before she embarked on the equally miserable task of pinning Martin Scirocco down in the *Cocktail.* Even if she declined this second bottle, he'd still come across as the sensitive and caring dude that he could be every now and then, so this seemed like a win-win. His instincts told him his life wasn't in danger anymore, but it was still a very real possibility that she'd walk away at the end of the mission and pretend she'd never met him. If he wanted *his* ideal ending to become reality, he needed to take advantage of every remaining opportunity to impress her. There might not be many of them left.

He finished his dinner about ten minutes later, at which point he was given a bill for twelve gold and change. He paid fifteen to the hostess, telling her as he did so that the place was worthy of his old chef's seal of approval. She told him in return that she hoped to see him again. He heard that a lot from women, but until he knew where he stood with the druid-sorceress, he couldn't afford to go on a dating spree. If he cheated on Kiralyn Frostwhisper, he'd probably end up needing that catacomb after all.

It sounded like the perfect hideout—assuming it wasn't well lit, his echolocation would give him as good a chance as he was going to get of eluding the druid-sorceress long enough for her to give up. The only negative was the three-kilometre distance between the city walls and the site. He could cover that distance in nine minutes at top speed, but Kiralyn's owl form was capable of sixty kilometres per hour or more, which meant she could cover the same distance in *three* minutes.

It wasn't as bad as it sounded, though. She'd have to spot him first in order to chase him, and it was within his power to make that very difficult for her. The evidence did strongly suggest that he'd be fine even if the worst-case scenario did come to pass.

So why don't I feel more confident?

Chapter Ten
The First Answers

20 July 1511N

"Rise and shine, sleepyhead."

Rufino awoke slowly, not knowing whether the voice he'd heard was real or imagined. With a concerted effort, he forced his tired eyes open, and after a short moment, they were able to tell him two things: that it was dark outside, and that the chandelier above him had been lit. The second observation told him he was not alone—he had a very clear memory of snuffing out the candles before going to sleep. "Didn't feel like knocking tonight?" he murmured into one of his pillows.

"Actually," Kiralyn corrected him, "I was out there knocking for almost three minutes before I decided to let myself in. I thought you might have made a run for it."

The little vampire heaved an exasperated sigh and rolled onto his back so he could see her. She was in a long black dress again, this time an asymmetrical single-strap design with her left arm in a full sleeve and her right arm bare. The sleeve had been done in lace, as had the top two inches of the diagonal neckline and also the fairly narrow stripe that ran around her tummy at an angle parallel to that of the neckline. It wasn't the starscape dress, but it was still a match for anything they had in this town. "If I was going to run away," he stifled a yawn, "don't you think I would have done so before now?"

"Under other circumstances, yes," she replied as she sat down at the desk across from the bed. "But this is different. Have you ever taken a life before?"

He shook his head. "Not unless you count kobolds."

The sorceress shifted her gaze toward the open window. "Are you prepared to have this eating away at your conscience for the rest of your life?"

Rufino sat up straighter and folded his arms across his chest. "Was that question intended for me," he inquired thoughtfully, "or for both of us?"

She remained silent, which told him he was on to something. "Haven't *you* killed before?"

"In self-defence, yes," she admitted with a sigh. "Not like this."

He saw an opportunity to strengthen the case he was making, so he took it. "Then it's not unreasonable for me to assume that your feet are feeling a bit cold, too," he pointed out. "You're undoubtedly going to tell me that your sense of duty is what's keeping you here, and it just so happens that *I'm* still here for the very same reason."

"You're not a druid," she reminded him.

"It doesn't matter," he replied with confidence. "If I bailed out now, I'd not only be betraying you, but I'd be sending myself back to the empty existence in which you found me." He paused for a moment, but when Kiralyn neglected to respond, he decided to fill the void with a question. "Were you in my shoes, what would you do? Would you hide in some corner of your hedge maze hoping never to be found, or would you try to recover some of what you'd lost?"

"I'm not the giving-up type," she needed only a second to come up with her answer.

"Nor am I," he rested his case. "Speaking of which, I haven't for…"

"I do have some information for you," she cut him off as if she'd known exactly what he was going to say, "but that'll have to wait a moment. We have a problem."

"I didn't do it," he declared reflexively.

Her serious expression broke for a short moment. "I'd be impressed if you did," she admitted easily, "since the problem began about eight hours ago."

During the middle of the day. "I guess I really didn't do it, then."

Kiralyn shook her head slowly. "Not this time. A woman's gone missing."

She let her words sink in for a moment before continuing. "Apparently this is the second woman to disappear in as many months, so foul play is all but assured. There are currently ten times as many police and militiamen patrolling the streets as there were at this time yesterday, and I've personally observed them giving escorts to isolated pedestrians of both sexes."

Rufino could see where she was going with this. "If they decide to give Scirocco a friendly escort back to his house tomorrow night…"

"…You won't be able to reach him," she completed the thought on his behalf.

That *was* a fairly serious problem. "What should I do if he *does* make it back to his house?" he blurted out the first concern that came to mind. "It won't look like a coincidence if I attack him there."

"I couldn't agree more," she told him. "Under no circumstances are you to attack him if he's given an escort, even *if* you still believe you can finish the job. Vampires aren't in the habit of stalking groups of people—they go for targets of opportunity."

Rufino nodded. "I'll hit a group of two if I'm desperate, but never three or more."

"Exactly," she agreed in return. "Now, there *are* one or two things I can do to discourage the patrollers," she went on. "It's going to rain tomorrow, and it just happens to be within my power to turn a light rainfall into a heavy one, which should keep some of the militia patrols off the streets. I ca…"

"I'm going to be out in your downpour, too," he reminded her.

"I know, and I'm sorry," she sounded genuinely remorseful. "It's also within my power to start a fire large enough to occupy every authority figure in the city, but I refuse to endanger innocent lives for the sake of a mission, no matter how important that mission may be."

"Heavy rainfall can be dangerous too, you know."

The druid-sorceress smirked. "Ever the thoughtful one, aren't you?"

He blinked a few times in surprise. She actually seemed *happy* that he was challenging her ideas, which was an attitude he'd seldom seen outside of Galensdorf. "What makes you say that?"

"I noticed the new bottle of cider sitting in the coat closet."

Rufino shrugged. "I figured you'd want some more cider before or after dealing with Martin Scirocco, so I pushed my way back to the *Cocktail;* defeated the orc in personal combat; then cornered the owner in his storeroom and told him, 'Your peach cider, or your life.' As you can see, he was quite accommodating."

"Or perhaps you bought it using that gold I left for you?"

Thus began the staring contest. Halflings loved staring contests, but it quickly became apparent that he was both out of practice and overmatched. After only thirty seconds, he could hold his expression no longer. "Okay, okay," he conceded defeat with a grin, "I didn't extort this bottle from that little wiener at the *Cocktail.*" He paused a moment for some dramatic emphasis. "I merely incited a riot and forever altered the political landscape of this town."

"A worthy cause if ever I heard one," she remarked in good humour as she stood up. "Anyway, the only real danger from heavy rainfall is flooding, and I'll make sure that doesn't happen. Now before you go and mention property damage," she raised an index finger to her lips in order to shut him up for a moment, "may I remind you that Nyobi is, statistically, the third-rainiest country in the world. If these people haven't waterproofed their homes by now, that's their problem."

That sounded reasonable. "When you said there were one or two things you could do to discourage the patrollers, what was the other thing you had in mind?"

She sighed. "The patrols will taper off as the evening progresses. The longer I can keep Martin inside the *Cocktail*, the better our chances will be."

Rufino wasn't sure he liked the sound of that, but he decided not to complain—it wasn't like Kiralyn would be having any more fun with Martin Scirocco than he'd be having with Mother Nature, after all. "What happens if I do have to abort?"

"Then things get complicated," she borrowed a line from Captain Obvious. "Veronica Pentaghast is scheduled to leave town tomorrow night, and Kiralyn Frostwhisper is also due elsewhere in the very near future." He still hated it when she referred to herself in the third person. "As I see it, we'll have three options if the hit fails: we could agree to meet back here in four or five weeks, I could summon one of the other druids to take my place, or you could attempt to finish the operation on your own."

The little hitman was surprised to learn that the third option was even on the table. "You'd trust me to stay behind unsupervised?"

She lifted an eyebrow. "Is there a reason I shouldn't?"

"Well," his mouth hung open as he attempted to find an appropriate response, "not really, no. I just wasn't expecting you to see it that way."

"I'm not especially eager to find out how well you'd get along with one of the others," she explained in a voice that was both casual and serious at the same time. "Besides, after I mark the target, you won't need us anymore."

Rufino didn't appreciate how she'd worded that. "I may not need you from an operational standpoint," he argued, "but I still don't believe that my questions can be answered as easily as you think."

"You have no idea how right you are," her opinion had apparently shifted quite dramatically over the past week. "The druidic vault of knowledge is replete with information about vampirism dating back to the very *birth* of vampirism, but even *it* can't explain you. I am prepared to share what I've learned thus far, but be warned: some of your questions are still over my head."

The little vampire thought back to their negotiations in Borallis. "I do recall asking for a second date," he pointed out rather brazenly.

The druid-sorceress shook her head immediately. "It would be too far out-of-character for us to go out together," she had her convenient excuse all lined up. "If you'd like, we could get some room service."

Rufino sighed and leaned back against his pillow. "To tell you the truth," he murmured, "I'm not hungry."

"Well, I *am* hungry," she informed him as she turned toward the door, "so I'm going downstairs for a few minutes. Are you certain you don't want anything?"

"A female O-negative on the rocks would be grand."

Kiralyn's face became uncharacteristically mischievous. "Well, this place *does* claim to have the best customer service in the city," she remarked as she stepped into the hallway. "Let's see how far they're willing to go to prove it."

Rufino knew she wasn't going to present his incriminating order to the staff, but he appreciated her joke nevertheless. Under other circumstances, she might have succeeded in calming his nerves, but unfortunately she'd made the mistake of telling him she was due elsewhere in the near future. He almost certainly wasn't welcome to come along, so tonight was shaping up to be his last chance to convince her to meet with him again at some point. He didn't know if what she'd shown him over the past three evenings was just another persona or if it was actually her, but he *did* know he wanted to see more of it. She'd have made an excellent halfling if she were about three feet shorter and a bit less frightening.

He pushed the thought aside and started working on an argument. One way or another, his future was about to be decided.

***

Kiralyn returned eighteen minutes later, by which time Rufino was out of bed and spruced to perfection, as ready as he'd ever be to make the sales pitch of a lifetime. His original intent was to wear the brown toupee, seeing as how it made him look a lot more sensible. At the last minute, though, he decided to go without it. *If she's ever going to accept me,* he reasoned, *I want it to be the real me. For better or for worse.*

When she did finally return, it was with a Bloody Mary that was obviously meant for him. He decided to play along for a bit, lest he discourage her from showing her playful side. The "blood" was supposedly courtesy of the brunette hostess who had a crush on him, which eventually led Rufino to question how the woman had ended up with a bottle of vodka in place of a heart. He then went on a tirade of sorts about the brunette and her use of the dreaded C-word, but Kiralyn didn't understand what all the fuss was about. How could she? She probably hadn't been called "cute" since she was twelve years old.

Rufino then tried to steer the conversation toward business, but the druid warned him to keep it casual until after her food had been delivered. He decided to respect her wishes by making a personal guarantee that her food would have tasted better if he'd prepared it himself. He sincerely doubted she was looking to add a vampire-chef to her non-existent personal staff, but the more he talked about his past life, the easier it should be for her to think of him as a person. They couldn't have been more different if they tried, but "different" did not necessarily mean "incompatible." If he could get her to regard him without prejudice for even five minutes, he was *certain* his fine qualities were capable of winning her over.

Unless, of course, Kiralyn was a lesbian. If she was, his negative side might never shut up again.

Her food arrived about ten minutes later. It consisted of relatively thick pasta noodles, five or six different types of chopped vegetables, and something called yeri sauce. The miniature chef had never encountered yeri sauce before, so his first order of business was to campaign for a taste. Kiralyn teased him a little about his credentials, but he didn't let this bother him—he knew he'd win a cook-off against the amateurs downstairs even if he *didn't* know what all of the ingredients were. Give him a halfling-sized stove or two and he became a magician in his own right.

His relentless mooching eventually got the better of her, at which point she permitted him to pilfer a sample of the sauce. It was delicious, of course, which necessitated that he ask her about its origins. All she knew was that it originated from somewhere in East Vendraca, where many of the people were vegetarians who used sauces to make their meals exciting. The word "exciting" didn't do yeri sauce justice, but unfortunately the stuff was quite expensive in this part of the world, so it wasn't going to become a staple at *Good Eats* any time soon. Halflings didn't want to spend more than four or five gold for a plate of food, and according to Kiralyn, this plate had cost five times that.

His culinary curiosity now satisfied, the little vampire changed the subject back to business by raising his biggest concern about staying behind on his own: he'd have to feed sooner or later, and doing so would attract vampire-hunters to Tundora like moths to an open flame. Kiralyn finished a mouthful before suggesting that she could leave two or three vials of blood behind to help him keep a low profile, but what she said immediately thereafter made him forget all about the prospect of free blood. "Frankly," she went on, "I don't think the hunters will give you much trouble even if they do make an appearance."

She sounded awfully certain of that. "They never have before," he agreed, "but…"

"Have you ever wondered," she cut him off, "*why* you've been able to elude the king's undead-hunters for so long? They *are* pretty good at what they do, you know."

He had wondered about that, yes. "I just assumed I was smarter than they were."

She finished a small mouthful of pasta. "You probably are," she threw his ego a significant bone, "but in this case, I don't think intellect has anything to do with it. Undead creatures possess auras that can be detected by those who've been trained to look for them. I can sense undead from up to a hundred feet away within direct line-of-sight, or from thirty feet away through solid rock. I once busted a vampire who was hiding at the bottom of a storm drain across the street from where I was walking."

Kiralyn paused for another bite of her food. "The king's hunters don't have to outsmart their prey," she went on after she finished chewing. "They detect vampires by following search patterns and utilizing their senses, which are normally up to the challenge. Their senses are worthless against you, though, because *your* aura is so weak that I didn't even know it existed until you touched my hand that first time. I'd been sitting with you for an hour at that point."

He hung his head in embarrassment. "That was when you suddenly became interested in sex," he recalled with way more clarity than he would have liked. "I feel like such a fool."

"You're not the first man to be taken in by that trick," she remarked mildly, "nor will you be the last."

Her words weren't comforting in the slightest. "Don't you feel even the tiniest bit guilty," he asked as he lifted his head again, "about crushing a poor vampire's dreams like that?"

She shook her head. "At the time, I didn't feel guilty at all," her words came as no surprise whatsoever. "However, if I'd known then what I know now, I might have used a different approach. I…"

"What in blazes is *that* supposed to mean?"

But Kiralyn was clearly unwilling to elaborate. "I've just told you that you're virtually undetectable," she reminded him, "and all you want to talk about is *this?*"

Rufino folded his arms across his chest and attempted to look miffed. "That aura thing is nice and all," he admitted with ill grace, "but it can only help me live a longer life, which is worthless to me without a corresponding increase in quality. I told you that back in Borallis, but I don't think you were listening."

The sorceress was shovelling food into her mouth with a bit more urgency now, which he took as a sign that she was going to leave if he didn't drop this subject soon. "Have I not proven the sincerity of my words by having come this far?" he asked.

Kiralyn finished chewing another mouthful before looking at him again. "The only thing I know for certain about you," she spoke slowly, "is that I know nothing."

Rufino blinked a few times as his brain searched for words. "What do you mean?"

"I mean," she set her plate down on the desk before folding her arms across her chest, "that what the vault of knowledge is telling me and what my own two eyes are showing me are two *completely* different things. The halfling thing alone is…"

"What 'halfling thing'?"

Kiralyn sighed through her nose. "Vampirism was designed to convert humans, but as everyone knows, it can also convert dwarves and elves due to the similarities between the three species. It's too weak to convert orcs, but unfortunately it's also too strong to convert halflings."

The little vampire didn't like the sound of that one bit. "You mean…?"

She nodded gravely. "It kills your people, Rufino," she told him, her voice filled with compassion. "The Nyobian vault of knowledge contains forty-three records of halflings being bitten by vampires. Seven of the victims were healed quickly; the rest died within an hour. There were no conversions."

Rufino felt as though he'd just been trampled by a horse. His gut told him she was telling the truth, but on this occasion, he might have preferred to hear a lie. She'd just taken everything he'd believed about his continued existence and thrown it into the trash can. *There were no conversions*, he repeated her words inside his head. Vampirism was a fate he wouldn't have wished upon his worst enemy, so on one hand, it was a relief to learn that none of his kin had experienced the misery of this existence. On the other hand, he still had a snowball's chance in the hells of a happy ending— the deceased did not. What made him so bloody special that he'd been spared when dozens before him had perished?

Nyobian halflings were no strangers to survivor's guilt. He'd been hit close to home, himself, when his best friend's girlfriend had been killed during a battle against the wretched kobolds. This was different, though—not only was he the *only* survivor, but he'd survived to become the very thing that had killed the others. He wasn't personally responsible for any of this, of course, but there was no getting past the fact that at least thirty-six halflings had died because of monsters like him. "Are those numbers re…" he attempted to force his question through a very uncooperative larynx, "…regional, or are th…"

The distressed vampire could maintain his composure no longer. He turned toward the mattress and buried his face in it, using his arms to obstruct the druid's view of his watering eyes. Unfortunately, his body was starting to tremble, too, and there was nothing he could do to hide that. It did occur to him to shift into his bat form—where his emotions would be far less visible—but the act of shape-shifting required focus, which was currently beyond him.

He spent the next minute desperately trying to avoid making a sound, as if Kiralyn didn't know exactly what was going on anyway. Halfling men weren't supposed to cry, but they weren't supposed to become vampires, either. This realization gave his mind something to latch onto, and within twenty seconds, he was back under some semblance of control. He was still shaking a little bit, but the flood gates had closed and he was probably capable of clear and concise speech again. He turned around.

Kiralyn was still there, of course, but not where he figured she'd be. He'd expected to find her near the desk, or perhaps in the library; instead, he found a black wig and a hair net sitting on the floor, and a beautiful snowy owl perched on the windowsill. This implied that she wanted to go for a flight, but to the best of his knowledge, she had no *reason* to go for a flight—not unless she believed some fresh air would calm him down. It was very obvious that she wanted him to come along—after ruffling her feathers for a moment, she turned her head to look at him, and then she did not look away. He was briefly tempted to initiate round two of the staring contest, but he quickly thought better of it. No self-respecting owl would ever lose a staring contest.

He changed into his bat form, at which point Kiralyn took off and ascended to about fifty feet. He didn't know if she had an actual objective or if she was just going to fly in circles for a while, but he appreciated what she was doing nevertheless. He might never fully recover from the shock of what she'd just told him, but knowing the truth about his existence should help him make sense of the rest of his life. That was how it went in the storybooks, anyway.

As it turned out, Kiralyn did have something specific in mind—she led him straight to the *Killer Cocktail*. He wanted to believe she was going to frog Grunk on his behalf, but instead of avenging the mistreatment of her favourite halfling, the druid-sorceress turned east and followed Plantation Avenue until they reached the border between the commercial and residential districts. He had a funny feeling that he knew where she was going, so when she turned north a few blocks later, he made a mental note that she'd done so on Willow Street. She followed Willow Street for two blocks before turning east onto Garden Avenue, then she turned north again after half a block. When he caught up a few moments later, he found himself above a cul-de-sac featuring five homes, and he also saw that Kiralyn had taken a particular interest in one of them. She landed on the roof of the house that was second from the right, and then she made a cooing sound in order to get his attention. It was unnecessary—he already knew he was looking at the home of Martin Scirocco.

By Tundoran standards, it was luxurious—two storeys, made of brick instead of wood, and probably pushing three thousand square feet. There was a topiary of a dolphin in the front yard—along with the customary flower garden—and there also appeared to be a huge model of an ancient warship in the backyard, complete with sails and cannons built to scale. There was a very good chance that Mr. Scirocco was only renting the property because of how often loggers were required to relocate, but the fact that he'd chosen to rent a house with such a strong nautical theme might be just as telling as if he owned it himself. *If you can hear me, Martin,* the little vampire directed his thoughts toward the quiet house, *there will never be a better time than tomorrow for quitting your job and becoming a sailor.*

Her objective now completed, Kiralyn took to the skies once more and started back toward the *Duchess*. With but a single coo—as if she expected him to know what it meant—she left him in the dust, which was initially somewhat puzzling. It didn't take him long to come up with a reasonable explanation for her action, though. Veronica Pentaghast couldn't break a nail without the entire staff of the hotel hearing about it, so if it was discovered that she'd somehow vanished within nine bloody hours of someone *else* going missing, there would be bedlam. Within minutes, the managers, hostesses and porters would be pointing the collective finger at the kitchen, because blaming the kitchen was the standard cop-out in the hospitality industry. Rufino didn't want to see his culinary colleagues bear the brunt of some more undeserved slander, so he wished Kiralyn well in her bid to avert a disaster. Or whatever it was that she was doing.

The druid wasn't in his room when he returned, which came as something of a surprise. Her plate was also gone, though, which told him that she'd simply taken it downstairs herself and that she intended to return in a few minutes. He took a few deep, calming breaths as he stood in the middle of the room, but they weren't necessary—he already felt quite a bit better, and he had her little distraction to thank for it. The way wizards and sorcerers were portrayed in literature made them seem quite helpless without their magic, but Kiralyn's social versatility was so strong that in his mind it *overshadowed* her magic. All druids could use at least *some* nature magic, but how many of them could earn the trust of a vampire?

She returned five minutes later. "Feeling better?" she inquired as she locked the door behind her.

"For the most part," he admitted. "I still feel a little guilty about surviving when so many others have died, but it's not like I asked for this dubious distinction. I'll be fine."

Kiralyn sat down at the foot of the bed once again, as though gravity pulled her toward that spot whenever it was available. "I'm glad you realize that," she told him. "Now, to answer your earlier question, the numbers I gave you were strictly regional. You may not be the first halfling in the world to survive a conversion, but until I can present the question to the global druidic community, I have no way of knowing one way or the other."

"How long will it take to ask everyone?"

"Seven months," she replied smoothly, with no hint of deception, "give or take a couple of weeks. In the meantime, I have two working theories as to how this might have happened, but first I need to know a little more about your background. This is a long shot, but do you remember anything about the vampire who bit you?"

How could I forget? "She was a black-haired human woman who stood about five-four. I didn't get her name, but she was still present when I woke up, and she ended up giving me a few pointers about how to survive as a vampire. Then she left."

"You were already a vampire by the time you woke up?"

Rufino nodded. "Yes, I was," he told her, "and yes, I know that's not typical."

She nodded. "It's also atypical for a vampire to remain at the scene of a crime."

He hardly needed a druid to tell him that. "What are you getting at?"

Kiralyn sat up a little straighter. "Before I answer your question," she began with a bit of apprehension, "I feel obligated to remind you that I'm currently operating on theory, not fact. I cannot absolutely guarantee that what I'm about to tell you is true."

Rufino shrugged easily. "Be that as it may, I trust your theories more than I trust a lot of people's facts."

It had seemed like an insignificant comment, but apparently it wasn't. "Why's that?" she asked with no small amount of interest.

He blinked a few times before deciding it was safe enough to give an unfiltered response. "Over these last few days, you've shown yourself to be perceptive and analytical, with an outstanding eye for detail—you'd make an excellent detective if ever you tire of the spy game. More telling than that, though, is the way you've been treating me, which has thus far been a helluva lot better than I was expecting. This tells me you're more open-minded than you let on, and since truth is a matter of perspective, it stands to reason that a theory borne from several perspectives will often contain more truth than a fact borne from a single perspective, yes?"

Kiralyn didn't respond verbally, but she did stand up and make a beeline for her new bottle of cider. Then, in a move that was apparently *very* uncharacteristic, she twisted the cap open and took a long gulp straight out of the bottle. "I thought you didn't do that," he remarked mildly.

She resealed the bottle and set it back down on the floor. "There are exceptions to every rule, Rufino," she delivered her excuse in a very strange voice, which told him her true meaning lay somewhere beneath the surface. As usual.

She didn't give him time to think about it, though. "To confirm my first theory, I need a brief summary of your medical history."

There wasn't much to summarize. "I was born premature after my mother was attacked by a stray dog," he explained. "As she tells the story, they almost lost me to illness twice during my first year, but I have no memory of that. What I *do* remember is how all of the bugs and viruses that hit Galensdorf during my childhood never seemed to hit me. I always chalked it up to good luck."

She shook her head slowly. "I think it's more likely that your infant body realized it was in trouble and decided to overdevelop your immune system in order to survive. I also think your overdeveloped immune system combined with my second theory is what saved your life six years ago."

Kiralyn was being cagey about her second theory, which told him he might have to jump through hoops in order to wrestle it out of her. "I hope you're not going to make me play twenty questions before you tell me what's on your mind," he grumbled under his breath.

She lifted her eyebrows. "I thought halflings liked games?"

"We love games," he admitted, "but this doesn't strike me as the time or the place."

Her eyebrows stood at ease. "It seems fortunate, then," she said in a tone that was suddenly very severe, "that I didn't intend to play one. I *was*, however, going to ask for your solemn word not to repeat what I'm about to say to *anyone.* If this reaches the citizenry, it will very likely cause widespread panic and probably violence."

The little vampire smiled as sweetly as a miniature man with fangs could manage. "I'm already keeping one secret for you, Kira," he reminded her. "A second one will make no difference."

"This is a lot worse than the Scirocco secret, Rufino," she replied, her voice having lost none of its severity. "I want a specific promise."

Rufino sighed theatrically and held up his right hand. "I promise not to tell anyone what you're about to tell me," he put his non-existent reputation as an honest vampire on the line. "But frankly, nobody would believe me anyway, so…"

"I think some sick bastard engineered a brand new strain of vampirism and turned it loose upon the world."

It was a long minute before Rufino found his voice again. "Couldn't it be a mutation?" he asked.

"That's what most of the arch-druids believe," she told him, "but I believe this new strain is the product of intelligent design because of how it does such a perfect job of increasing suffering across the board. For example: the old vampires have most of their humanity burned away during a conversion, but the new vampires seem to be retaining their feelings and memories. To me, a vampire who feels remorse and regret is worse off than one who doesn't feel anything."

"Two weeks ago, I probably would have agreed with you."

She rolled her eyes. "Until I walked into your life and fixed everything with a wave of my magic wand, right?"

It did sound like a pretty cheesy pick-up line, at that. "So far you've fixed only one thing," he corrected her calmly, "but it was the most important thing you could have possibly fixed: my attitude."

She didn't respond, but at least her eyes weren't rolling anymore. "I know you didn't believe me when I said that meeting you had stirred my dormant spirit," he hadn't put it so eloquently at first, of course, "but what's most important here is what *I* believe. When I realized it was still possible for me to have feelings for another person, it made me think about what *else* might be possible, and I've since come to the conclusion that it *should* be possible for me to build a brand-new life for myself. So you see, Kira," he started to wrap things up, "the fact that I've retained my humanity isn't necessarily a bad thing. In fact, I now consider it a blessing, because without my feelings, I'd have nothing to look forward to."

The sorceress was certainly paying attention now. "That doesn't disprove my theory," she argued passionately. "I think the creator of this strain *intended* for the negative feelings to overwhelm the positive ones, and he simply underestimated you personally."

It felt really good to be in the thick of an argument right now. In Galensdorf, this sort of thing was practically foreplay. "You insist that it's intelligent design, yet creatures all around us have evolved in all sorts of crazy ways in order to survive. Why can't viruses do the same?"

"They can," she admitted, "which is why I'm not dismissing the possibility that I'm wrong. I don't think I'm wrong, though—if the original strain was capable of altering itself in this manner, I strongly believe it wouldn't have waited three thousand years to do so. I also know that such a virus couldn't have mutated overnight, so we should have found *some* evidence of a more gradual change. To this date, we haven't."

"Why do your people still believe it's a mutation, then?"

She favoured him with a smile. "That is an excellent question," she buried him in praise, "and again, I can't give you a definitive answer. My theory, however, is that my people simply can't bring themselves to believe someone would *want* to duplicate the damage caused by the original strain. I, on the other hand, have met more than a few "people" who'd get off on doing something like this if they could. Fortunately, a vampiric virus is so incredibly complicated that even *beginning* to understand the actual construction of it is beyond all but a handful of people."

"Are you one of those people?"

She shook her head. "Don't put me on a pedestal just yet, my little anomaly," she spoke the words with what almost sounded like affection. "Genetic engineering is beyond me, as are many other things."

"Like what?"

She didn't respond verbally, but she did give him a funny look. "Oh, come on," he protested innocently. "You know everything about me, but I hardly know anything about you. I want to learn."

Kiralyn's expression became unreadable as she exhaled softly through her nose. "As I said earlier," she spoke slowly, "I don't know you nearly as well as you think I do."

This was probably as good an opportunity as he was going to get to bring this up. "So why don't we meet up again at some point in the future?" he made his bold proposition whilst the opportunity existed. "We can call it a study session if you don't wanna call it a date—I don't care. I just really want to see you again."

Once again, the stinging remark didn't come—at the rate she was warming up to him, they might be married by this time next week. "I fully intend to come find you again once I've had a chance to ask the global druidic community about halfling vampires," she explained, "but…"

"You said that would take seven months!"

She seemed a bit taken aback by his sudden outburst. "I'm afraid so," she nodded. "Due to the way the community communicates, we ca…"

"You're missing the point," he interrupted her quite brazenly. "I don't *care* if I'm halfling vampire number one or number fourteen. What I want is to see…"

"I know, I know," she swiped the reins from him in return. "You want to see me again. That's sweet, in a bizarre sort of way, but I don't think you've taken into consideration how busy I am on a day-to-day basis, or that I spend the majority of my time undercover. I am not the girl next door, Rufino Endicott—I'm a druid, I'm a spy, and I lead a life that is more complicated and more dangerous than you…"

"Actually," Rufino cut her off with a triumphant grin, "I realized all that about four hours after I met you. It doesn't bother me—my life is pretty dangerous in its own right, and any halfling will tell you that 'complicated' is just another word for 'interesting'. You *really* don't understand the halfling psyche if you think I'm going to give up just because the road ahead will be difficult. I…"

"Your halfling psyche is going to have to accept the fact that my schedule is crazy," she returned his interruption with casual grace. "You're also going to have to accept that I have no choice but to keep people at arm's length—mostly for my own sake, but in this case for yours as well. Has it occurred to you what would happen to a certain green-haired halfling male if it was discovered that he was associating with Nyobi's Most Wanted?"

"I imagine most of your associates would be in trouble if they were caught," he responded after a brief moment of hesitation.

The druid-sorceress shook her head. "Most of them wouldn't be in as much trouble as you think," she told him. "Augustus V doesn't want me dead; he wants to make me an offer he thinks I can't refuse. He would track down and *reward* just about anyone who could help him find me—anyone except you, of course. His men would eventually discover your secret, and then you'd die." There was a brief pause. "Now tell me something else: what do you think would happen to my people if word got out that we'd been associating with a vampire?"

Rufino hung his head. "It would be front-page news for a decade."

He looked up in time to see her nod. "That about sums it up," she agreed. "Every time I meet with you, I'm playing with fire. I realize we're both very good at concealing our true natures, but when the consequences of failure are so cataclysmic, it only makes sense to be cautious."

"We could still meet tomorrow," he suggested impulsively. "Nothing would seem out of the ordinary."

She started toward the hallway. "We could," she agreed, "but I'd rather not do so unless Scirocco still lives. I'm going to be in a hurry to leave town, and you'd only get in the way."

He sighed, and he exaggerated it for her benefit. *Whether she's doing it on purpose or not, she certainly has this hard-to-get routine down to a science.* "What's so bloody important that you can't even live up to the agreement you made with me?"

Kiralyn folded her arms across her chest. "I tried to get someone else to verify your discovery in the *Bog*," she explained with some obvious frustration, "but he refused to believe that you could be telling the truth. That means I have to head out there myself before something happens to the evidence. I also have to keep an appointment right after that, so…"

How bloody convenient. "What about my reward?" he demanded with some irritation of his own. "Room service doesn't count as a date, lady."

She rolled her eyes. "I've answered every question that I'm capable of answering. If you can find the patience to wait for me to do my homework, the result will be a much more satisfactory 'date' for both of us."

"Seven bloody months from now," he grumbled under his breath, "or maybe longer. How can I trust that you'll come back in seven months? 'Use him and lose him' might have been your plan all along."

"I give you my word," she replied simply.

Rufino scrutinized her features for an entire minute, trying to find even a hint of deception. It was a waste of time, for once again there was nothing but the perfectly neutral expression of a professional spy. There was something about the way she'd spoken those words, though. "I make a point of not questioning a person's word until I have reason to," he sighed in resignation, "so I'm gonna give you this one. I do, however, want something in return."

The druid-sorceress rolled her eyes again, and for one brief, shining moment, he felt as though he knew *exactly* what she was thinking. "Nothing outrageous," he hastened to assure her, "but from my point of view, there's a very simple way for you to knock a bit of time off my wait."

"By not leaving just yet?" she drew the correct conclusion.

He nodded. "Your 'crazy' schedule doesn't seem to be all that 'crazy' right now."

She sighed and leaned against the right angle where the hallway and reading room walls met. "Actually," she corrected him, "I'm supposed to meet with another druid in fifteen minutes, and then I'm supposed to go to sleep. Don't let my owl form fool you—I like to be in bed by midnight."

Her actions were not in alignment with her words, however. Whilst Rufino was still scrambling for a response, she stepped past him and once again took a seat on her favourite corner of the bed. "Ummm," Rufino was understandably confused, "didn't you just sa…"

"He's a jerk," Kiralyn interrupted him with a conspiratorial smirk on her face. "He can wait."

Chapter Eleven
Points of No-Return

Kiralyn stayed with Rufino for fifty-eight minutes, which was about fifty-five minutes longer than he'd been expecting. One wouldn't have believed that a vampire and a druid could make small talk for such a lengthy period of time, but they managed, covering every topic from Galensdorf to the king's hairstyle and back again. She was still extremely reluctant to reveal anything about her background, but she did throw him a bone by admitting that her starscape dress was a gift from her father, not from the druids. That made her a noblewoman, whether she'd admit it or not, because none but a noble family could have *possibly* afforded that thing.

Rufino was also certain she was a foreign noble, since there was no way in the hells that a Nyobian noblewoman of marrying age could have become a druid without *anyone* in the Nyobian nobility connecting the dots. She wasn't going to tell him where she was from, though, so he decided not to ask.

She left just before midnight, which left him with a lot of idle time and nothing to fill it with. He eventually decided to kill some time by reading a book from his suite's little library, but what he had the misfortune of pulling from the shelf wasn't actual literature so much as it was insidious propaganda. All that was missing was the stamp of approval from the secret police. It was called *Over the Mountains*, and it told the story of two young lovers who were so dissatisfied with their miserable lives that they decided to take a chance on migrating to a neighbouring country. Separating these two countries, of course, was a treacherous mountain range, and for dozens of merciless pages, those peaks beat the crap out of the protagonists and the readers alike. Despite being ill-prepared and under-geared, the heroes miraculously survived the mountain crossing, only to discover that their new home was a socially backward cesspit of corruption from which they could not escape. They died young, wishing they'd been wise enough to fully appreciate their country of birth.

Rufino wished he'd been wise enough to close the book after page seven. It *had* helped him kill four hours, though, so that was something. 04:00 was an early bedtime for him, even in the middle of summer, but he didn't particularly feel like staying awake any longer. He climbed into bed, closed his eyes, and tried not to think. Alas, his runaway mind refused to cooperate, and it wasn't until after noon that he finally managed to nod off.

21 July 1511N

Rufino awoke seven hours later to the sound of heavy rainfall. This was both expected and disturbing. The elements themselves he could handle with his usual grace, but this wasn't a storm so much as it was a *stage*. His point of no-return was fast approaching.

Maybe. Things didn't always go as expected, even for Kiralyn Frostwhisper. Maybe Martin Scirocco had taken one look at the weather and decided not to visit the *Cocktail* today. Maybe Kiralyn hadn't been able to keep him at the *Cocktail* long enough to set him up for The Chomp. If so, Rufino hoped she'd do him the courtesy of calling him off *before* he rushed off to drown in this little storm of hers. He didn't know her moods well enough to know what she'd do if she was pissed off.

The bedside clock displayed 19:22, so the little vampire had about an hour with which to prepare for the hit that was probably still on. He required only five minutes of that time. He still didn't *want* to kill Martin Scirocco, and there was no way for him to verify much of what Kiralyn had told him; but Earl himself had said that Martin had been the head foreman in Tundora for four years now. That the troublemaker was still around after all this time did strongly suggest that the druids had tried to go through the official channels first. Rufino took great comfort in this.

He didn't want to just sit around for an hour doing nothing, though, so he fetched his hairpiece; left the window precisely one inch open, so that he'd know if someone had used it; then locked his room and made his way downstairs. The hostess with the foul tongue was nowhere to be seen, but the good times ended as soon as he located the dining area and opened one of the menus. The *cheapest* dishes were twenty gold each, and the dishes that were listed in a different language all cost forty or fifty. Was foreign cuisine really that much better than Nyobian slop?

Rufino didn't know, and he wasn't about to find out—he didn't have forty freakin' gold to spend on a plate of exotic food that he didn't need anyway.

He spent the next twenty minutes spying on the kitchen in an effort to learn the great secrets of foreign cuisine. There weren't any. The stuff was prepared using pots and pans, as was the case with domestic slop; it required special attention at pre-determined intervals, as was the case with domestic slop; and several cooks were involved in the preparation of each meal, as was almost always the case in large commercial kitchens. That settled it, then—by ordering a few exotic sauces and writing your menu in another language, you automatically became a fancy restaurant and were thus entitled to double the price of everything.

The little spy now felt ready to return to his room, but he'd not taken four steps toward the staircase when the brunette hostess appeared at the end of the hallway. She held a piece of paper in her left hand as she approached, but her attention was completely and unmistakably on him. That was bad—the dining area had no exit of its own, and the kitchen contained far too many well-armed cooks to be a suitable hiding place. Maybe he'd get lucky and she wouldn't be in a mood to talk.

"Hello."

Or maybe he wouldn't get lucky and she would be in a mood to talk. "Hi," he croaked in response.

"May I be of assistance?" she asked as she stopped a few feet away.

Sure, he snarled in silence, *you could leave.* "Not really," he bit his tongue instead. "I can't afford to order this food, so I thought I'd just stand here and smell it for a while."

He realized his error the instant she began to giggle. *Gods, give me strength.* "Maybe I *can* be of assistance, then," she offered after a moment. "There's a restaurant called *The Spice of Life* at the southwest corner of Main Street and Plantation Avenue. Their menu has almost everything that ours does and they charge about half of what we do."

"Really?"

She nodded with conviction. "Really. It's the best restaurant in the city, bar none. Every man I've ever dated has taken me there."

Rufino wanted to scratch his noggin whilst he assembled this puzzle in his mind, but it occurred to him at the last second that doing so might displace his hairpiece. The hostess might realize that a green mohawk had no place on the head of a noble's servant, but it seemed far more likely that she'd think it was *cute* and decide to tell him as much. There'd be nothing left for him to do at that point but to walk into the kitchen and ask one of the cooks to put him out of his misery. "While I do appreciate your insider's knowledge," he replied cautiously, "I have to ask:

does your manager know you're undermining your own kitchen?"

"I don't see how she could," the young woman shrugged, "since I haven't done it before."

"I see," the little vampire murmured with a sigh. She'd obviously taken an interest in him, and the bone-chilling C-word was just as obviously one of her reasons for doing so. He only needed to think back to their brief conversation from two days ago, though, to realize there was more than one thing on her mind right now. "I'm afraid I'm still not at liberty to discuss the specifics of my work," he discouraged the inquiry before she could bring it up again, "but perhaps I can be useful in some other way. Am I correct in my observation that you don't seem to be happy here?"

She looked away for a brief moment. "Don't get me wrong," she eventually replied, "the money here is pretty good, and I really like having an excuse to dress up and stuff, but…"

"But," he cut in smoothly, "something's missing, and it's significant enough that you're considering other lines of work."

It was a reasonable hypothesis—from what he knew, little girls didn't grow up dreaming about being welcome mats. Her immediate response was to step past him and disappear into the kitchen, which gave him the golden opportunity to flee that he'd been craving a short moment ago. He didn't take it, and a moment later she rejoined him in the corridor. "So are you a mind-reader or something?" she answered his question with a somewhat flirtatious question of her own.

"Not at all," he assured her, hoping to discourage any such moods of hers before they could spiral out of control, "but I am perceptive. I have to be, with these muscles."

She started to giggle again, so he decided not to say anything else that was even *remotely* funny or cute. It did strike him as damning, though, that he had yet to react to this woman on a more basic level. The young hostess was about six inches shorter than Kiralyn and was noticeably curvier, both of which were pluses as far as most halfling men were concerned. She also seemed to have a much less conservative sense of style, for she was currently wearing a snug, sequined purple one-piece dress that cut off about twenty inches higher than anything the druid-sorceress wore. This fairly risqué dress on this *very* pretty woman would have lit Rufino up like a firework six years ago, but in the here-and-now he felt absolutely nothing. Nothing but a distant memory of the way he used to be. "What's your name?" he asked before the silence could become conspicuous.

She seemed surprised and pointed at her upper chest. "My name is rig… oh, blast, you can't see it from down there, can you?"

That was correct—she was a well-endowed woman and Rufino was not far enough away from her to overcome these angles. "I'm Crystal," she told him. "What's your name?"

"I'm Bryce," he borrowed the name of his partner at *Good Eats*, "and I'm going to tell you straight up that the money in my line of work isn't worth the pounding my self-esteem endures on a daily basis. You can almost certainly do better for yourself."

"But you don't believe the same of yourself?"

That was actually a pretty good question, which necessitated that he treat it as such. "Quite the contrary," he decided to say. "In wanting something more for ourselves, you and I have something in common. As soon as I have the money to open another business, that's exactly what I'm going to do."

Crystal looked surprised again. "You had a business?"

Rufino nodded. "I co-opened the first restaurant in my home village of Galensdorf, and when I left home, it was doing very well for itself."

"Why did you leave home?"

The little vampire wanted to glower at her for being so bloody nosy, but he supposed it was his own fault for telling a story that invited such questions. "Personal reasons," he shut down her line of inquiry. "I'd rather not get into them right now, please."

"Sorry."

Her quick apology left him with the impression that he was successfully pushing her away. The only problem was that getting rid of her no longer seemed to be his goal. "Don't apologize," he offered her a reassuring smile. "There's no need—I just have a few old scars that're really difficult to talk about."

"I completely understand," she still seemed to be apprehensive for reasons he didn't fully comprehend. "Is your new business going to be another restaurant?"

"I'm an excellent chef," he boasted just a little, "so yes, I was planning to open another restaurant."

"I'm a good cook, too. Would you consider hiring me?"

Now the reason for her apprehension was as clear as her name. "It's not just about being competent, Crystal," he warned her. "You have to *really* like cooking in order to hack it in a professional kitchen—chefs work miserable hours and endure way more than our fair share of criticism. Passion for our craft is what keeps us going. Do you have that passion?"

Her silence told him all he needed to know. "You've asked a few questions of me," he went on, "so now it's my turn. I'm going to ask you one question, Crystal, and I want you to answer it as quickly as you can. I want to know what's in your heart, not in your head. Are you ready?"

She stood up a tad straighter and nodded, so he went ahead with his question. "If you could have any job in the world, what would it be?"

"Queen of Nyobi," she blurted out before giggling again.

The little career counsellor sighed and folded his arms across his chest. "I realize that position is currently vacant," he conceded with mild irritation, "but perhaps I should rephrase my question. If you could have any job in the world that *doesn't* involve marrying into the ruling class, what would it be?"

"Veterinarian."

That was more like it. "So you're an animal lover?" he asked.

"I am," she agreed. "I have a horse, two huskies, and a very foul-mouthed parrot. When I was younger, I had a beagle, three hamsters, and a snake. Snakes and hamsters don't mix, in case you were wondering."

If his day in the *Bog* had taught him anything, it was that snakes and halflings didn't mix, either. "What's stopping you from pursuing your ambition, then?" he asked. "Grades?"

"My younger brother," she told him. "He has a severe disability and my parents are both dead. I'm the only one left to look after him."

"I see," he murmured.

"Not as simple as you thought it would be, is it?"

A potentially awkward question, but Dr. Endicott was ready for it. "Actually, I do have a possible solution for you," he replied, "but it would mean moving to Strelas and signing up for one of the University of Nyobi's study-at-home programs. You'd only have to go to school for the tests and the lab work."

"If I only had myself to think about, I'd have moved to Strelas years ago," she told him. "But I'm not confident my brother could handle moving to a city that size."

"Have you asked him?"

"It's not that simple," the young woman was starting to look very fatigued. "His language skills are very poor—he communicates more with feelings than with words. Even after all these years, I'm still not certain what he's trying to say a lot of the time."

The little vampire reached out to hold one of her hands, the C-bombs from two days ago all but forgotten. "Maybe I can help you fill in some of the blanks," he suggested gently. "No matter your brother's condition, I'm certain that on some level he knows who you are and what you're doing for him. I'll also bet that his feelings are just as strong as ours, and that he loves his sister very much."

She was starting to get misty-eyed, which told him his argument was having the desired effect. "Moving to Strelas may be difficult for him," Rufino went on, "but, were I in his shoes, I'd rather face that difficulty than watch my sister miss out on the life she should have had. That life is yours for the taking, Crystal. These high-paying hostess jobs will only last for as long as the industry thinks you're young and beautiful, but I'm betting that'll be long enough for you to work your way through veterinary school. Once you do that, you'll be set."

"This plan of yours is heavily dependent on my ability to get a good job in Strelas," she pointed out. "If I can't, I'm sunk."

"Again, have you tried?"

She hesitated briefly. "No," she admitted, "I…"

"How long have you been working here?"

The hostess needed only a second to collect herself. "Three years," she told him.

Three years was an eternity in her line of work. "Would your manager give you a good reference?" he asked.

"Well, she wants me to marry her son," Crystal replied with a sigh. "So I guess that's a 'yes'."

"Then I'll bet some serious coin," Rufino filled his voice with confidence, "that when you step into Strelas, you'll have a job offer faster than a halfling child can get into trouble. I've been to the *Empress* a few times—with my mistress, of course—and I see no reason why they wouldn't want you. No reason at all."

In actual fact, his first-hand knowledge of the *Empress*—the most prestigious hotel in Strelas—was limited to a handful of flybys whilst on his way to or from the seedy parts of town, where his coffin was usually parked. But she didn't need to know that. "Really?" her big brown eyes told him she was buying it.

"Absolutely," he assured her. "With your looks and an upscale hotel on your resume, you'll…"

"So you think I'm beautiful, do you?"

Rufino wanted to smack himself with a spatula. He'd miscalculated, and Crystal was no longer thinking about the *Empress* or about vet school. Now he had to find a way to escape without hurting her feelings, lest she decide to ignore his advice for no better reason than because it was part of a painful memory. "Well, yes," he began the very delicate process of disengagement, "but…"

"But what?"

He sighed. "But I never intended for this conversation to be a prelude to asking you out. The mistress and I are leaving town as soon as she gets back from her meeting."

The young woman was starting to look very confused. And upset. "What *was* your motive, then? A man always has one."

That was true, but men had more potential motives than she was giving them credit for. Halfling men, in particular, might give advice simply for the pleasure of hearing themselves talk. She wouldn't understand if he told her as much, though, so he decided to tell her something sensitive and thoughtful that also had the virtue of being more or less true. "I haven't always been this pint-sized pillar of wisdom, you know," he explained quite humbly, "I've made a couple of really, *really* bad choices in my life. Again, I'm not willing to discuss the specifics, but I've decided that the only way to give my own struggle some meaning is to share my experience with others. Where I made a bad choice, I want you to make a good one, so that you don't go where I've been."

"And you share this wisdom with everyone you meet?"

She had him there—if she'd been some greasy sailor at the *Salty Squid,* their conversation would have ended about five seconds after it had begun. Maybe he wasn't quite as far gone as he thought. "No," he admitted, "I don't." He took a deep breath, and as he did so it occurred to him that this could be an excellent time for a bagel on a stick. Sometimes a world of difference could be made by a few well-placed words. "I have no say in when the mistress and I leave town this evening," he repeated his earlier claim, "but I *can* leave you with something to hold onto. As I said, I accompany my mistress to Strelas on a semi-regular basis, so if you do relocate to the capital, then there's a pretty good chance that we'll bump into each other again. If and when that happens, I will be delighted to see you building a better life for yourself, and I'll express that delight by taking you to *The Lion's Den*, where I will probably ma…"

"That's the best restaurant in the country!" the significance of the proposal was not lost on the Tundoran girl.

"Until I open my new establishment, perha…"

"But the wait list is three months long," the realization dulled some of her excitement.

The little vampire clasped his hands behind his back and smiled. "That three-month wait for you or me is about three minutes for Lady Veronica. She can get us a table on short notice."

Crystal seemed a bit taken aback. "Would she do that?"

He made a show of scanning the corridor for eavesdroppers before responding in a hushed voice. "Upper noble or not, she has her weaknesses," he embarked on an *extremely* misguided tale. "One masterfully timed 'sad-puppy face', and we'll have our table."

The young woman started to smile again. "That may be the cutest thi…"

He tuned out after that, in the name of self-preservation. He wasn't upset, though, because deep down he knew he'd had that one coming. He wasn't actually a semi-regular guest of the high-end hotels in Strelas, so it was all but certain that he and Crystal were never going to see each other again. On the off-chance that they *did*, there was absolutely *no* chance that he'd be able to live up to his promise of a date at the *Den*. Still, despite having made a lying snake of himself for the gazillionth time in the last six years, he didn't think he had a whole lot to apologize for. By the time she realized he wasn't coming, she'd be up to her neck in homework and wouldn't have time to worry about one little halfling. A jackass move this may have been, but he'd done it for the purest of reasons.

Unfortunately, his next jackass move wasn't going to be so easy to excuse. Good intentions or not, a man was going to die before this night was done—an event that would have far-reaching repercussions not unlike a drop on a pond. If it were up to him, Rufino would have put this execution off long enough for the city to make some progress in tracking down those missing women. He didn't want them to remain missing because the town was too busy trying to track down an undetectable vampire.

Unfortunately, the timetable was out of his control—he returned to his room at 20:18, only to discover that the window had not been disturbed during his absence. A crappy feeling in his gut told him Kiralyn wasn't going to cancel in the seventeen minutes before sundown, so it was too late for second thoughts. It was time to act.

***

Not quite time to act, as it turned out. Thank the gods that his bat form was more or less waterproof, because he'd been sitting on the roof of the building just south of the *Cocktail* for almost two hours before something finally decided to happen. When it did, it happened quickly. A really wet horse and carriage rolled to a stop just outside the *Cocktail*'s saloon doors, at which point two very different figures appeared from inside the establishment. One of them was a five-seven human man dressed in brown work boots, brown cargo pants, and a brown vest over a white shirt. He still had most of his short brown hair, and he possessed no scars or tattoos or other distinguishing features. *A man who could lose himself in a crowd of three people….*

The second figure, of course, was a freak of nature. Kiralyn Frostwhisper had promised a red dress, and she hadn't disappointed, appearing now in a full-length garment that came really close to matching her magnificent natural hair colour. The leg slit and neckline were still on the conservative side, of course, but *conservative* was seldom an appropriate word to use when describing a red dress. Red was the colour of confidence, and confidence was the sexiest trait of them all.

The lovesick vampire watched, adoringly, as the raven-haired lady in the blood-red dress climbed into the coach—the taxi-man holding an umbrella over her head all the while. There was definitely a guilty pleasure in being the only non-druid in Tundora who knew who "Veronica" really was. There was also a strange logic behind his inexplicable attraction to her—the two of them really were cut from the same cloth. She was wanted by the Crown; he was wanted by the Crown. She hid in plain sight; he hid in plain sight. She could get the opposite sex to dance to whatever tune she wanted; he could get th…

…And Martin was now half a block away. *Crap.*

The little hitman leapt into the rain-soaked sky and gave chase, his wings flapping faster than they were ever designed to. Fortunately, the foreman seemed to be having some difficulty remaining upright, so he wasn't moving fast enough to maintain the lead he'd established. Score one for the manipulative druid-spy: she'd obviously decided that getting Scirocco completely smashed would improve the odds of him meeting an unfortunate end on his way home. Rufino wasn't sure if he should be grateful for the extra help or offended by the insinuation that he needed it, but it would definitely come in handy.

Within a minute, the predator was thirty feet above his unsteady target. There were no police patrols within his perceptive range, but common sense told Rufino that he should wait until Martin was out of the main commercial area before he did anything. He hadn't gotten a good look at the man's neck yet, but it was entirely possible that he'd have to break out his larger humanoid fangs in order to reach the man's jugular—some veins ran deeper than others. He wasn't lucky enough to have Mr. Scirocco randomly duck into a dark alley of opportunity, but during last night's tour of the neighbourhood, he'd noticed that Plantation Avenue was very poorly lit around where the commercial and residential districts met. Unless Scirocco managed to get himself killed in the next few minutes, the attack would take place there.

Unfortunately, getting there wasn't going to be quite as easy as Rufino had anticipated: some gusts of wind were starting to come out of the north. They weren't very strong gusts by humanoid standards, but having a flight form that weighed one pound gave a person a unique perspective about wind. It was the enemy, to be loathed with every spare thought of every waking day. It didn't like him much, either—in spite of his supreme effort to remain above Plantation Avenue, he was steadily being pushed to the south. *Kira, if you can hear me,* he sent a desperate thought into the stormy night, *there will never be a better time to rein in this storm of yours.*

There was no immediate response, so he was left with but a single option. Once he'd been pushed a full block to the south, he descended to ten feet and used this new avenue's buildings as shields. He then raced to the east as fast as his little wings could propel him, gauging the crosswind at every intersection. By the time he'd reached the eastern edge of the district, there had been jack all in terms of weather improvement, so now he had to choose between aborting the mission and using his humanoid form to overcome this natural obstacle. When it occurred to him that he could still abort if someone took too much interest in a halfling sprinting north on Spruce Street, he decided to chance it.

Seconds later, Rufino was on foot, struggling to keep his hood in place as he dashed into the wind. Nobody passed through the intersection of Spruce and Plantation during his approach, so at the last second he ducked into the service alley on the south side of the avenue and used his bat form to gain access to the rooftops. The roof at the southeast corner of the intersection was flat, so he landed on it, shifted back into his humanoid form, and then raced at top speed to the edge overlooking the avenue.

Martin was nowhere to be seen.

The panicked vampire double- and triple-checked his findings, but there was no mistake: Plantation Avenue was completely lifeless for three blocks in both directions. He had failed, and now he could either make a run for it or he could grovel at the feet of the most dangerous person in the country and pray that she was in a good mood. A good mood that wasn't bloody likely after she'd spent the last four or five hours schmoozing with her hated enemy. *The sensible choice,* he realized, *is the same as it has been all along: stow away on a boat to Minta Cadra and don't look back.*

Rufino heaved a long, drawn-out sigh as the rain continued its relentless onslaught. Apparently, he wasn't all that sensible, because his desire to return to Kiralyn was once again stronger than his desire to flee. He almost certainly had some form of punishment coming, and he had no way of knowing what it would be until it was unleashed upon him. Would she be content with some exquisitely chosen words of scorn, or would he be spending the next few hours as a frog?

Either way, he stood to learn something about her. Anyone could be pleasant when things were going smoothly, but when carefully laid plans were disintegrating, some people stayed as cool as ice and some people snapped. There was perhaps no single more important thing a person could learn about a prospective mate than how he or she responded to bad news, so he owed it to himself to go back and man up. Vampire or no, the word "accountable" still meant something to him, and…

His train of thought then jumped the rails. Down on Plantation Avenue, two blocks to the west, a short and slim figure stepped out of a small alley between two buildings. It wasn't possible to make out colours at this distance, but from the overall shape of the man and from the way he was fidgeting with his zipper, Rufino decided it had to be

Martin Scirocco. The man had stepped into the alley to relieve his distressed bladder—a perfectly natural consequence of having a few too many—and Rufino had missed out on that absolutely *perfect* opportunity to strike because Mother Nature was conspiring against him.

But this was no time to curse—the target was the only person in sight, and the wind was beginning to die down. There were six streetlamps on the northern sidewalk west of the intersection, but the second- and third-closest ones weren't lit. With those two lamps extinguished, there was a fifty-metre gap between lights on that side of the street—a window of opportunity if ever there was one.

Batfino took up a position thirty feet above those darkened streetlamps and watched with great interest as his prey approached. Scirocco's condition had deteriorated in the last ten minutes, to the point that he might no longer be capable of finding his own house. To a vampire, this was a double-edged sword: on one hand, a person who had to concentrate so hard on remaining upright wasn't going to spot a sudden threat from above until it was too late. On the other hand, a target that was as unsteady as this one could be quite difficult to land on. Fortunately, Rufino retained the option of performing a controlled crash landing in cases like this. Crashing would be as painful as the word implied, but it would get the job done—his tiny claws were wonderfully effective at getting themselves tangled up in hair and clothing.

A minute later, at long last, Mr. Scirocco staggered his way into the little vampire's chomping ground. Rufino had been expecting some last-second jitters, but when they didn't come, he concluded that either his resolve was stronger than he realized or that his negative side had simply given up on him. Either way, it was time to put his money where his mouth was. He spread his wings as far as he could and then pitched down into a dive like a hawk in slow motion. He had five seconds to figure out how best to land on this obnoxiously unstable man.

He decided to aim for the man's starboard breast because he knew from experience that when it came to crashing, fat deposits were good and collar bones were bad. Unfortunately, in hyperfocusing on his landing zone, he completely missed the bigger picture, and it wasn't until the very last instant that he realized the target was starting to fall over sideways toward the street. This realization came as such a surprise that he hesitated when he should have been pulling out of his dive.

***

Rufino had no memory of the collision itself, but when he came to a minute later, he immediately realized two things: that he was lying in a puddle on the sidewalk, and that his tiny body was *very* unhappy about the mistreatment it had just been subjected to. There wasn't a single part of him that didn't hurt right now, but under the circumstances that was probably a good thing. If a body part *wasn't* in pain after crashing into something almost two hundred times its mass at roughly thirty kilometres per hour, then that body part would probably never feel anything again.

Groggily, he took in his surroundings, trying to decide whether or not he was in any danger. It didn't appear that he was—the logger foreman was prone and unconscious a foot and a half away, his head resting in a puddle of its own. There was no one within two blocks to come to the distressed man's aid. That could change in a hurry, though, so amid significant protests from his battered body, Rufino got back to his tiny feet and tried to concentrate on his objective. Unfortunately, there were a few drops of male B-positive inside his mouth, which suggested that Martin might already have a couple of fang-sized holes in his face or neck. If so, Rufino might have no choice but to abort the mission, since drawing blood from two different wounds did not fall into the realm of typical vampiric behaviour.

He needed to inspect the damage. Maybe this blood was the result of a scratch—a glancing blow instead of a bona fide puncture. Such a wound, if present, would suggest that a struggle had taken place and that the vampire had bitten the jugular by accident. Maybe he'd gotten lucky.

He had. And he hadn't.

Rufino was preparing to roll his prey over when it occurred to him that the puddle beneath the man's neck didn't look quite right. He couldn't explain it in this dreadful light, but something told him that he needed to investigate this. He was right: a somewhat ill-advised taste test revealed that the anomalous puddle was in fact male B-positive blood, not water. Not only was it blood, but from the rate the puddle was expanding, Rufino estimated that Martin was going to run out of the life-giving fluid in a matter of minutes.

So why didn't he feel better? The druids would be thrilled—they'd wanted a phony accidental death and they were about to get a real one. The sharpest investigator on the planet wouldn't be able to implicate them. None of that seemed to matter at the moment, though—all Rufino wanted to know was whether Martin had killed himself or if he'd had some assistance. Rufino had yet to explain how he'd regained consciousness with blood in his mouth, and he would never get another opportunity to answer this particular question. *No self-respecting halfling would shy away from the truth.*

He had the truth a moment later, and it was going to be a difficult truth to live with. There were two fang holes in Martin Scirocco's left jugular vein, and it was from these small but perfectly placed wounds that the man was bleeding out. This made Rufino's skin crawl, to the point that he felt an overpowering need to put some distance between himself and his victim. A moment later, he was on the nearest roof in his bat form, being assaulted by *both* sides of his mind who, for once, were in complete agreement with each other. *This* was much worse than a deliberate act because *this* had the potential to happen again. Chomping necks was dangerous business, he knew, but to the best of his knowledge, he'd never missed his mark in six years as a vampire. That streak was over now, and never again would he be able to dive at his prey without wondering if *this* was about to happen again.

A very large part of him wanted someone to come along and save Martin's life so he'd be off the hook, but it didn't happen, and after about five minutes, the pool of blood beneath the man's neck stopped getting bigger. Rufino cried for a few minutes thereafter. On one hand, he was grateful his victim hadn't suffered—the man was going to wake up in the afterlife without the faintest idea how he got there. On the other hand, the little vampire wished the collision had killed him, too, because death seemed a more merciful fate than having to live with this experience. A predator without confidence was a dead predator, so not only did he have to find a way to come to terms with what had happened, but he had about twelve days in which to do so before he starved to death.

Over the span of the next minute, Rufino's incalculable misery morphed itself into anger, both toward himself and toward the manipulative shrew who'd gotten him into this mess in the first place. It was not the halfling way to keep such strong feelings contained, so he took to the sky and set a course back to his suite at the *Duchess*. Whether she wanted it or not, Kiralyn was going to get a piece of his mind.

Chapter Twelve
No Good Deed...

The druid-sorceress—still clad in her blood-red dress—was cleansing their safe-house of evidence when Rufino returned to it, and her attention was on him the instant he flittered his dripping wet way through the open window. "So it's bad news, then?" she surmised calmly.

Very calmly, he noticed—almost as if she'd been expecting her undead henchman to screw things up. "Actually, I'm here to thank you," he informed her upon his successful reversion to halfling-form, "for all the *confidence* you showed in me this evening."

His sarcasm seemed to have her at a disadvantage. "I beg your pardon?" she demanded frostily.

A woman like Kiralyn was probably used to having people wilt whenever she used that tone of voice, but Rufino was far too upset to be intimidated right now. "If you'd liquored that bastard up any more than you did, he might have died all on his own," he snarled up at her.

"The liquor was his idea," she replied without hesitation, though of course Rufino could hardly verify the claim now that the man was dead. "I told him he was about to receive a substantial performance bonus, and he felt like celebrating." She took a slow breath, and he got the impression it was more for his benefit than for her own. "What happened?"

The little vampire spilled his guts about the accidental murder, and as usual, she gave him precious little in the way of readable responses. The one thing that *was* clear was that she didn't seem to understand why he was so upset. "If you want to beat yourself up over a freak accident, that's your prerogative," she ended up telling him as she returned to the task of junking out the desk, "but trolls will stop eating meat before something like this happens again. The odds…"

"Halflings have no use for odds," he cut her off with a frustrated snort. "By your own admission, I shouldn't exist and this shouldn't have happened, but I do and it *did.* And if it hadn't been flying fangs-first into a jugular vein, it could just as easily have been something else. Has it ever occurred to you how many ways a person can get hurt during a vampire attack? One twitch at the wrong time and it's…"

"One twitch at the wrong time and my spell of silence becomes a spell of poison," she pointed out. "You aren't the only one who can inflict great damage by accident, you know."

He wasn't particularly interested in letting her make this about her. "I know that," he insisted, "but *you* weren't the one who was out there attacking that logger tonight."

"No, I only masterminded the conspiracy to kill him," she argued over her shoulder. "Many would argue that I am more responsible for this crime than you are."

"I'm not one of those people, druid," Rufino shot her down with another angry snort. "This conspiracy was, in your own words, a 'theoretical long shot' until I came along. I could have stopped this at any time, but I *didn't.*" He balled his hands into fists in another futile effort to expunge his negative energy. "Right now I wish I had. How am I supposed to go on with the knowledge that every time I attack someone it could end in a pool of blood?"

The sorceress posted her hands on her hips and turned back to face him. "Fortunately, you won't have to."

He almost made a smart remark before he realized what she might be saying. "What?"

"You are one of only five people who know what happened here tonight," she explained, "and the other four are druids. I've been instructed to clamp your mouth shut. Permanently."

Rufino almost laughed. *Just when I thought my evening couldn't get any worse.* "So you're going to kill me, then?" he demanded incredulously. "One murder wasn't enough for you?"

Kiralyn seemed to be game for a Final Argument. "Actually," she explained calmly, "as the arch-druid of my branch described it, we're going to 'lay your corpse to rest', thereby granting your spirit the peace that was cruelly denied to it by undeath."

He folded his arms across his chest in a gesture that went beyond communicating how unimpressed he was with her rationalization. The remaining capsule of flash powder was still tucked away inside his breast pocket, and his right hand was now positioned so that he could pinch the capsule with his thumb and index finger as soon as opportunity knocked. If he could get her to avert her gaze for even a *second*… "I imagine Krexin Vath used similar euphemisms to justify his depravity," he spoke up before it could become obvious that he was up to something. "From where I'm standing, your 'act of mercy' is no better than whatever he called his murders to make them sound better."

Her gaze remained steady, as did her expression. Blast her, anyway—the comparison to a mass-murderer should have been worth at *least* a flinch. "I will take no more pleasure from this than I took from Martin's death," she assured him, as if he would somehow be comforted by her words, "but we druids are duty-bound to fight undeath wherever we encounter it, and I take my responsibilities as a druid very seriously."

The little undead beastie, armed with a confidence that he couldn't explain under the circumstances, rolled his eyes and shifted his weight. "What do you see when you look into my eyes, Kira?" he demanded. "Do you not see the spark of life that your people claim to protect?"

"I see a living spirit trapped within a dead body," she answered his question with conviction. "You…"

"For a dead body, this one is surprisingly animated," he was quick to challenge her belief. "It's also quite mouthy, wouldn't you say? Have you ever seen dead lips that moved this much?"

She finally averted her gaze for a moment, allowing him to pinch his capsule of flash powder without being observed. Unfortunately, the two of them were currently standing on an exquisitely soft carpet, so he couldn't simply smash the capsule on the ground between them. The wall to his right was the closest hard surface, but since he was right-handed, he wasn't in a position to throw his capsule at that wall with any significant velocity. He needed to reorient himself without arousing suspicion. "You're not answering," he spoke into the silence after an entire two seconds had elapsed. "Could it be that this new strain of vampirism isn't undeath so much as it's an alternative form of life? Wouldn't your people be obligated to protect it in that case?"

"Policy is dictated by the arch-druids," she found her voice again, "not by me. I…"

"Fine," Rufino saw an opening and half-turned toward the window. "Take me to your arch-druids. If you want to prove to them that your theories about the second strain are accurate, I'm the most compelling evidence you could ever have."

"I…"

Now that his foe was well and thoroughly distracted, Rufino cocked his arm and hurled the capsule of flash powder at the wall with as much force as he could muster. Kiralyn's instinctive reaction, of course, was to track and identify the projectile, which *should* have bought him the handful of seconds he needed in order to make a clean getaway. Sadly, he neglected to close his eyes before the capsule hit the wall, so the blinding flash of light ended up working its wonders on him as well.

You bloody idiot, he cursed himself for his error. The window had been about four feet in front of him and one foot to the right when last he'd seen it, so he shifted into his bat form and leapt toward the opening in one very hurried action. One rather violent encounter with the window sash later, he was back out in the rain.

There was just one small problem: he had no plan to speak of. Oh, he had his destination all picked out, but there was a *lot* of space between here and there. Under other circumstances, his tiny black flight form would have been more than up to the task of hiding him from pursuit; but if *anything* could spot a black bat at midnight, it was the snowy owl that Kiralyn's flight form just happened to be. *Why couldn't she have been a chickadee or something?*

His grace period expired as his vision returned to normal, so he made a snap decision and flew over the roof to the front of the building. He then made a ninety-degree turn to his right and dove until he was between the building and the hedges that surrounded it. His original intent was to hold this course until he'd left the *Duchess* behind him, but before he could do that, he spotted something in his path that got the cogs spinning inside his fiendishly clever mind: another open window. *Bingo,* Rufino smiled to himself, *she'll never expect me to go back inside the hotel!*

The self-satisfied genius zoomed through the open window, this time without smacking his noggin on the sash. He wasted no time in setting down on the floor and shifting back into his natural form, at which point he pulled the window closed before Kiralyn had a chance to see it. In doing so, he'd bought himself some time—time he could use to develop the plan he'd negle…

PFFFFFFFFFFFFF!

Rufino was really not in the mood for PFFFFFFFF! He whirled toward the noise and dropped into a defensive combat stance, ready to fight a desperate hand-to-hand battle for his life if need be. But in a harmonious blending of both good and bad fortune, the noise turned out to be just a naked fat man passing wind in his sleep. *Peeeeyewww,* Rufino winced as he looked back at the window with new understanding. *No wonder it was left open.*

In response to being insulted, the sleeping man's backside exploded again, this time sounding more like a wet gurgle. Rufino was starting to feel sick. *What in the hells have you been eating, man? Garlic and ice cream?*

There was definitely garlic in there somewhere—Rufino Endicott was never wrong about garlic. Fortunately, the smell of the gods-forsaken stuff wasn't enough to do him any serious damage, so he was out of harm's way for the moment. He crawled under the bed and started to work on the plan that he should have had by now. It was briefly tempting to try to hide under this bed until the following evening, but since every authority figure in town was going to be searching for Scirocco's killer later that day, Rufino decided—reluctantly—that it would be best if he skipped town before then.

After half an hour of making a supreme effort not to breathe, Rufino emerged from his hiding place, re-opened the window, then shifted into his bat form and hopped onto the windowsill. The storm was still out there, of course, but the wind had died down, and now that the elements were working in his favour, he was far less inclined to complain about them. In fact, if he could make it past the city's north wall, he should be home free, since there was absolutely *nothing* between that wall and the catacomb. No matter how good Kiralyn's owl-form eyes were, they were still eyes, and in the complete absence of light, they were as worthless as his own.

But even in his wildest dreams, he wasn't going to have an easy time getting to that wall. The owl part was bad enough, but the druid-sorceress was by her own merit an experienced hunter and a very smart cookie—she would know as well as he did that his options were limited. East and west were out of the question—to the east was a large residential district full of burning streetlamps; to the west was a forest full of homicidal druids and monstrous snakes. He could go south, but he'd flown past several farms on his way into town, and if any of those farmers were working late, they might give Kiralyn enough light with which to spot her prey. North was the obvious choice, so she'd undoubtedly be watching the north wall more closely than the others. He'd have to be *extra* sneaky in order to get past her.

He was game. He was a vampire who'd once been a halfling child—he could sneak with the best of them. Though he hadn't the faintest idea where Kiralyn was at the moment, he *did* know she didn't know where he was either, so his mood was much improved over half an hour ago. He was still frightened, of course, but there was something to be said for always knowing where the target was. For all Kiralyn knew, her prey was ten kilometres away by now.

Rufino followed the hedge wall around the *Duchess* to the hedge maze out back. Beyond that hedge maze was Pandxes Park, which would give him some cover as he began his trip north. He didn't have the faintest idea what he was going to do once he reached the far side of the park, but there was no other way to buy himself even this much relative safety. He'd just have to make up the rest as he went along.

The park cut off at Donovan Avenue. Donovan Avenue was so well-lit that it was practically on fire, so instead of continuing north, Rufino flittered two blocks west over to Oak Street. He then worked his way north and west—crossing streets only in the poorest-lit areas—until he found himself above Arbour Street in the industrial district. There, where the infernal streetlamps were few and far between, he made his beeline for the wall.

He was safely over that wall two minutes later. Supposedly that nice catacomb was three kilometres directly ahead, but since he could barely see the ground beneath his claws, he was going to have to take the map's word for it. Rufino never enjoyed flying blind, but there was a great deal of comfort to be derived from the knowledge that he could just keep on going if for some reason he missed his destination. He could easily put thirty kilometres between himself and Tundora before dawn, and once he'd done that, not even the *gods* would be able to find him. He could then stow away on a boat, start wearing toupees in public again, and skilfully evade any woman who was five-eleven or taller. Kiralyn probably had better things to do than to chase him to the ends of the earth, but one could never be too careful about such things.

The little vampire put his head down and concentrated on his flapping. Another fifteen minutes—half an hour at the most—and his ordeal would be over.

***

Rufino was about two kilometres clear of the north wall—and was just starting to breathe normally again—when the suffocating darkness behind him suddenly became a whole lot brighter. He pulled a 180 out of curiosity and discovered that twelve orbs of bright light had appeared in the sky above Tundora. By his estimate, they were about a hundred metres off the ground and spread out enough to light up the entire western half of town. Those who were still awake back there probably believed this was an act of the gods.

Rufino knew better. Those lights could mean only one thing: that Kiralyn had gotten sick of relying on streetlamps and was now taking matters into her own hands. If she got it in her head to create a few of her magical lights in this field, she'd probably be able to spot him, even at this distance. It did occur to him, in that moment, that he was probably far enough away from Tundora for one of his holes in the dirt to elude detection for twenty-four hours. Kiralyn supposedly had a schedule to keep, so there was an excellent chance she'd be long gone by this time tomorrow, at which point he'd be home free.

That was good thinking—he probably should have acted on it. He didn't, though, and one minute later, Kiralyn did exactly what he'd been afraid she'd do: she cast one of her obnoxiously bright lights a few hundred metres to his left. A few seconds after that, a horizontally oriented bolt of lightning scythed into the ground not five metres to his right. That was a damned good shot from over two kilometres away, and Rufino *really* didn't want to find out what she could do from close range. The catacomb complex was now visible in the distance, so he corrected his course and started flapping his wings like his life depended on it.

His flight path was slightly irregular, due to the uneven strength of his wings. In a perfect world, this little detail would render him a more difficult target to hit, but magic was not archery and he hadn't a clue whether or not his erratic flight would be of any benefit to his cause. It didn't seem to be hurting, though, because after three minutes of frantic flight, he reached the complex's perimeter fencing and he was still alive. His work was far from over, though—there were four small buildings above ground and, of course, the one that housed the entrance to the catacomb was *not* appropriately labelled. He'd have to open the doors to find the correct one, and the instant he returned to his humanoid form, Kiralyn would have a *much* larger target to shoot at. Rufino had never thought of his fine halfling body as a giant bulls-eye before, but suddenly it was impossible to think of it as anything else.

Before he made it to the first building, however, he spotted something off to his right: a small construction of stone that had been built into the earth. After increasing his altitude for a better perspective, he saw that the structure was, in fact, a ten-foot-wide staircase leading fifteen feet down into a tunnel with an iron palisade gate. Rufino couldn't see anything beyond that gate, but it was obviously the entrance to the catacomb, and whatever was down there had to be infinitely better than what was out here. He steered himself toward the staircase and said a silent prayer to the gods for his luck to hold out just one minute longer.

Rufino could hear Kiralyn's beating wings behind him now, which meant she was close enough to see what her prey was so interested in. On cue, a flickering orange light of some sort appeared at her approximate location and started moving toward him at a high rate of speed. He'd barely had time to realize it was a fireball before the projectile roared past him and slammed into the grass just in front of the staircase. Ten square yards of that grass went up in raging flames, and now there was a second flickering orange light coming up fast behind him. This was an undeniably lousy predicament for a vampire to find himself in, but the fact that she was attempting to cut off his escape route was enough to breathe some life back into his enthusiasm. *She doesn't want me going in there!*

With single-minded purpose, he drove toward the entrance to his chosen refuge; and with single-minded purpose, Kiralyn continued to lob fireballs in his general direction. None of them came particularly close to hitting him, but by the time he reached the staircase, it was completely surrounded by a raging wall of fire. To reach his promised land now, he'd have to go *through* all that vicious black smoke—an idea he wasn't exactly in love with. He needed only a moment, though, to decide that his fears were probably unwarranted—he likely did more damage to his lungs every time he stepped into a human tavern, so in love were the skyscrapers with their cigars, cigarettes and pipes. He'd gone to a tavern in Meridian one night tha…

Another lightning bolt shot past him—two feet to his right—and not three feet in front of him, it split into ten separate bolts, *all* of which had enough charge to do significant damage at their points of impact. Rufino wanted to swear, but he couldn't think of a word that was profane enough to be adequate. If Kiralyn found the range with *that* spell, he'd be skewered and cooked over a campfire; so without further hesitation, he plunged himself into the menacing wall of smoke. The idea was to hold his breath until he made it to the other side, but after five minutes spent at panic velocity, he was too oxygen-starved to do so.

The little vampire emerged from the obstacle after the longest two seconds of his life. His lungs were full of smoke and his eyes were watering too badly to be useful, but with a presence of mind that was quite remarkable under the circumstances, he made a seamless transition to echolocation and acquired his palisade objective. Without a millisecond's hesitation, he pitched down into a desperate dive and barrelled through a gap between two of the thin iron bars.

He'd made it.

Sort of. Kiralyn's snowy owl form was too fat to fit between the bars, but that disadvantage wasn't going to keep her at bay for long. Not far into the tunnel was a ninety-degree turn to his right that he was all too happy to take, but he found himself with a decision to make immediately thereafter. There were two door handles—on opposite sides of the passage—ten metres ahead of him. What lay behind those doors was anyone's guess, but surely Kiralyn wouldn't expect her prey to stop running until he was a good deal farther underground than this. Oh, how satisfying it would be to use the predator's own ego against her!

But if she checks all the doors, just in case....

For the second time in as many weeks, Rufino was paralyzed by indecision with his life on the line. *Damn it,* he scolded himself viciously, *she could be right behind me. Make up your mind and ma…*

That was when a really, *really* obnoxiously massive fireball slammed into the wall a few metres behind him. Rufino took off again at top speed, having hastily decided that the only defence against Kiralyn was distance, and a lot of it. Maybe it wouldn't matter—maybe the druid's claim that he was undetectable had been a lie meant to lull him into a false sense of security. Maybe she'd find him no matter where he hid.

It didn't matter. He was still a halfling in his heart, and a proper halfling was far too stubborn to roll over and die. The treacherous tree-hugger was going to have to work for this kill, and if he could make her late for her next engagement, so much the better.

As he put more and more distance between himself and the entrance, he was dimly aware that the gap between himself and Kiralyn was likewise growing larger. Sound carried incredibly well within the confines of these tunnels, so he believed he'd know it if the palisade gate had been breached. Unless he was sorely mistaken, it hadn't been. Did this mean her intention was not to follow him down here, but to have a fellow druid stake out the entrance until the king's undead-hunters showed up to take care of the dirty work?

If so, he could live with that. Not only would his enemies be giving him a day or two in which to calm himself and come up with something brilliant, but he doubted they'd want to waste an important druid on a stakeout. *That* was a job for a flunky, and Rufino could handle flunkies. By this time next week, he'd be on a boat to Minta Cadra, and his enemies would still be upstairs waiting for him. Minta Cadra was a prosperous nation, so it was reasonable to believe he'd be able to find another mobile coffin there. A newer one, perhaps, with some actual shock absorption….

With a concerted effort, he dragged his wandering mind back into the present. Kiralyn might yet decide to enter the catacomb, so his priority was still to find the best hiding place known to man and then stay there for about eighteen hours. That sounded simple enough: a six-hundred-year-old civil war catacomb had to have an abundance of hidey-holes to choose from—large cracks in the stone; rodent nests; hundreds, if not thousands of sarcophagi; and so forth. Hiding in someone else's sarcophagus was a rather morbid prospect, so Rufino was quick to catalogue that one as a last resort. Not only was he anxious to avoid *burying himself*, but he also had no particular interest in learning what the inside of a sarcophagus smelled like after all this time.

Speaking of which, this tunnel didn't smell all that great, and the pungent scent was getting stronger as he worked his way deeper into the complex. Perhaps some looters had been through here recently and had neglected to put the corpses back where they'd found them. This place supposedly had a keeper—Lionel's old friend, Edal—but best sellers had been written about crazy cryptkeepers, and this one could easily be worth a book or two of his own. *Why was I so eager to come down here again?*

After another minute or so, the little vampire came upon a room at the end of the tunnel: a large rectangular room—perhaps thirty metres wide by ten metres deep—with a ceiling that was one foot higher than it had been in the tunnel. There was zero light with which to see, but he was able to echolocate half-a-dozen door handles and another tunnel that—like the one he'd just emerged from—did not have a door. This was worth getting excited about, in spite of the seriousness of his situation. What could a pursuer possibly hate more than a seven-way fork in the road? *Nothing!* Nothing at all. If he played his cards right, he should be able to turn this room into an *incredible* headache for his enemies.

Then he noticed it: a very faint light, coming from behind the door furthest to his right.

For a moment he just hovered as well as he could, uncertain as to whether he should be intrigued or frightened by this latest development. There were *magical* candles, he knew, that could burn for incredible lengths of time, but it didn't seem likely that one of those had been set up in a burial site for soldiers. It seemed far more likely that the light's source was an ordinary candle struck by someone who was currently in need of it. Was it Edal, perhaps? Performing janitorial duties, hopefully? No matter—Rufino wanted nothing to do with this person, and he was certain the feeling was mutual. There were six other directions to choose from, so he selected a door at random, landed on the cold stone floor directly in front of it, and shifted back into his humanoid form. The wooden door was locked, of course, but they had yet to invent the lock that could befuddle a halfling. Rufino's personal kit just *happened* to include a paper clip, with which he…

"Who the devil are you?"

The little vampire whirled toward the noise, to discover that the candle behind the door was a mystery no more. A man *was* using it, and that man was now standing in the doorway staring directly at the intruder. This came as no surprise whatsoever—the way Rufino's evening was going, the only *surprise* was that the man *wasn't* pointing a weapon at him. Yet. "I'm lost," were the first words that came to mind.

The new threat, who stood about five-three and wore a hooded brown robe, folded his arms across his chest. There was insufficient light to make out the finer details, but from the way he moved and from the sound of his voice, Rufino surmised he was an older man, possibly in ill health. That did fit with what little he knew about Lionel's friend, but he didn't have enough for a positive identification just yet.

"Are you, now?" the man replied, and this time there was no mistaking that his vocal chords had been around for a while. "Went straight on Main Street when you should have turned left, hmmm?"

"Something like that," Rufino agreed with a healthy amount of caution. "I didn't mean to intrude."

"No worries, no worries," came the response as the man took a few steps into the junction. He then he raised his left arm and pointed toward the tunnel that currently had a human siege weapon at the end of it. "Follow that tunnel back to the surface, then turn left and proceed for about three klicks until you run into the big wall. You're welcome."

The helpful man then did a very peculiar thing—he walked back into the room from whence he'd appeared and closed the door behind him, leaving a rather dumbfounded little vampire in his wake. *What the heck just happened?* Had it not occurred to the man to ask himself how the supposedly innocent halfling had bypassed the palisade gate at the entrance? Had it not occurred to the man that his visitor might actually be a cunning looter, or possibly even a desperate vampire being pursued by treacherous nature freaks?

Maybe these things *had* occurred to the man; maybe he simply didn't give a damn. That *would* be congruous with the fact that he hadn't done anything about the smell around here. Still, Rufino couldn't in good conscience allow the man to remain oblivious to the danger upstairs, so he walked over to door and gave it a quick triple-knock.

Following some disgruntled murmuring about "tourist season," the old man answered the door and looked down at Rufino in apparent surprise. "You again?" he demanded in disappointment.

"Me again," Rufino nodded. "I…"

"My directions were very clear."

The little vampire took a moment to remind himself that patience was a virtue. "Oh, finding the way out isn't the problem," he explained from behind a mask of calmness that he most certainly did *not* feel. "My…"

"Then what is?" the other demanded again.

These interruptions were getting really annoying, really fast. "My problem is with actually *getting* out. The…"

"My gate didn't stop you the first time," the old man cut in again.

Rufino would have been irritated by that interruption as well had it not given him two valuable pieces of information: the man thought of this place as "his," which all but confirmed that he *was* the keeper, and his brain still worked well enough to extrapolate. "I was actually referring to the lynch mob that will soon be setting up on the other side of that gate," Rufino informed the other. "They…"

"But my memoires aren't finished yet!" the old man spun and stomped back into the room.

Rufino blinked a few times. Again, that was the last reaction he would have expected, for the man had just implied that a lynch mob would be here for *him* and not for the evil undead beastie. Was this an example of advanced senility, or was there actually something behind his seemingly irrational concern? Intrigued in spite of himself, Rufino stepped through the doorway.

What he found was a study of moderate size, with seven-foot-tall bookcases lining both of the side walls all the way to the back of the room. Against the far wall was a desk, upon which sat the burning candle that was the sole source of light and heat for the room. The man had taken a seat at that desk and was now hurriedly scribbling something onto a piece of paper. At the left edge of the desk was a stack of paper at least four hundred pages thick—a helluva lot of memoires, if that was in fact what they were.

But what was on the papers seemed unimportant in light of the fact that the man kept his office was down *here* instead of inside one of the surface buildings. *That* registered as a nine point eight on Rufino's weird-o-meter, and the one thing keeping it from being a perfect ten was the lack of nudity. "Nice place," he murmured out loud.

He'd spoken the words very softly, but apparently not softly enough. "It would be a nicer place," the keeper spoke tersely, "if all the heat wasn't escaping through that open door, hmmm?"

What the man lacked in social graces, he made up for in quirky logic, so Rufino stepped the rest of the way into the subterranean study and closed the door behind him. "Sorry," he said for reasons he didn't understand. "Why wo..."

"If you want to be useful," Edal cut him off yet again, "fetch me some more ink—second bookcase on your right; third shelf up."

Rufino had no burning desire to be "useful," but if he was going to have to share a catacomb with this man for a day or two, then it couldn't hurt to build some rapport. The ink was right where the man said it would be, so Rufino grabbed a bottle, then tootled over to the desk and presented his offering to the Lord of the Catacomb. "Why would an angry mob be after you?" he inquired again.

The old man snorted and turned to face his visitor. "You're not from around here, are you?"

Up close, the little vampire could make out some of the man's finer details, and one of them was very alarming: the helixes of his ears were pointed, and much more so than Kiralyn's had been. The man was a full-blooded elf, and in this ginormous subterranean echo-chamber, he stood a *very* good chance of realizing that his uninvited guest had no heartbeat. Rufino needed to keep things noisy from now on. "Is it that obvious?" he asked in response.

"You'd know of me if you were," the old man told him simply.

Such words could usually be chalked up to an overdeveloped ego or a stratospheric blood-alcohol level, but Rufino already knew from Lionel that something had happened—something serious enough to turn a bookkeeper into a cryptkeeper. "Sounds like there's a story to be had, here," he invited the man to elaborate.

Edal wasn't biting. "No time, no time," he replied in haste, "I must commit these thoughts to paper before I die."

Such determination was quite commendable—Rufino was almost sorry to have to derail him. "There isn't going to be any mob justice upstairs, you know," he told the man as gently as he could.

The man turned to face the vampire again. "No mob?"

Rufino shook his head, which prompted the other to stare at the wall in either confusion or contemplation—he wasn't sure which. What he *did* know was that things had gotten way too quiet for comfort, so he started to hum the opening verse of an ancient dwarven drinking song. "Hmmm mmm mm mmm HMMM mm mmmmm." He wasn't exactly doing justice to the masterpiece that was *One Last Keg*, but surely the composer would forgive him under the circumstances. "Hmm MMMMM…"

"Why did you say there would be a mob?"

"Why are you so disappointed there won't be?" Rufino asked in return.

The man's gaze returned to the wall behind his desk. "A man tires of the journey after a time," he spoke softly. "But you didn't answer my question, hmmm?"

Rufino had been hoping the keeper would overlook that little detail. "There is someone who might come down here in the next few minutes," he admitted, "but she'll be looking for me. You never saw me, okay?"

"But I *did* see you," the old man picked a really bad time to become obtuse.

Rufino sighed, and he made certain the other was aware of it. "I know that," he said, "but nobody *else* needs to know that. All I wa..."

"Men of my breeding do not lie," the man declared in the self-righteous tone that Rufino had heard all too often from pointy-eared bas... elves.

"Do men of your breeding get smashed enough to wake up with short-term memory loss?" he suggested as an alternative.

"Not unless you have a bottle of Siddurnan wine hidden under your shirt," the old elf stated his terms over his shoulder. "I'm guessing you don't, hmmm?"

That was a pretty safe bet. "No, I don't," Rufino admitted, "but you must have *something* worth drinking in this massive wine cellar of yours. Allo..."

"This cellar is bare," the keeper cut in again.

Rufino blinked a few times in disbelief. "You're kidding."

Edal stood up from his chair and started shoving his guest toward the door. "Hey!" the halfling exclaimed. "Wha..."

"The green hair was a nice touch," the old man remarked, "but I know entrapment when I see it, hmmm? You may inform my parole officer that Old Man Edal is continuing to behave himself, and that he look..."

"*Parole officer?*" Rufino repeated incredulously as he continued to resist being pushed. "Look, friend, I don't know what you think is going on here, but..."

"...He looks forward to his review next month," the keeper completed his thought. One second later, he pulled open the door and shoved the "parole-office spy" back into the junction.

Rufino stumbled to a halt a few feet away. "Wait!"

But the old man was no longer listening. He slammed the door in Rufino's face, leaving the latter right back at square one. After taking a moment to kick that door with all of his strength, Rufino returned his attention to more urgent matters. He still had to find somewhere to hide, but before he could start picking locks, he decided it was necessary to get the last word in. "She'll betray you," he called into the darkness, knowing damned well that the pointy-eared parolee could hear him, "just like she betrayed me!" The acoustics in this place were unbelievable—he heard the word "me" about six times before it finally faded away. "Don't say I didn't warn you."

He was about to shift into his bat form—in order to regain his echo-sight—when the door to the study swung open once again. "Betrayal, you say?" Edal's voice came through the doorway.

"Oh, don't mind me," Rufino brushed him off in frustration. "I'm just trying to find my way back to the parole off…"

"What sort of betrayal?"

The man's interest was genuine—of that there was no doubt—so Rufino decided to humour him in a very nonspecific kind of way. "I was hired to do a job," he delivered a highly filtered version of the truth. "I finished the job and now my employer is trying to finish me. It's the oldest story in the book, really."

The old elf nodded gravely before extending an arm into the study. "Come, little one," he was suddenly sounding a whole lot friendlier, "let's talk. Betrayal is a mistress with whom I am on intimate terms."

Those were the first words out of his mouth that hadn't sounded bonkers, so Rufino took him up on the invitation. A moment later he was back inside the study, scrutinizing some of the titles on the shelves as Edal slid back into his seat at the desk. One of the more prominent hardcover volumes was entitled *Seize the Day: A Self-Help Guide*, which implied that the keeper was working to correct a flaw or to otherwise improve himself. Quite admirable, really. "You went to prison?" Rufino asked after a moment of silence.

"Yes," the keeper hissed in response. "I was imprisoned six years for a crime I did not commit."

The halfling had heard many protestations of innocence during his time—nobody in Galensdorf ever seemed to know how all the cookies kept vanishing. "Who was your accuser?"

"The mayor of this worthless town."

Rufino *hadn't* heard that one before. "Really?"

Edal nodded gravelly. "Really. He was embezzling funds from the treasury, and I had the misfortune of being the first to discover it, hmmm?"

"He framed you?"

The old man nodded again. "It wasn't even that good a frame," he explained, "but there was nobody in Tundora willing to look past his charisma to find the truth. Certainly not for a crotchety old elf like myself, hmmm?"

Rufino didn't want to touch on the subject of old prejudices right now. "Can you hide me for a day or two?"

Edal nodded. "Or longer, if necessary, but first I need to know what you did on your employer's behalf. You can be honest with me—nobody hates the Tundoran establishment more than I do, hmmm?"

One more "hmmm" and Rufino might decide to take his chances down here on his own. "Why are you so eager to know?" he asked, uncertain how to proceed. On one hand, Kiralyn couldn't possibly expect him to honour his vow of silence after she'd tried so hard to terminate his existence. On the other hand, he wouldn't exactly feel good about himself if he broke the first promise he'd made in years. This was a difficult position to be in.

"I just need to know if I can trust you, is all," the other man made a very reasonable-sounding claim.

Rufino sighed in resignation. Maybe, if he gave only one or two details, he could earn the man's trust without compromising what was left of his principles. "I killed someone."

Edal lifted his eyebrows. "You're a hitman, then?"

"Something like that."

"How delightful!" the elf exclaimed with glee as he stood up from his seat. "Who did you kill? Was it someone I know?"

The bloodthirsty old man was *way* too interested in this subject matter for Rufino's liking. "Can't we talk about something else?"

"Was it the mayor? Or Judge Gates?"

Edal didn't seem to know when to back off, so Rufino decided to teach him a thing or two about boundaries. "No, it wasn't either of those people, and no, I'm not going to tell you who it was." He turned his back to the other in defiance and added, "I just want to pretend this whole evening never happened."

There was a moment of silence before the keeper spoke again. "There shouldn't be any secrets between friends, you know," he hissed softly.

"We're no…"

"Shinzado ax'gala pen ramu-mindac!"

Rufino turned back to the old man, his face full of suspicion. The last time he'd heard gibberish like that was when Kiralyn had used a nature spell to create an ice pack for him. "What are y…?"

"Tell me who died," the man repeated his request as a command.

"I told you no… aaAAHH!"

Rufino was on his knees a moment later, clutching his cranium with both hands, as if that would do him any good. There was now something inside his head that was *squeezing* the life out of his brain, as one might wring water from a sponge, and the sensation was uncomfortable to say the least. As quickly as the active pain started, though, it ended, leaving its victim on his hands and knees with a headache that wasn't going to go away any time soon.

"We can do this the easy way or the hard way," Edal spoke up again, quite casually under the circumstances, "it's up to you."

Rufino found the strength to meet the old elf's gaze. "Wha…" he took another laboured breath, "what the f…"

"A simple domination spell," the man's conversational tone continued to belie the sinister implications of his words. "It compels you to tell me the truth and to obey my commands, and it prevents you from taking any hostile action against me."

The little vampire hauled himself to his feet and favoured his tormentor with the most sarcastic sneer he could muster. "Now why would I possibly want to take hostile action against you?"

The mysterious spellcaster smiled a bit in response. "I can't imagine," he returned the sarcasm. "Now: your victim's name, if you please?"

"Go to the he…aaah!"

Just like that, Rufino was on the floor again, writhing in agony as the spell heaped its punishment upon him. This time, however, he noticed the direct relationship between the strength of his resistance and the strength of the pain. Though it went against every one of his halfling instincts, he made a conscious decision to relax his struggle. As he relented, so too did the spell.

Unfortunately, the spell's caster didn't give up so easily. "The name?"

Rufino was powerless to prevent the confession. To nobody's surprise, the old man had an opinion about it. "Druids are perfectly capable of doing their own killing, hmmm?" he pointed out once the story had been laid bare. "Why did they bring you in on this one?"

Rufino wanted to resist some more, but a moment of mind-crushing pain reminded him of the folly of doing so. "They wanted Martin Scirocco's death to look like a random vampire attack gone bad," he blurted out in resignation, "so the king wo…"

"You're a *vampire*?!"

Knocking the wind out of the old bastard's sails was immensely satisfying. "I am."

"That's impossible."

The impossible halfling vampire sneered up at his captor. "So certain, are you? Would I not be on the floor right now for telling such an egregious lie?"

There was a very long pause in the conversation as the elf struggled to wrap his mind around what his senses were telling him. "Everything I've ever read has told me that halflings are too small to survive a conversion."

It was nice to know that Kiralyn had told him the truth about *something*. "I'm tough to kill," he declared with pride. Such words were oft-spoke by men of all shapes and sizes, but after surviving a few dozen kobold attacks, a one-sided relationship with a crazy halfling female, a conversion into a vampire, and now a firefight with *Kiralyn Frostwhisper*, modesty was no longer an option. He had more lives than a freakin' cat.

"Well," the spellcaster spoke after another moment, "this is a fortuitous turn of events. For both of us, hmmm?"

Rufino wasn't so sure about that. "Excuse me?"

Edal picked up the candle from the desk, then stepped past his visitor and opened the door to the junction. "Come," he instructed, "and you will see."

Rufino didn't have a choice, so he followed the keeper into a room on the opposite side of the junction. It was a large rectangular room that seemed to be serving no purpose other than storage, but he didn't think Edal would have brought him in here for no reason. He was right. "There's more to this complex than meets the eye," the old tour guide explained with a rather smug look on his face. "The royal family was none too pleased about the Civil War Resolution, so it took the liberty of constructing several hidden bases as part of an ambitious plan to re-conquer the nation. That plan never came into fruition, but some of the bases still exist, and one of them…"

He set the candle down on a very old table and then pushed his hands against two very specific points on the back wall of the room. "…Is right here," he finished.

Rufino heard a faint clicking noise, followed shortly thereafter by the soft sound of stone rubbing against stone as a portion of the wall swung open like a door on hinges. Behind that perfectly camouflaged door was a hidden passage, and Rufino had already seen enough to know he wasn't going to like whatever was in there.

"Don't be frightened," Edal must have sensed his apprehension somehow. "You're among friends now."

Rufino didn't respond, so the two of them proceeded into the abandoned base without conversation. About fifty metres past the door and probably another ten metres deeper into the earth, the secret passage emptied into a large square room lit by torches mounted to the left and right walls. The room looked the part of an alchemist's workshop: a huge cauldron sat smack in the middle of the room, and one could barely see the walls past all the workbenches and cupboards. There were four exits, including the entrance, and if this had been designed as a military base, then there had to be quite a lot of space down here. At the very least there would be a briefing room, as well as storage rooms for weapons and food, some sleeping quarters, and…

There was movement in the corner of his right eye.

He turned toward the doorway to his right and his eyes fell upon a young human woman, or rather what was left of one. She had no hair; she was missing her left eye, and her face featured several prominent cuts that couldn't have been more than a day old. And there was more where that came from—the underwear she wore did a rather poor job of hiding the other abuses that had been heaped upon her. Portions of her abdomen had been slashed to pieces and then stitched back together again for reasons he didn't even want to imagine, and the same thing had been done to the left side of her chest. If the paleness of her skin was any indication, her heart no longer beat; in fact, it might have been cut out completely.

It was a banshee, a higher form of undead: a woman murdered—brutally in this case—and then reanimated before her spirit had a chance to escape. Like a vampire, a banshee still thought for herself; unlike a vampire, a banshee could not survive without the assistance of dark magic. That made Edal a necromancer, often referred to as a shadow priest—a twisted, evil, sadistic old bastard who desperately needed to die in the most expedient way possible.

"Welcome to my army, little one," the shadow priest interrupted his thoughts with palpable malice. "You'll be a useful servant."

Army? What army? Rufino was about to ask that very question when he noticed a figure standing against the wall in the room behind the banshee. It was a human male in shape and size, but it was just as certainly no longer human—it had a mortal wound in its abdomen, and it also appeared to be suffering from about six hundred years' worth of decay. It was a zombie—a reanimated body that no longer housed a spirit.

He could see four zombies now—four mindless puppets standing in place, awaiting instructions from their puppeteer, the shadow priest. And there could be thousands more of them just around the corner—there was nothing stopping the old man from reanimating every corpse in the whole bloody complex. That sounded like an army, all right, and though the little vampire didn't know what the general had in mind for the troops, he *did* know it wasn't going to be anything palatable. Zombies weren't used for peacekeeping, and no man with even a shred of decency or compassion would create a banshee, whose only purpose was to suffer.

Rufino had to do something. Hopefully he had another life or two to spare, because it looked like he was going to need them.

To be continued…

About Joshua Rem:

Joshua Rem is a professional driver based out of Vancouver, Canada. His true self—the storyteller—only comes out at night, which probably explains why he is so interested in vampires. His fondest wish is that his stories will bring laughter and inspiration to those in need, as they have done for him.

Acknowledgements:

The author would like to take a moment to offer thanks to those who contributed to the creation of this story:

To Kathryn: my grandmother and first editor, without whom this project may never have gotten off the ground. I love you.

To Mom: it may have been the road less travelled, but we got there in the end.

To Ali: my first fan who wasn't a relative. You're the best.

To Solstice Publishing: for taking the Leap of Faith on me.

To Dane and the crew at Ebooklaunch.com: for the unique and beautiful cover art, and for putting up with me. I'll be back.

Made in the USA
Charleston, SC
15 September 2016